Books by Peter De Vries

NO BUT I SAW THE MOVIE

THE TUNNEL OF LOVE

COMFORT ME WITH APPLES

THE MACKEREL PLAZA

THE TENTS OF WICKEDNESS

THROUGH THE FIELDS OF CLOVER

THE BLOOD OF THE LAMB

REUBEN, REUBEN

LET ME COUNT THE WAYS

THE VALE OF LAUGHTER

THE CAT'S PAJAMAS & WITCH'S MILK

MRS. WALLOP

INTO YOUR TENT I'LL CREEP

WITHOUT A STITCH IN TIME

FOREVER PANTING

THE GLORY OF THE HUMMINGBIRD

I HEAR AMERICA SWINGING

MADDER MUSIC

CONSENTING ADULTS, OR THE DUCHESS WILL BE FURIOUS

SAUCE FOR THE GOOSE

Sauce for the Goose

Sauce for the Goose

Peter De Vries

Little, Brown and Company — Boston – Toronto

The author is grateful to the following publishers for per-
mission to quote material noted below:
Bourne Co. for lines from "Music Maestro, Please," words
by Herb Magidson, music by Allie Wrubel; copyright © 1938
by Bourne Co., copyright renewed, used by permission.
Houghton Mifflin Company for lines from "L'An Trentiesme
de Mon Age" in *New and Collected Poems 1917–1976* by
Archibald MacLeish; copyright © 1976 by Archibald Mac-
Leish, reprinted by permission of Houghton Mifflin Company.
Alfred A. Knopf, Inc. for lines from *Collected Poems of
Elinor Wylie*; copyright 1932 by Alfred A. Knopf, Inc., re-
newed 1960 by Edwina C. Rubenstein, reprinted by permis-
sion of Alfred A. Knopf, Inc.
Viking Penguin Inc. for lines from "Vigils" in *Collected
Poems* by Siegfried Sassoon; copyright 1918, 1920 by E. P.
Dutton & Co.; 1936, 1946, 1947, 1948 by Siegfried Sassoon,
reprinted by permission of Viking Penguin Inc.
Warner Bros. Music for lines from "Valencia"; © 1925
Francis Salabert; © 1926 Warner Bros. Inc., copyright re-
newed, all rights reserved, used by permission.

LIBRARY OF CONGRESS CATALOGING IN PUBLICATION DATA

De Vries, Peter.
    Sauce for the goose.

    I. Title.
PS3507.E8673S2   813'.52   81-8124
ISBN 0-316-18202-8   AACR2

Designed by Susan Windheim

*Published simultaneously in Canada
by Little, Brown & Company (Canada) Limited*

Now let no charitable hope
Confuse my mind with images
Of eagle and of antelope;
I am in nature none of these.

I was, being human, born alone;
I am, being woman, hard beset;
I live by squeezing from a stone
The little nourishment I get.

In masks outrageous and austere
The years go by in single file;
But none has merited my fear,
And none has quite escaped my smile.

Elinor Wylie

Sauce for the Goose

· 1 ·

FORTUNE, when not smiling on you, may be grinning at you. It's hardly the next best thing, as we all know, Daisy not least of all. Sometimes, however, it's the reverse. Fate seems to be mocking us when all along it has rewards in store, often unearned. Life has a way of showering us with diamonds for nothing, having just exacted our blood for paste.

Children are said to be devastated to learn they have been adopted, but Daisy Dobbin couldn't have been more delighted. Then the nice freckled man who wore socks to bed, who snacked on pigs' feet and ate his breakfast grapefruit last, as dessert, who snored when he was awake — Daisy later knew it was called stertorous breathing — was not her father? The oblong lady who loved her but seemed equally to love cancelling subscriptions and snitching on big corporations wasn't really her mother? The couple with a horse's name who were seen strolling at five-thirty into restaurants where the posh crowd didn't eat until half-past six, maybe a quarter to seven, and who emerged an hour later fondling toothpicks, their charge between them, these were not her real parents? The bliss. The reassurance, the freedom now to soar into imaginative recapitulations of her true begetters: her father, say, a dashing subaltern killed in battle after getting with child the belle of the ball, a Boston beauty of at least patrician if not royal blood. Dazzlers they were both, who lived in a milieu and had met in a purlieu and danced in an ambiance. Butterflies briefly aflit in a summer garden before reality tore their wings and crushed them to earth, leaving a love child to be set afloat amid bulrushes on the stream of humankind.

Mr. Dobbin limped, a war wound contracted on the way to a Selective Service examination. He was inducted anyway and served creditably enough, though the slight hitch in his gait remained, less noticeable on his way to the local bar than when homeward bound from it. "*This* isn't your father's dish of tea," Mrs. Dobbin told Daisy, archly indicating the pot of oolong from which she would pour them each a cup, for a winter night's gossip while her father was hitting the suds. Once or twice a year he asked somebody to step outside, returning home with a black eye or swollen lip vividly supplementing the limp. Mommy invited Daisy to join her in wondering where the beer drinkers roosting till midnight at Carmody's put it all, ceaselessly washing the tongue, the throat, the bladder. "Such people have nothing within themselves," she said. "Quite the contrary," her father said, and guffawed. Sitting at bar height, her mother submitted, was so universally satisfactory because it reminded us of our high chairs — a point she bet every psychologist had missed. But the kidding between them was good-natured. "Your mother's so dumb she thinks the charge of the light brigade is the electric bill. Heh-heh," he laughed, his grin enriched by a missing incisor. He took them on regular vacations, once to New

York, where he and Daisy stood in a long queue for tickets to a Broadway hit, inching forward until he could read the prices beside the box office window, when he pulled her out and started back to the hotel, a paving contractor from Terre Haute.

That was all part of the rough chrysalis temporarily encasing the caterpillar destined for the butterfly she would herself one day become. Free to find her rightful parents, pray God; at least free to imagine them as they were, bent not over ham hocks and sauerkraut, but chicken Kiev and dead-white asparagus, bandying pleasantries of the kind one heard in drawing room comedies or television films, before which she sat hugging her knees in anticipation of her own ascent into the beau monde they called it. She saw herself in a gown of ice blue like her mother's, while a man in faultless tweeds like her father's crossed the room to bring her a demitasse. And the talk! "Eating kedgeree is like meeting a man named Murgatroyd. We shall never do it again." The bliss. To think that someday men with eyes glittering like the studs in their shirtfronts would say stuff like that to you. Epigrams they called them. "Have you seen Peewee's play? He writes as though he majored in drama." Conversational sprigs from the movies she saw and the grown-up books she read were grafted onto her own life's tree, as vividly envisioned. She saw her set dabbling in séances, and when the medium produced a manifestation her suave date remarking, "That's the spirit." She could hardly breathe, for thinking of it. She lay awake at night, throbbing with expectation. Absolutely on fire.

"Daisy, will you marry me?"

"No."

"But you say you love me."

"Love, my dear Bruce, is to marriage as the forest is to the lumberyard. I shan't be sawed into planks."

The ecstasy of it, and on top of it knowing you didn't have to get married if you didn't want to. She could hardly wait. She would know men with names like Hilary, Chrétien, Maurice. Meanwhile she could, she must, bear with: "Let's not tell your father about the rat in the piano until he's had his winky-pooh. Here he comes, after another day of asphalt."

Neither, then, was she related to relatives like Aunt Frieda, who lived in Bloomington and was married to an Irishman *manqué*: he didn't drink, he didn't fight, he couldn't quote any Yeats. And he a poet, of sorts, himself. As a versifier he stank, though not, perhaps, on ice. It was how Mommy fairly put it. She would dutifully read the "serious" work he sent — he made a living writing rhymes for a greeting card company. She discussed his things openly with Daisy. " 'Safe in the nest is folded every weary wing.' Close, but no cigar." Suddenly this Uncle Pat entered a "black" period, when his birthday jingles for the Felicity Card Company became steeped in existential despair and cosmic nausea. "Roses are red, violets are blue, stick your head in the oven, it's the best thing you can do." That could not even go in the "Insulting" category of the drugstore racks. Then there was one about the recipient's birthday cake having so many candles on it she'd best have a fire marshal on hand when she blew them out — "if you've got the breath, you asthmatic old bag you, or is it emphysema?" The front office told him he'd simply have to lace up if he wanted to keep those paychecks coming, so he went back to grinding out the old "heartfelt crapola," as he called it, each week complaining about the Monday morning blahs until well into Thursday.

So Daisy was twelve when told her relatives were no kin

of her'n, as their cleaning woman would have put it. The courier was little Effie Sniffen, a playmate, blurting out the story in the course of a spat they had. "You're not even real — you're adopted!" she'd exclaimed as she made off on one roller skate — presumably spilling a secret the Dobbins had been precariously keeping for all that time. Daisy was shocked, of course, at first, and immersed in the melancholy normal to children thus uprooted — until the compensations began secretly to collect themselves. And she took a rueful pleasure in shielding her parents from the fact that she *knew*, just as they had all those years been safeguarding her from the truth now unveiled. Like Daisy herself once, they must Never Know.

"Tell me more about Mrs. Sniffen," Daisy asked her mother, egging her on to the bouts of backbiting that had once privately grated on her, now no more since the character trait behind them could be safely ruled out as any part of her true heritage — certainly ruled out as typical of the lady from whom she'd got her aristocratic nose and swanlike neck. Daisy sat on the floor watching Mrs. Dobbin shell peas in a pan resting in a crater made of the lap of her skirt, her legs spread wide, like those of the cello player Daisy might herself one day become. Daisy hugged her own drawn-up legs, her cheek resting on a knee, gazing upward in a thoroughly feminine if slightly theatrical posture associated in her mind with young women who "made brilliant matches." She was really hugging her Mom for not being that at all, and had just been fantasizing a marriage she *might* briefly have with a man met in Cannes, a fashionable architect seeing whom in evening clothes was like hearing a gong struck. And the crackle of dialogue when the split-up came!

"Derek, I want a divorce."

"Why?"

"This thing is bigger than both of us."

Daisy tried to imagine her parents' courtship, and then what the wits in her set, like Derek and Chrétien, would have made of the marriage. "Was it a civil marriage?" "For a few weeks." No, that was about another couple, one of their own snobbish crowd, and could not really be said of the Dobbins, who probably got along as well as most people. Still, it was hard to visualize them "pitching woo," as they apparently said in the olden days; harder still to figure her mother and Effie's mother as the romantic rivals they were known to have been, a fact that made them lifelong enemies — and her mother easy to egg on about the other. "Go on, badmouth Josie Sniffen some more," Daisy urged, settling a cheek against her clasped knees. "Go ahead, pour it on, Mommy."

"Now, now, mustn't be catty. My, look at this customer, nine plump little peas in one pod." Mother wedged them out with a thumb. "Why, I don't know what makes Josie Sniffen, née Clapesaddle, so feisty, such a tartar they call them, unless it was that once in the dear dead days beyond recall, when on the world the mists began to fall, she was crowned Miss Congeniality of the Cooking Apple Division of the South Carolina Apple Festival of 1941. There, wasn't that worth waiting for?" She patted Daisy on the head and opened another pod. "I don't know how many other virtues got coronated before they got around to that one, let alone the Queen probably surrounded by a court you could also get lost in. It must take a lot out of you to be decorated amid the rumble of that many specifications." Daisy gave a wriggle of delight; what a lip on Mom! No wonder Josie Sniffen was overheard remarking, "Any daughter studying to be an ixenvay can go to school to her all right." Mom generally got her own back, with interest. "Well, my dear, that was by no means the end of her honors. The next year she was crowned Miss Soil Erosion of 1942, or maybe it was '43, and Miss Lake and River Pollution, because we had environment already then, way ahead of our time."

You were never sure what was fact and what Mom was cooking up, she being famous for her improvisations they called them, more of the ixenvay Daisy need now have no fear of blossoming into herself. Shifting the pan of peas in her lap, Mom gave the humorous twitch to her mouth that telegraphed another send-up, so that Daisy gave another anticipatory wriggle of pleasure. Supplementing the twitch before, was the humorous sniff that came after, when Mom had driven her zinger home.

"You got to give credit for her community activities. She works for Birth Defects, Cancer, Multiple Sclerosis and Muscular Dystrophy, and rumor has it that she's against all of those things. She won't take silver for door-to-door contributions. 'I don't want any currency I can hear,' she'll say. 'I want noiseless money, it comes in sheets.' She's honestly earned the harried look she's got, the right to tell how much everybody gave. She's your original Meddlesome Matty." More than merely talking prose without knowing it, like the Molière character of whom Daisy was to learn in later college years, Mom spoke in alliterations without knowing it. If somebody wasn't a Meddlesome Matty he was likely to be a Paul Pry. If neither of those, then surely a Fidgety Phil, Dapper Dan or Nervous Nellie. She didn't know any Caspar Milquetoasts.

"You've got to take people for what they are," a mutual friend once said. "On her mother's side Josie's shanty Portuguese."

"And that after a lifetime of upward mobility." Sniff.

"She gives her all for worthy causes. She does everything on a big scale."

"Especially weigh herself." Sniff.

"She keeps her nose to the grindstone."

"You should of seen it before she started." Sniff.

Mrs. Dobbin tried to imbue her daughter similarly with standards of wit and discrimination, setting wherever possible an example above which Daisy must, in her turn, rise, as she had risen above her own parents. One summer two local oafs literally named Hunt and Peck opened up a typewriter and office-supplies store, of all things. So there was this bustin'-laughin' Grand Opening night. Mrs. Dobbin was disgusted. "I've got to get out of this cornball town," she said. She thought she was absolutely right in purging from Daisy's father the baser elements in his own makeup, such as made him think that furtively slipping merchandise into other people's supermarket carts when they had their backs turned was justifiable human jollification. But Hunt and Peck indeed! It was the sort of thing that made her despair of Terre Haute as the end, the boonies, from which she must periodically escape to Grand Rapids and *breathe*. That had come into living possibility thanks to a new friend there, Lolly Schramm, the acquisition of whom had opened vistas. This was in 1960. "These men are Neanderthals, my dear," she said, piloting Daisy past the offensive shop-front after an ice cream, their faces, under parasols, averted from threatened glimpses of the partner clods doubled over with guffaws in a back room. "It's like those Ketchum and Kill undertakers in Chicago — you remember we saw their sign as we drove by?" "Yes. How awful for you, Mommy."

Daisy in her white organdy was drawn round the corner to a museum, actually a department store of which a corner was set aside for local artists. There was a fish still life; men kneeling in a crap game; some tuckered camels disposed over a title, "Where My Caravan Has Rested." Mrs. Dobbin had a passion for pictures. She was especially fond of the Impressionists, hospitable to a surprising amount of what had come tumbling after, but disliked chair-splat constructions, numbered improvisations, and balls of twine eight feet high. Not that she was averse to artifacts per se, or blind to the esthetic potential of debris. When in Grand Rapids she and her friend often went looking for found objects, equally available, of course, in Terre Haute, such as the hubcap which, its dents hammered out and its chrome scrubbed to a gleam, enjoyed reincarnation as a fruit bowl on the Dobbins' alcove table. Such ideas for creative living, the new casualness, were obtained from magazines with smooth complexions like *Vogue* and *Cosmopolitan*. If not subscribed to, their pages might be profitably turned while waiting to have a molar drawn or a flu shot given.

"When I'm in Grand Rapids with Lolly Schramm, I'm a new person. Unused parts of me come alive. I seem to breathe my native atmosphere, to spread my wings. She's a piece of work, that one." Mod receptivities to fresh winds and pivotal trends were echoed by her prompt seizure of the latest expressions. Widowed Lolly now had a widowed gentleman caller who explained that "piece of work" came from *Hamlet*, and who said things like, "Come sit beside me, my dear, and bring out the worst in me." Grand Rapids was where it was at.

Mrs. Dobbin enjoyed listening to symphonic concerts on the radio. One Sunday afternoon, Daisy found her asleep on the parlor couch, a half eaten apple in her hand. An intermission commentator was interviewing a guest.

"Dot goes bag to de tays when I was studyink under

Schoenberg, und he taught me abbresiashun of Bruckner's zymphonies. It is my regollegshun zat Schoenberg spoke rather more of Mahler zan Bruckner, but he did help bring Bruckner to ze fore, until now he is a growing part of ze zymphonic repertory.

"Bruckner was a great diver. He would make his friends frightened by diving down deep in ze water und never comink up again. Zen he would come up again, smilink. Dot was ze horseplayer in him, you zee. But ze abbresiashun of him is growink steadily. You have in New York ze street named after him, an important highway."

"I'm . . . not sure I . . . Street?"

"Ja, ja, Bruckner Boulevard."

"Yes, well, thank you very much, Doctor von —"

Snapping the radio off, Daisy eased the apple, yellow with neglect, from her mother's fingers and drew a coverlet up to her chin. She returned to the composition of her first short story, "Beets Make Your Spit Pink," which her third-grade teacher said was well within the mode of current realism.

But strongly as Daisy's mother urged the finely shaded life upon her, she warned her equally against the pitfalls of chic. There was always for example the cautionary gullibility of the supposed smart set, how they could be rooked like rubes by external frills. Once the two saw a long line of people waiting to enter a larcenously expensive new fish restaurant. "You know why they pull them in, like salmon in a net? They put panty hose on their lemon halfs, so you won't get pips on your shrimps when you squeeze the juice out. People are sheep. I've got to get out of this burg."

Snitching on big corporations. Nearly every one from General Motors down had been reported to Better Business or consumer groups, or been excoriated in letters to the editor, for defective merchandise, poor service, or surly per-

sonnel, or any other offense or shortcoming of which a
business could be guilty. Mrs. Dobbin was even known to
report Better Business Bureaus to *other* Better Business
Bureaus, addressing complaints about local agencies to
state, or vice versa. The Terre Haute bureau became
noticeably more effective when joined by Jennie Dobbin,
who became the scourge of neighborhood merchants as
well as giant octopi such as General Motors.

Josie Sniffen claimed that marriage to Jennie Hurlbutt,
her rival, had cost Frank Dobbin his sense of humor.
Which Mrs. Dobbin said was just as well if what Josie inspired when Frank had briefly courted her was any example. There was a snapshot in Josie's possession showing
Frank swimming to shore with a mallard in his mouth, like
a retriever. He was a crazy kid then, this youth with the Joe
E. Brown face, always horsing around for the girls, and God
only knew the hysterics on the riverbank out of sight of
the camera's range, that picnic day long ago, as he paddled
to shore with the wild duck in his jaws. No one knew who
had shot it. There was just the picture. Had there been any
such shenanigans, Daisy wondered, in her mother's courtship days, or were their memory the exclusive property of
Mrs. Sniffen? She'd heard the tales of her father's pranks
as a young groom, like the supermarket japes. Willing in-
formants told how he would watch from cover as shoppers
into whose carts he had slipped wares plucked from the
shelves at random, when they weren't looking, pulled into
the checkout lane to find they had in their circuit of the
store mysteriously acquired cans of sardines, pudding
mixes, denture adhesives, bottles of chow-chow and God
knew what else they'd had no intention of buying. Neutral
observers said that Jennie Dobbin had at first equally
enjoyed the customers' consternation and the ensuing
scenes of confusion, or at least connived at his snickering

relish of them; for it must be borne in mind that the didoes were never conducted solitarily but always for her benefit, Dobbin telegraphing with a wink when another was about to begin. Reports on the degree of bridal complicity varied; but all narrators agreed that early on Jennie discouraged such tomfoolery as unsuited to one hoping to make a name for himself in asphalt. That would be in character for one coming down all that hard on Hunt and Peck — texturally dissimilar as the two forms of drollery were. "She killed the card in that man," was, in any event, Josie Sniffen's taut-lipped judgment. His muse was dead. He had become a husband; his bride, a wife. Those mountain pines had been sawed into planks, lying, as in state, in the lumberyard that was holy matrimony.

Mrs. Dobbin had once read an article on humor in one of the magazines with smooth complexions, which analyzed satire by sorting its practitioners into two classes. Satirists were either soft-mouthed or hard-mouthed. They both brought their prey back dead, true, but some mangled it in purveyance while others did not. Retrievers — such as Frank had been hilariously imitating in the snapshot now rued as in Josie Sniffen's everlasting grip — retrievers were soft-mouthed, so trained. "Josie isn't," Mrs. Dobbin said, leaving Daisy to ponder the question of which her mother might be.

By one of those odd coincidences that checker our lives from time to time, Daisy's childhood in that period was full of dogs, and all of them retrievers or setters to boot. There was the Hinkles' black Labrador forever tipping over their garbage cans. The contents of three were once worried about the driveway, on a day when in addition the kitchen drain had stopped up, the refrigerator broken down, and an orange rolled downstairs. "A maid would quit," Mrs. Dobbin said. In midafternoon of the next day, Sunday, Mr. Dobbin was to be seen seated outside in the backyard with a camera, firmly determined to get some home movies of the Ghookasians' setter tearing up their flower beds, as was its wont, damning footage with which he could successfully confront a neighbor delinquent in letting his dog roam through surrounding properties, and bullheaded in his refusal to believe the damage it did. Daisy's mother beckoned her to the dining alcove from which the yard in question was visible.

Together they would watch the show, seated at a table on which reposed the *objet trouvé*, the burnished hubcap now serving as a fruit bowl. In it were a few pears and a declining banana. Mr. Dobbin sat on a terrace chair waiting for the dog to show up and muck about among the dahlias, in keeping with the afternoon schedule during which the bitch was let wander. He had his back to them, but sensing they were watching, he twisted about and waved, his face gashed in the grin that had been so favorably compared to Joe E. Brown's. Wide as the mouth was — after all, it had accommodated a wild duck — it was satisfactorily absorbed in a broad face, with large handsome blue eyes under a dark shock of hair. Daisy had once had a dream in which a circus lion had put his head into it. The canvas chair in which Mr. Dobbin waited was evocative itself of Hollywood associations, even without the camera in his lap.

Mrs. Dobbin took the banana from the hubcap and gestured with it at the wallpaper, woodland scenes in which birds peering from deep foliage abounded. "Josie Sniffen doesn't like this pattern, and there's no higher praise than that."

They waited, two spectators watching a third keep his vigil. The vandal to be trapped on cinéma vérité, so to speak, was a red setter named Polly Esther. "Polly Esther." Mrs. Dobbin loved to repeat it, shaking her discriminating head. It went with Hunt and Peck and Ketchum and Kill — to say nothing of the other stigmata driving her to Grand Rapids such as a local knittery threatening to open up under the name the Darn Yarn Shoppe. "Mr. Ghookasian is in fabrics, but does that excuse him?"

"Not in the least, Mommy."

"That's my girl." The bananaless hand reached across the table to give a caress. Kindred spirits. The banana was waved in a broad arc encompassing innumerable constituents in a world of nincompoops, people strictly from hunger concerning whom it was best not to hold one's breath while waiting for them to evolve. "My dear, if all the cornballs in this town alone were to be — But soft."

Polly Esther was seen rounding the end of the hedge separating their property from the Ghookasians'. Mrs. Dobbin rose to alert Mr. Dobbin with a rap on the window, but he had already sprung into action. Crouched behind a tree, the camera cocked and ready, he waited for the dog to come closer. Then he began the take, panning in a long shot as he followed her from the hedge to the dahlia bed, the dog pausing now and then to sniff something on the ground. The watchers were as tense as Mr. Dobbin himself, a common current of excitement charging them. If all went well, they would have dead to rights a citizen reprehensibly indifferent to telephone calls, complaints to the dog warden, and even protests lodged at the police station. Confronted with the evidence for which they hoped, Ghookasian would have to keep his dog chained or build a run for her.

But at the flower bed nothing happened. The scene stalled. The dog snuffled about the soil, that was all. Little was pawed, let alone torn up. Threatened with nothing for his pains but some inconclusive footage showing Polly Esther loping innocuously enough along the privet and harmlessly nosing the ground here and there and now starting to romp off, Mr. Dobbin emerged from cover and called her over. "Polly Esther," he shouted, "here girl! That's a good girl."

He stopped to pat the dog, who began to caper and spring about, wagging her tail as she dashed off, crouched down, then scampered playfully back again. Mr. Dobbin pointed to the flower bed. "Dig, that's a girl. *Dig*, damn you!" he could be heard exclaiming. "Like you always do. Dig — *you dig?*"

"That's wit as it was meant to be," Mrs. Dobbin told Daisy, pointing a thumb. "His true potential. Never fully realized." Then she became gently ironic. "And what he really should do is direct." It was affectionate joshing. She had her sunny side. Once when Mr. Dobbin in the course of an argument shouted, "You're wearing me thin!" she had poked him in the tum and replied, "And high time someone did."

Polly Esther was now so baffled, and Mr. Dobbin so exasperated, calling her a dumb sonofabitch and so on, that he set the camera down to demonstrate exactly what he wanted in this scene. Getting down on all fours, he began to paw the flower bed with his "front paws" and shoot the dirt backwards between his "hind legs." The animal still showed no signs of comprehension, much less of following suit, but instead came around and mounted Mr. Dobbin from behind, as bitches will in imitating what they see males do. With a disgusted roar Mr. Dobbin heaved about, flinging her off his back with a jab of his elbow, then climbed to his feet once more. Apparently seeing no alternative, he took the last resort for which he had come prepared, determined to get the goods on Ghookasian on an end-justifying-the-means basis.

Glancing around toward the Ghookasians' property, to make sure he was not being observed from enemy quarters, he took a roast beef bone from his coat pocket, held it out for the dog to sniff, and proceeded to bury it among the dahlias. Having done that, he drew back a bit for the shot now to be presumed inevitable — which it was. The dog immediately began to shovel the bone up with both front paws, a scene Mr. Dobbin was quick to get on film. It would have to be edited of course, in that the actual unearthing of the bone itself would have to be cut, leaving only the setter scrabbling about in the garden bed. Otherwise it would be useless as evidence, or at least highly dubious. The rest would be proof positive of what he had seen the dog doing *anyway*. Thus there would be no ethically vulnerable "dishonesty" in the stratagem.

"The footage will be the lie that tells the truth, as Picasso said of art, my dear," Mrs. Dobbin explained to Daisy.

Alas there was a snag. Ghookasian himself popped from a cleft in the privet, squinting through a camera of his own. He presently flourished it with a triumphant whoop. He had got his own shot from the beginning, showing Dobbin rigging his by burying the bone. The obscenest imaginable shouting match ensued. It began with a laughing Ghookasian, a thickset man in a green cable-stitch sweater, dancing a victory jig. Daisy was to remember it years later when with college friends she attended a campus revival of *The Treasure of the Sierra Madre*. It was the jig Walter Huston dances over the gold he alone of the three prospectors has recognized on the mountainside, his partners unaware of the fortune at their feet, laughing and yelling as he kicks and scuffs the dirt. "Aha!" Ghookasian taunted. "Caught you in the act! Got the goods on you! What good's your evidence now against mine? So sue me! Sue me! Ha!"

"Why, you slimy bastard!" Dobbin retorted, charging at him with his camera held aloft, as though he was going to brain him with it, as well he might have had Ghookasian not taken to his heels, the dog in his wake. "She's been doing exactly what I said so this was perfectly — I'm perfectly within my — Come here, you crummy, cruddy weaseler!"

Panic seemed to make Ghookasian fleeter of foot than rage did Dobbin, who, seeing him crash through the underbrush for home, began to pick up rocks and hurl them at him. "And those loud parties of yours," he yelled, broadening the base of his charge. "Did you know there's a law about that after ten o'clock? Noise pollution, not that you give a damn, you lousy . . . And giving a dog two names, the affectation. With a woman it's bad enough. Sally Ann!" he shouted, pitching stones. "Patty Sue, Helen Mary . . ."

As an island of sanity in a world gone mad, Mrs. Dobbin with measured movements peeled down the banana, smiling faintly at Daisy as she bent off and handed her a piece, as though to say, "Take, eat, this is my body which is broken for you. This do in remembrance of me. The only thing is, my yoke is not easy and my burden is not light, it's only fair you should know."

The two sat soberly munching away, each her half of the divided banana, in a sort of silent communion terminated when, sighing heavily, Mrs. Dobbin tossed the skin over her shoulder into the hubcap and said, "I've got to get to Grand Rapids."

· 2 ·

DAISY'S MOTHER took her to Grand Rapids when she was
fifteen. Mrs. Dobbin had bought Grand Rapids cheap. She
had discovered it long before Gerald Ford had blazed his
meteoric trail across the political skies, certainly before the
Calder stabile had been commissioned by the city. Around
that now swirled the Babylonian "New Ferment," as it
was called, for the yeast of self-expressive individuality in-
herent in the quickened life-style that had suddenly, for-
tuitously, seized Grand Rapids. Its Dionysian beat was
heard not only in the inner city but beyond the town
limits, where under fluttering pennants self-styled mad-
men sold previously owned cars, rather than used ones as
hitherto, and out into the urbanized rusticity of a country-
side where, supplanting the "lovely homes" of a squarer
day, were to be seen converted barns in backslidden com-
munities. The furniture with which the city's name had
for generations been platitudinously linked was now radically free-form; the symphony played not only Satie, but
Cage and Stockhausen; people ate out more. Church at-
tendance, long since dwindled to a trickle even in congre-

gations merged and remerged, now consisted largely of dispirited clergymen preaching sermons to one another. This in a place once famous as a city of churches — denominations with numerous congregations were not unheard of. The buildings in most cases still stood, of course, though put to different uses. One housed the annual Meatloaf Writers Conference. It was in this that Daisy enrolled for three weeks.

Now, Mrs. Dobbin had never severely objected to the obscurity of contemporary verse; indeed, she was grateful for an opacity which, if penetrated, usually revealed meanings baleful in the extreme, turning out psychic pockets without a penny of faith in them and flourishing sensibilities so pained that one became nostalgic for boys on burning decks and snows that began in the gloaming. She even hurriedly skimmed Daisy's poetry for fear of catching its drift, content that her high-school teachers had seen merit in phrases like "the sea's unceasing saliva," and rhymes like "When you are either too fat or too thin, and I shall have pieces of cork in my skin." The teacher at Meatloaf liked what she turned in, thinking "pieces of cork in my skin" vastly more interesting than "moles."

Mrs. Dobbin and her friend Lolly Schramm dropped Daisy off for her first class session in Lolly's Chevrolet, then set out for a nearby junkyard to look for found objects. They stumbled on an old auto horn the bulb of which might be squeezed at table to summon servants for the next course, if one were ever staffed. One of the magazines with creamy complexions had pictured a New York hostess doing precisely that by tweaking a row of teambells suspended on a wall beside her, cut from a horse harness also of olden time. Rating that as an *objet trouvé* was based on an interior decorator's having "found" it in an antiques boutique and paid through the nose for it, or through the hostess's nose. Mrs. Dobbin had legitimately unearthed the period horn in the scrapyard, practically under the nose of an owner who sat in his office shack with his stocking feet up on the desk, poring over a copy of *Penthouse,* and occasionally with bravura accuracy emitting a jet of tobacco juice through a hole in the window. The women, not to say the New York hostess, might very well have wanted to take *him* home, for the admiration and envy of guests reduced to exclaiming, "Where on earth did you ever find him?" "Well, my dear, there was this window in this dump, and I simply looked through a hole in it — that was all you could see through, the glass itself was so filthy — and there he was." "My dear, you must never put shoes on him, promise me you won't spoil Lafe."

Daisy in a handpicked seminar of nine was listening to their teacher at Meatloaf, a young man named Scudder, knock everything since Baudelaire. He dwelt at some length on the early-modernist motivation to *"épater le bourgeois."* He gave a rather nasty little chuckle as he tossed a stub of chalk up and down in his hand, the presence of which seemed to baffle him since there was no blackboard in this former consistory room. "Now then," Scudder put to the class, smiling maliciously, "what would you have to do to shock the bourgeoisie today?" The pickle the modernists had quite written themselves into, only themselves to blame, appeared to amuse him. He read aloud a specially succulent bit of filth from a novel currently on the best-seller list, fazing, as expected, no one. He closed the book with a clap like a gunshot and repeated, "What would you have to do to shock anybody today?" He shrugged, and for a moment had a look like Baudelaire himself sensing infinite weariness. "You might take a hush-hush attitude toward sex. That might outrage some."

Daisy raised her hand. "Or you might say marriages are

made in heaven," she piped up. "That ought to raise a few eyebrows."

Scudder gave her a speculative look. This child had possibilities. He picked up a submitted manuscript, a section of a novel in progress which depicted an act of bestiality in a brothel, a fable in which the animals talked. When he had finished, there were suggestions for making it more vivid, of galvanizing the reader with details more graphic than those adduced. Again Daisy raised her hand. "As long as the animals talk, he might have the sow turn and accuse the man of the double standard. Or no. Call him a male chauvinist pig."

So. A brat. It was what Scudder, as an English teacher in a Massachusetts college called Kidderminster, always looked for in a new class. He found them usually tart about the other students' work, rarely with the teacher himself, though even that lent some relief among the apple polishers. Some bore wanted to talk about the role of the artist in society, and when Scudder woke up about a thousand years later it was to hear a student mention Emily Dickinson, who, so far from occupying the human arena, was known to fly upstairs and hide in her room at the sound of callers. Up again went the little Dobbin creature's hand. "Anything to be the center of attention," she said. A real minx. He must get her to come to Kidderminster. What malicious little conferences they would have. He would tell her about the lines Emily stole from other poets, research showed it, almost as many as that old pickpocket Coleridge.

He invited her for a stroll after the class. There was nothing unsavory about it, as he was homosexual, a course from which he was not likely to deviate. They struck out toward town with some possibility of encountering open-air diversion to vary whatever conversational pleasures might eventuate, for the city was that week hosting a Pan-theatre Festival. Dramaturgy of every conceivable species and shade was being given free rein, with street theatre, by then almost old hat, the least extreme of the avant-garde varieties then in the wind. Sure enough, after a few blocks of chatting about poetry, they saw a scene being enacted on someone's front porch. A small troupe, motley in the sense that a pinstripe or two could be glimpsed among the more picturesquely costumed mob boiling about the steps, had so dedicated itself to "bringing theatre to the people" as to do so whether they wanted it or not, the people. If citizens could not be lured from the stupe-faction of their living rooms, a form of death, then force must be used, and so one or two of the strolling players were banging on the front door demanding that whatever cottagers stagnated within come out and hear their offer-ing, a mélange of Ionesco bits soldered together by the director. Their raps being unavailing, they began to thump ever more loudly with their fists, shouting at the tops of their voices and bringing their arms back so far for each successive blow that when at last the door was jerked open by an occupant he was dealt a punch in the nose that brought a spurt of blood from it. The resulting brawl, with the resident holding a handkerchief to his face, supplied an exchange that fit nicely into the rather episodic scene the company had prepared. Our two friends watched from across the street for a few minutes before moving on.

"I was interested in what you said about what you'd have to do to shock the bourgeoisie today," Daisy re-marked. "In poetry, what about a few four-letter words, like fain and doth."

How fast the child learned, Scudder thought to himself. And her poetry, the scraps he'd seen of it, showed a sense of the antipoetic remarkable in one so young, combined with a bracing cynicism also precocious. He might get her to tighten these qualities even more; get her to change that marine line to "the ever-slavering sea." Or maybe even "the ever-slobbering sea," with its sense of cosmic disgust. What the current scene needed was a real harridan, no more of these half-baked Medusas with their hair a nest of worms, forever turning up on the chat shows. Of course men made the best bitches, as they did the best cooks, the best everything if it came to that — today even the best mothers — but here was the potential for a topflight vixen, provided she didn't turn out to be happy in love, or some sonofabitch didn't do her a good turn and sour her cynicism. Otherwise, a few more years of marinating in life's bilious realities and she'd be just fine. He knew she was wellborn, having seen the mother. He had only talked with her a few minutes, but it was enough.

"Were you ever born in Terre Haute?"

"No," Scudder said. "What's it like?"

"Living there is all I know — I don't know where I was born. I was adapted in the Midwest. Did you get that slip of the tongue? I said adapted. My parents don't know I know I'm not theirs, so don't say anything."

"Of course not. Our secret."

Alas, the mother's genes could not be counted on, then, and the father? A paving contractor had he heard? Weekly Rotary lunches, vestryman in an Episcopal church. Still, she was a waif, like himself. They must wander the earth together, a platonic Humbert Humbert–and–Lolita pair. He would give up teaching. No more pencils, no more books, no more students' vapid looks. Never again yet another dissertation on Mallarmé's silly vaporizings, no more of Rilke's mystic slush to wade through. No more poets in Creative Writing 203, Frostbitten or Swinburnt.

A jogger scuttled by along the curb, like a rat along the wainscoting, hitchhiking as he ran, glancing over his shoulder.

"He's keeping his options open," Daisy said.

"Not sure he wouldn't after all rather be riding in comfort instead of puffing along half-naked like a damn fool." Scudder felt an exhilaration, almost unwilling, at how their minds meshed, responded instinctively to one another. Soul mates they might be. Already were. My God, what was happening to him, that he wanted to sink to his knees then and there and girdle the flower-stem waist in his two arms? He was coming unwrapped, turning normal.

"Or just thought of something he ought to do."

"What?"

"Him. The jogger. Like make a phone call that slipped his mind."

"Or the refrigerator repairman is coming." Oh, my God, my God. He could smell her soap, his head reeled . . .

A car stopped for the jogger and he climbed in and was borne swiftly from view, gesticulating to the driver from the backseat as though directing a chauffeur. Scudder plucked up the nerve to satisfy a curiosity Daisy had piqued.

"Then you have no idea where you were born?"

"Oh, yes. I've got it all worked out." She tapped a temple with two fingers. "My father was a concert pianist whose shirt-cuffs just showed beneath his sleeve, and my mother a member of the French aristocracy who need never have bathed —"

"Like you." He was going mad. Mad.

"— and they conceived me in a château in the south of France called Domblémy. Do you like the name? I made it up."

Like it, he loved it, with its sense of bleating self-justification, the eternal bone-draining recriminations between the sexes living in all that mucilaginous intimacy. Ugh! Devised by a deity nothing if not devilish. Indeed, the gods themselves are depicted as spending their time in little but petty bickering. What an imagination the child had. "How did you ever think of it? Domblémy." He rolled it on his tongue, shaking his head in wonder.

"It just came to me, all of a heap, as Mommy used to say. Still does."

"Oh, Mommy always says that, does she? What else does she say?"

"She used to say 'pert nigh but not plumb.' That's regional for almost but not quite. But the name, it just popped into my head as I woke up one night. I may have dreamt it. I *saw* the word, accent and all."

It fitted in with the general sense of *her* fitting in with him, of their sharing utterly the feline mystique. The chit would never be satisfied with her lot. Could she be kept soaring, and not brought down to earth to grub in something like journalistic crusading? An investigative reporter busybodying the days away at consumerism, say, or, God forbid, feminism? Horrors, might she become one of those? Scudder thought, with a clairvoyance he little suspected.

Daisy snapped his train of thought by staying him with a gesture. Another kind of theatre was on display, this time with strolling spectators detained by performers themselves fixed. Again a front porch was the scene, a couple sat on rocking chairs as they read. The woman was bent over a copy of *Dorian Gray*, the man smoked a pipe as he turned the pages of *The Skin of Our Teeth*.

> WOMAN: You've driven me Wilde.
> MAN: You've driven me Wilder.

Scudder said, "Your caretakers for Domblémy. I can absolutely see them there, grousing in the last of the evening light, their chores done. Shall we pop down this street here?"

"My father goes to restaurants where he orders dinners without looking at the menu, and he would never park by a meter with somebody else's unexpired time on it without feeling a little *de trop*."

"More than a little *de trop*. What is this? Methinks mehears voices." There had been insanity on his mother's side, appearing suddenly in early middle life. An uncle and a girl in his Sunday school class. Something about putting his head under her skirt at a church picnic, and pretending he was a photographer taking pictures. No warning.

Coming toward them along a maple-shaded sidewalk was a company of townsfolk on all fours, devotees of a cult called the Quadrupedalists, publicly demonstrating their conviction that our physical ills date back to that time in the dim past when our ancestors elected to walk upright, thus seriously dislocating the bag of guts that, essentially, we are. Entrails had been designed over mind-numbing millennia to depend from a supporting flagstaffed, spinally horizontal posture, and that to expect them in a relatively puny span of time to hang otherwise is to invite the disorders and malfunctions that, in fact, have resulted to the alimentary thruway — to say nothing of the irremediable mischief done to sinal drainage. The nasal hydraulics are by now so hopelessly mucked up that even a daily period of return to hands-and-knees locomotion is but a poor palliative, helping us slightly to muddle through as the repellently drizzling lot we have become in consequence, schlepping along to our appointed graves as best we can on eucalyptus, Primatene Mist, Neo-Synephrine, and whatever else we can find to squirt, spray, drip and fizz up our misbegotten snouts.

Meanwhile, the doughty Quadrupedalists experience nothing discommoding to the arts of human intercourse in their mode of travel, as a few of the conversational passages bystanders might pick up proved. Two men bringing up the rear of the group, totalling some sixty adherents, were deep in a discussion about the decline of religion in this former "city of churches."

"Yet the fact remains, my dear Tolliver, that those rigidly indoctrinated in childhood will go to every semantic extreme to retain some identification with a belief not to be scrapped without a grievous wrench to the psyche," one was saying to the other. "Unable to break the umbilical cord, they stretch it, for yards and yards of the most far-fetched liberal interpretation."

"So that the cord — one might call it the umbiblical cord, don't you know, Overholt old chap — becomes a kind of tether. There are those, a school, even now trying to reconcile, in fact equate, the Freudian principle of imperative Dionysian release from repressed sexuality with the Christian resurrection of the body. Fact. The so-called millennial 'rapture' of the church united with Christ returning as the bridegroom coming."

"So that the conception of the Second Coming would have veritably erotic, even orgiastic, overtones, and the conception a true one in every sense."

"These guys are all right," Scudder whispered to Daisy behind his hand. "It's no malarkey about the Freud-Christ stuff, as you'll find when you're assigned Brown's psychoanalysis of history in college. I do hope you'll come to Kidderminster. Let's tag along for a bit, do you mind?"

Scudder seemed about to crouch down and stroll along on all fours himself beside the two discoursers, the better to catch their exchanges, possibly even to join them, when, alas, another diversion deflected everyone's attention. The street theatre just then rounded a corner on its enormous flat truck and stopped there, seeing a captive audience. A performance of Ophelia's Mad Scene was given a kneeling ovation, and then the actress was taking much-deserved bows when gathering clouds suddenly emptied a downpour on the city. Everyone scurried into the lobby of a nearby hotel, the players themselves boiling down off the truck to join the general pell-mell.

Here there was to be another confluence. As the last of the now uniformly bipedal bags of guts bolted into the lobby, some thoroughly drenched from their sprint through what was in fact nothing less than a cloudburst, a door in an adjoining corridor opened, and out of it poured six characters in search of an author, from a matinee production of Pirandello in progress in a little theatre located in the basement of the hotel. That their identities, already elucidated as fluid, were now totally dissolved in the mass confusion that followed was hardly detrimental to the Festival as such, enriching discoveries being inevitable in the melee. An encounter group taking a breather from another direction further quickened the mass tempo.

"Look, bud, who do you think you're bumping into?"

"That's just it. I don't even know who *you're* bumping into — who I am myself."

"Watch it, mister," a woman elsewhere warned. "Keep your hands to yourself."

"I was only trying to emit warmth. Trying to relate —"

"And now this one. Help, I'm being molested, I think."

"I'll call a cop. There's one. Officer!"

"I'm only a cop in a play."

"You're the one who's molesting me, I bet."

"He pinched you for loitering? Heh-heh."

A further embroilment was now inescapable. An intermission in a surrealist drama running in a theatre across the street sent additional streams of people into the lobby, braving the rain in an attempt to elbow their way toward the only bar in the neighborhood. The work there being both audience participation and, perforce, improvisational, few patrons were surprised by what happened, onstage or off, or to themselves. A couple holding hands so as not to become separated in the swelling jam as they fought their way by inches to the cocktail lounge were speaking of the man's disappearance during a previous intermission, not surprising in itself as the theatre interior was undergoing carpentrics themselves rather sketchily free-form, not to say impromptu. "I had to go to the men's room," the husband said. "What happened in the second act?"

"You were in it."

Daisy and Scudder had long since become separated, as had Mrs. Dobbin and her friend Lolly, who had also turned up, not entirely voluntarily. They had tried unsuccessfully to stop for an ice cream, their *objets trouvés* locked up in Lolly's car. Daisy caught the merest glimpse of her mother's head bobbing on the crest of a human tide being swept along in a kind of Armageddon of the Arts. The last contingent to join the scene was a small group emerging from a banquet room in which there had been a luncheon symposium on comedy to which they had been an audience, finally listening over their sherbet and coffee to the mandatory intellectual analysis of humor by a college professor.

"Doctor Didisheim?" said a woman who had been waiting by the folding doors for the professor to squeeze himself through. She held a sheet of paper in her hand.

· 31 ·

"Yes?"

"I heard your analysis of humor."

"Oh? And what did you think of it?"

"This." And she smacked him in the face with a recipe for custard pie.

"I told you this is where it's at," Mrs. Dobbin said to Daisy as they bowled homeward to Indiana on a Greyhound bus. "I expect you got a lot out of your classes. Mr. Scudder seemed odd, but nice. Did he give you plenty of pointers?"

"Yes. We may correspond. Or maybe not. He's rather epicene."

"What's that?"

"Neuter."

"This could go on all day. Lolly claimed she was ravaged in an intermission of that play. One of her jokes. She's a blast."

"You'll have a lot to tell Josie Sniffen."

"The gross-breasted rosebeak."

At about that time, as closely as could be reconstructed, Mr. Dobbin was going into the house garage with a length of rubber hose, which he fitted to the exhaust pipe and then ran through the front window of his car, wedging the end securely between the top of the glass and the frame, by giving the crank an extra quarter-turn. He had been despondent over the loss of an important city paving contract, as well as other things, including, perhaps, that the rose once blown forever dies. He climbed into the front seat, started the motor, and settled back to await the end.

The motor had not been running long when he ran out

of gas. He got out of the car with a growl of disgust, slamming the door. This proved his point: that life was one frustration after another. He went around behind the car to the other side of the garage where the lawn mower stood, and, after a few pulls of the rope and some fiddling with the lever, got that started. It ran for a somewhat longer time, but the meagre fumes did little but give him a nasty headache and a feeling of nausea, necessitating a sudden bolt through the door into fresh air.

The whole experience depressed him further, in a sort of vicious spiral leaving a cumulative sense of futility so abysmal that he visited a local sporting house. There he contracted what their cleaning woman called "one dem funereal diseases." The whole story came out in a stream of scandal, itself curiously purgative, not the least precipitated by admissions on his own part and a penitential outburst that was not without its orgiastic elements. Mrs. Dobbin herself, though beating the air, wallowed in Forgiveness. "Tears ran down his cheeks," she later reported, "and him high up in paving." Dobbin himself protested complete bafflement with his behavior. None of it had been like him. He was powerless to explain it.

"You've been working too hard," his wife said, sympathetically, "under too much of a strain. What you need is a break, cut loose a little. I know just the thing. I'm going to take you to Grand Rapids."

·3·

WHETHER CAUGHT UP in the New Ferment, as such, or just another husband in a mid-life crisis ripe for a fling, facing the panic of the closing door, Dobbin in Grand Rapids became madly infatuated with Lolly Schramm. Mrs. Dobbin was stunned, but remained again stoutly understanding.

"When did you first realize there was something between you?" she asked him.

"When we were taking a shower together."

"It was then that it struck you all of a heap. Gazed at each other with a wild surmise they call it. Oh, if I could only believe that."

"Jen, as God is my judge. Until then it was only horsing around. Like a couple of crazy mixed-up kids, doing things for a lark."

"This is still my *saison en enfer*." It was a term she had got from Daisy, telling her about some of the French poets. "Trite as the best-friend syndrome is."

Dobbin sat with his elbows on his knees, his head in his hands, with the look of cowed contrition that for some curious reason makes a man's face seem dirty — like a boy who hasn't washed. He slowly raised his head, like a dazed boxer. "What did you say about Cézanne?"

"I didn't say anything about Cézanne," Mrs. Dobbin said. Pacing the floor, she gave her skirt a corrective tug. "I said *un saison en enfer*. It means season in hell."

"Don't say that. It'll all come out in the wash." The seeds of remorse were already being sown, in mid-transgression, the orgiastic harvest of penitence imminent. He rose and walked the floor with her, so that for several paces they marched in step across the hotel room. He threw his arms into the air, accused her of being too long-suffering. She didn't deserve this, nor he her. Once more he professed total confusion over what he had done, absolutely flabbergasted at his conduct, as incomprehensible to himself as to others, possibly more so. Like a bewildered sleeper thrashing in a collapsed pup tent, he didn't know what came over him.

"It'll blow over," he assured her, as, of course, it did. "It's never too late for the turmoils of adolescence," was how Daisy put her own estimate of the foolish susceptibilities of middle-aged men, which perhaps aren't all that foolish. Even after the affair had well gone out to sea, Dobbin kept asking for forgiveness with his air of voluptuous regret, throwing his hands into the air, spinning around some. Among others it was all fairly well resolved and even forgotten by the time Daisy was ready for college.

She did go to Kidderminster, but Scudder was no longer there. No one knew where he was. He had said only that he was sick of bookworms, and vanished in his battered Buick. Effie Sniffen went to Kidderminster too, and, their wobbling friendship back on course, the two girls became roommates. The memory of her childhood chum's "You're adopted!" as she roller-skated off with a parting moue, was a queasy one for Daisy, who didn't bring the subject up again, and had never asked for more details. Maybe Effie had no more to give. Maybe it had been the wildest hearsay of her own. Maybe she had completely forgotten having tossed it off. Naturally Daisy longed to know more about her birth and antecedents, while at the same time fearing to learn inclement truths deflating to the rosy fantasies she had evolved, as the young girl the older Daisy now looked back on with wistful amusement. The whole thing was a sleeping dog she figured she had best let lie.

Together they made another friend at Kidderminster, Roberta Diesel, who was to play a role in Daisy's life so pivotal as to determine, in fact, her destiny. That was owing to the cut of Bobsy Diesel's jib, disclosed early on to any acquaintance, male or female.

That as a militant feminist Bobsy might be beating off men who weren't trying to get to her was a view with which even many of her crusading sisterhood would have agreed, at least in their secret heart of hearts. Daisy it was who put it that way, though once and only once, in a moment she herself speedily regretted, despite the observation's having been made less in malice, God knew, than in a kind of rueful sympathy for the Diesel, widely expected to prove a George Sand without talent.

Daisy had wisecracked from an advantage enjoyed as one of the class beauties, and wanted to bite her tongue even as the words crossed her lips. To do her justice, Daisy would never have uttered them had Bobsy Diesel been plain; she was in fact handsome enough. That made her fair game. That and the fact that she seemed willfully to cancel out the good looks that might have gained her her share of dates with prospecting weekenders down from Dartmouth and Harvard, by dressing like a stevedore and smoking panatelas. Then there was the schnecke eternally crowning her head, the ropes of brown hair twisted into a coil like that of the German breakfast pastry of which it always reminded Daisy.

She and the Diesel teamed up in a sorority revue originally planned as a feminist lark, those being the early days of what came to be known as Women's Lib, but their writers produced few creditable antimasculine sketches and jokes; and so the routine the two settled on was simply a sort of abrasive-nostalgic lampoon of the vaudeville fare dominated by male performers of the era, seen in retrospect as clowns in the unconscious sense. It was a patter delivered with Bobsy Diesel dressed in baggy pants as the comic, and Daisy as the straight man in a tight suit and straw skimmer.

"My uncle is a mad scientist."

"Oh, yeah? What's he mad about?"

"The Ford Foundation cancelled his grant."

"Oh, yeah? What's he working on?"

"Now he's working on the Guggenheim people."

Daisy got Bobsy blind dates for evenings she might otherwise have spent curled up with an apple and George Sand. Promiscuity has a way of driving standards up, since everyone will have acquired a broad background of experience from which to judge palatability and performance, and the Diesel was so unsatisfactory in bed that she became known among local wags as the *Lay Misérable*. One Dartmouth junior telephoned Daisy afterward to thank her for fixing him up with a fine American dame with the guts and balls of a government mule. He had just been to the Netherlands and had his fill of dikes for a while. "It's the first time I ever had a goodnight kiss with a knee in my groin. But my doctor says if I wear this truss for a month I'll be O.K. Of course my horseback riding days are over."

"She wasn't quite herself."

"That's why I'm alive today?"

"She'd just got out of the hospital."

"Oh, yeah? What was she in for, a prostate operation?"

It was rather like the patter itself, and Daisy was glad to hear the last of a chap of whose humor she didn't think much.

The following Saturday it was Effie — or rather Effie's friend, a native she had met at a dance — who fixed Daisy up with a blind date. They had dinner and took in a film — *The Treasure of the Sierra Madre*, in which Walter Huston's victory jig reminded her of Mr. Ghookasian's in the home-movies feud — and then went on to a roaring party Effie's friend knew of. He told a story about a cannibal who made superb finger sandwiches, at which everybody laughed except Daisy's date, whose response was an increase of the pained expression chronically worn. A slender, sandy-haired fellow, he was at one point seen backing up to the cold fireplace, as though to scratch himself between the shoulder blades on the mantel edge. "Taste is the morality of the senses," he said. Oh, my God, Daisy thought, one of those. Epigrams. And not even eleven o'clock — a good hour to go before she could gracefully disengage herself. Sometime later he was saying: "The female mentality is like a bar of bath soap — constantly eluding our grasp." Daisy howled like an animal, in spirit. That did it. She would definitely be a feminist. And celibate to boot. Let rhapsodists hurtling inexorably toward breakfast rant about the divinity of the Pair. She would have Emily Dickinson's long, ascetic upper lip, and write to the Reverend Wadsworth in 1855: "At half-past April of my life . . ." Hey, not bad. She would snatch back the little conceit after the cleric's death and smelt it over into a poem ending, let's see, "When you my something something / May ruefully remember; / And I my something something / At a quarter to December."

"What are you smiling about, Daisy? A woman's smile is like a Phillips screwdriver. It —"

"I know, I know!" What am I doing here? she asked th'unanswering welkin. He asked if he might phone sometime. Daisy said she guessed she'd be around, and advised him to shave off his mustache.

"Why?"

"It makes you look effeminate."

But he has a beautiful head of hair, Daisy thought. He probably brushes it after every meal.

But as though there were a God in heaven after all, the Diesel was the first of her class to — abhorrent cliché — snare a man. Or hook a hubby, as her mother even more horrendously put it. And, of course, divorce one. Daisy heard about both, three years apart, when working as a columnist for a Long Island weekly, a job she took soon after graduation. Amateur psychoanalysts in the class had no trouble knowing that only a recessive ectomorph like Horton Pew would want to make the Diesel his; and two and a half years of cohabiting with the merchant marine was apparently enough for *him*. There would be, day piled upon day, the swinging gait of the approaching bar bouncer, the trencherman's appetite, the auburn schnecke nightly disassembled and diurnally recomposed — to say nothing of the smell of cigars no doubt by then firmly installed in the draperies. Still, they must have had their sport in bed, grotesque as the thought of it seemed to the scattered faithful comparing notes, by now, by letter or an occasional phone call. But then the thought of any two people conjoining, when one of them is not oneself, is grotesque. And the divorce was amicable. The wedding presents and the household goods were divided so equitably that even the stereo was dismantled and the components split fifty-fifty, Horton Pew taking the amplifier and speakers, Bobsy the turntable and Empire cabinet in which it had all been custom-built. This was also true of one jointly favored album, each taking three of the six records of Chopin's piano music as played by Rubinstein, then no longer available. Bobsy went back to being Ms. Diesel, which had, for her evangelical purposes, admittedly more resonance than the name lately shed. She had for five years been associate editor of an emancipationist magazine called *Femme* when Daisy, who had been largely out of touch with her since the tearful dispersions of graduation day, suddenly and to her surprise heard her voice on the phone.

"This is Bo."

"Bo?"

"Bo Diesel, silly. How *are* you, Daze? I want to tell you how impressed I've been with that series of yours in the *Long Island Watcher*. Both the consumerism and what you sneak in for the Cause. I wonder if you'd like to do something for *Femme*. I have an idea buzzing in my noodle for a series. Can you meet me in Manhattan for lunch tomorrow?"

Bo. She had bobbed her nickname, then, bringing it as far down from the original Roberta as it could get without being discarded altogether. Daisy forced herself to think new friends had done the pruning, not Bobsy herself, certainly not in the light of movie stars currently flashing across the glamour skies. Driving into the city the next day for the appointed lunch, she groomed herself for decency, vowing that while they chatted she would not think *schnecke,* and would not, *not* keep marking Bobsy's weird resemblance to Will Rogers. Something about the mouth and chin, provoking notions that she had a lariat concealed somewhere on her person, with which she would suddenly do tricks. Instead she would remain alert to new evidence of aplomb, of polemic derring-do, of sterling worth. Would the expiation for her wisecracks never end? Guilt traipse forever in her wake like a homeless dog? As a liberal she hated herself for a connective memory of their old cleaning woman, Mrs. Dexter, who had audibly wondered, one day at her chores, whether a neighbor marching past the house in mannish tweeds was "one dem 'lezibethans." Five Hail Marys.

She paused a moment in the restaurant doorway, having caught through a pane in the glazed vestibule a glimpse of the Diesel already seated in a snug favored corner of a place where she probably cut some local ice, elbows cocked on the table as she drew composedly on a Schimmelpen-ninck. She looked the intervening five years older, yet at the same time slimmed down and chiced up — as though she might have got *soignée* by dint of having been taken firmly in hand by a capon with a sense of physiological decor. She wore a blue wool dress, decent makeup, and her hair had been felicitously lightened. Oh, this kind of voyeurism was really deplorable, though we all engage in it, sometimes against our will, one shouldn't really be constantly, oh, my God, not *two* schnecken! Yes, each smaller than the remembered single crowning Danish —

half the size perhaps, tightly coiled — one on either side of the head, so that the front view gave the effect of an ill-fitting set of earphones. And the resemblance to Will Rogers eerier than ever. Ten Our Fathers.

The Diesel's grape-green gaze wandered to the front of the Straw Hat, as the restaurant was called, and Daisy swept through the inner door in the beige pants suit she thought Bobsy would dig, in such a gust of eagerness that she caught a whiff of her own perfume. "Bobsy!" as the Diesel rose as well as could be for one of those not-quite-kisses women exchange so as not to smudge each other's cheek. "Jesus, it's good to see you, Daze!" "And you too, Bobs, you're looking great. Minus a few pounds too," Daisy answered as she was shoehorned in behind a table the size of a throat lozenge.

They talked over old times, such as the sorority parties at which Bobsy sat at the piano and sang duets with her-self. Some laryngeal fluke enabled her to sing in two registers at once, so that she could single-handedly produce at least rudimentary harmonizations of simple melodies like "Tea for Two" and "My Bonnie Lies Over the Ocean." Dramatically, she would wrap a towel around her head when doing so; something about the resulting acous-tics made it possible for her to combine her normal con-tralto with a falsetto soprano. "We can all glissando from one register to another," she said, "the way a pianist glis-sandos a chord, but that's in sequence, one note after another, oh, let's talk about something else." She punched out her little cigar. "Have you heard anything from Effie? Married to an ophthalmologist named Colby. He does a lot with lasers."

They traded such gossip as they had over bloody Marys, Bobsy plunging into each subject in turn with the ravenous interest in personal detail to be expected in someone with a passion for kumquats. She ordered the chicken salad because they served it with kumquats there, as they did at the Algonquin, and when told by the waiter they didn't have it today, she switched to the available tuna salad, asking that they throw in some kumquats with that. Daisy ordered the same, and then they got on to Bobsy's divorce. She laughed about it, in the main good-naturedly. "Marriage is an unnatural condition," she said. "Almost a perversion. The rape of privacy. Once I caught him eating piccalilli per se. *Straight*. A dish of it, with a spoon. Or maybe it was a fork, it doesn't matter. He agreed with me about all the togetherness being too much. Never again for either of us." But Rats and Snails and Puppy Dogs' Tails had already remarried. "To the Amazon River," she said. But on to the business at hand.

"I want to run a series of articles on sexual harassment in offices. It will be frankly expository — I know I'm using the word wrong, but there's no adjective for exposé. That'll be the nature of the thing, flat out. You'll have to infiltrate places as an employee and get the firsthand goods on how women are expected to perform sexual favors, have affairs with the men in power, put it any way you want. This is a known fact about men running the shows there, and a few things *have* of course been said and written about it, but nothing in the way of a solid body of data. The woman as victim. The woman as sexual nigger. A female employee having to sleep her way up the corporate ladder."

"Would I be expected to actually do that?"

"No, no." Then laughed Bobsy — to recall a fad when they'd all for a time talked in inversions, like poets. Then shrugged Bobsy. "Of course you might find somebody you . . . But in the main it will be about sexist exploitation told from the woman's point of view. Refusing to put up with it. The threats, cajolings, propositions, the harassment as *such* would be all we'd need. You'll be ideal for it. You're attractive —"

"So are you, Bobsy." Handsome amends at last! "Why don't you be your own undercover agent?"

"Not in the way you are, come on now. And you write a sharp, pungent style. Plenty of pepper. That's what the thing needs. And of course I have to stay on the job at *Femme*."

"That brings up another question. Even supposing I'd have a taste for espionage, and a girl *would* be a spy, where would I get a job likely to pay off in the kind of intelligence you want — to use the polite word?"

Their food had come, and Bobsy ordered a carafe of white wine for them to split. Frowning as she picked up her fork, she said, "We already have intelligence *on* just that. A list of the companies with known leches on the prowl in them, seeking whom they may devour. So there's been plenty of preliminary undercover work. Don't ask me who my contacts are," she went on, lowering her voice as though they were CIA operatives within earshot of known double agents, "but I have three offices I'd like to put you into, and *can*, tomorrow. Secret personnel connections." Bobsy turned suddenly more sober still. "You *can* type, can't you? I mean not just hunt-and-peck. I seem to remember your learning it in your high-school days or something."

"I can type. Even take dictation." Daisy laughed in her turn. "Or resist it."

"Good. Really swell. Because we'd want you to start at the bottom, doing the white nigger work like in the stenographic pool. That's where the leches first feed, I understand, like Parisians seducing the little seamstress." The Diesel swallowed a mouthful of tuna salad, looking solemnly straight at her friend. "There's an opening right now at a wholesale stationery outfit called Pembroke Papers. I think with a phone call this afternoon I can pop you in there first thing Monday morning. Well, what do you say?"

"Oh, that's too soon. I'd have to give the *Watcher* a few weeks' notice. I wouldn't think of this if I wasn't getting fed up there — not a pleasant place to work."

"Done and done! Now let's talk salary."

Polishing off the Chablis, they came to terms in a suitably mellow frame of mind, and when the check came Bobsy would not hear of splitting it, as though they were still college classmates. Daisy asked assurance that she was on an expense account, and *Femme* was paying for this. "Oh, as to that!" the Diesel exclaimed, as though she were a heroine out of Henry James.

·4·

IT WAS IN FACT a full month before the Diesel smuggled
her into the Pembroke Papers offices, away over in west
midtown amid rather grimy warehouses and trucking
garages, by pulling strings about which she continued
clandestine, so that Daisy had no idea who her fellow operative was, or whether he or she was another plant on the
premises. The undercover hugger-mugger seemed by turns
sordid to her, and something legitimately spicing up em-
ployment dreary enough in all conscience. During her first
days, there was little doing in the typing pool to which she
was assigned, so she spent a good deal of time hanging
around the water cooler waiting to be harassed. When
nothing happened outside of an occasional coemployee
stopping to wish her well, or hurrying by with "Keep ya
thirsty, kid?" or some similar sally, she decided to ginger
her clothing up a bit. She came to work in a red silk dress
that showed some cleavage, wobbling about in what she
thought her "most senseless shoes," pumps with four-inch
heels that helped show off her ankles and calves, in them-

selves prettily hewn enough, to even more aphrodisiac advantage. Mrs. Deepshade, the iron-bosomed woman who rode herd on the white niggers in the typing pool (not a few of whom were black), cast some admonitory glances in her direction, and once, sniffing censoriously, murmured something about not having been aware she was running a brothel. Still nothing happened. The reportedly macho, or at least red-blooded, middle-aged executives bustled by on their chores, pausing to nod and smile when they stopped for a drink of water, but that was all. Where were the wolves she had been promised? So far the only grievance on which she could count was the knowledge that as a college-educated woman she was earning less than the average only-high-school-trained male, a familiar enough statistical American scandal.

But one morning molestation was forthcoming.

A thin, pink-haired young man with white eyelashes, phantasmagorically enlarged behind thick-lensed spectacles, came out of an office near the water cooler where Daisy again loitered, prolonging sips from a paper cup as though water were some kind of stuff she was "on," to be imbibed by the addict with systematic care in order to keep hazards to a minimum, so she would not o.d. on it. She had noticed him watching her before, but had ignored him as one hardly in a position to offer promotional perks in return for sexual favors. Out of the tail of her eye she had been aware of him again, observing her through his open door as she paused to chat with this man or that. Now he rose from behind his desk and, in shirt sleeves rolled up two cuff-lengths, sort of slithered through the door into the hall, smiling in a manner Daisy took to be definitely that of a man about to make a pitch. At last someone was *accosting* her!

"Have you made a decision yet?" he asked, drawing a cup from the dispenser tube.

"Decision?" She lowered her eyes and smiled demurely, as though denying any implication that she had in mind making a selection from the available males. "I don't understand. What do you mean?"

"For Christ." He held a thumb pressed against the faucet button till his Dixie cup overflowed, water streaming over its sides and down his fingers. "See that? That's how your cup will run over, when you accept Him. I found that out personally. You will too, if only you give your life to Him."

Whenever buttonholed by zealots, Daisy found it much the wisest course simply to say that you were already saved, much as you would tell a door-to-door salesman you didn't need anything today of whatever he was peddling. That usually stanched the evangelical flow, long enough to make one's escape. Not so here.

"I get the feeling — vibes as we say today — that you're spiritually empty. Impoverished. Living in a vacuum that wants to be filled. You'd be surprised what happens when you let Jesus rush in. I'm full of it."

"I know. I already go to a church," as though he was selling memberships in one. Maybe he was.

"You attend divine worship?"

"Regularly." On Easter and Christmas, like most tepid adherents of that admittedly most tepid of denominations, the Episcopal. Those Hail Mary routines were something picked up from a former boyfriend who was a lapsed Catholic for whom, nevertheless, the "umbiblical cord," as the crawling Quadrupedalist wit in Grand Rapids had put it, had not been completely cut, judging from the fact that, though intellectually emancipated blah blah blah, he was still emotionally blah blah blah with the church;

otherwise how explain his habit of muttering "Ten Hail Marys" after rising from a thrash in the sack with her, the guilt running out of his ears as he knotted his tie at the mirror? Or sometimes "Fifty Hail Marys" if it "was a good one." The Episcopal church of all bland diets! She'd recently had a dream that it had been bought by Minnesota Mining in a much-touted takeover. Twenty-four board members in charcoal-gray vested suits — no doubt representing the four and twenty elders in what? Revelation? — were sitting at a long table slicing up a melon, and at the head a pug dog smoking a meerschaum —

"Oh, if I could describe the change that came over my life when Jesus came into it. What a difference it made."

"That won't be necessary. I mean we all know the . . . that comes over . . . in people who. Well, I have to get back to the typing pool or Mrs. Deepshade will have my hide."

"I know you're in the typing pool, and new here. I hope you're happy. My name's Arthur Hearst. You're Daisy Dobbin."

Then had he in fact been casing her, one of those outwardly pious people beneath whose righteous surface intense lusts forever pulse and throb? What used to be called psalm-singing stinkers?

"Maybe we can have lunch sometime. Compare experiences. I know that for my first three years here, of course that was under a different management, because you know we've been just taken over . . ."

Visually roaming from one feature to another of Hearst's, who was not bad looking once you got past the cotton candy hair, Daisy was struck by a truth that had occurred to her before: namely, the difficulties involved in looking at somebody who is talking to you. You cannot focus on a face qua face at close quarters, only on this feature, then that, and so as Hearst dilated on his preconversion stresses she rambled over his chin, his teeth, of which the canines were set forward like Mickey Rooney's, finally with a sudden eyeball type of headache beginning to count his lashes, of which the lenses, acting as magnifying glasses, made a tally insanely possible. Any moment now she would scream. Who would come to her rescue? Where were the middle-management roués in which large corporations were said to abound? Where now when she needed them most?

At last she got away and hurried back to the pool, where Mrs. Deepshade, a herring keg rising and falling rhythmically inside a shirtwaist of Kelly green, was waiting for her with a report to type. It had to do with roadmen bagging their quarterly quotas, or not, as might betide.

To avoid Hearst and the threat of having to break bread with him, she switched to another water cooler, one away at the other end of the office, at a bend in the corridor where the foot traffic in men was thinner, to be sure, but choicer. Yes, distinctly so. She was being ogled. She felt it. She struck up acquaintance with three or four roughly departmental-head chaps in their seasoned forties. They often stopped to chat. Then finally one, a black-haired account executive named Leo Pocus, asked her to lunch. But that was all. No hanky-panky. No overtures. Nothing remotely resembling a pass, let alone threats of eternal stagnation on the stenographic level unless one played ball. He even showed her snapshots of his wife and three kids when he took out his wallet to pay for their weight-watcher fruit plates. He pored with special fondness over his youngest, a cherubic boy still crawling around on his hands and knees. "He gets into everything," Pocus chuckled. "We're having him baptized next Sunday."

"Don't you ever have any desire to break away?" Daisy asked.

"Break away?"

"I mean stray a little from the straight and narrow. Have a spot of sexual adventure on the side."

He looked at her with wide eyes. "Why, of course not. I would never think of cheating on the little woman. She's a jewel. I thank God for her every day of my life."

"But sleeping with only one person, the same one, all your life, don't you ever find it like eating the same thing for dinner every day? Or reading the same book over and over? Man is not by nature a monogamous animal, you know. The best psychologists recognize that. The natural need for variation leads, when permanently repressed, to all the neuroses that rack us."

"Really?" Pocus shook his head thoughtfully. "No, I'm happy with my Bertha." Here he did become a little lewd. "I sometimes hurry home for lunch."

Daisy sighed as, gathering her coat about her, she watched Pocus leave a tip so small she was half tempted to slip a coin or two herself onto the plate, and might well have had she not sidled out before instead of after him. The last of the heavy spenders bought a couple of apples from a sidewalk vendor as they strolled back among the warehouses to the office, giving her one to break her afternoon up with, snackwise.

She got herself up still more provocatively, wearing a pair of white linen slacks which were not only skintight, in a tradition now acceptable enough, but of which the seam was sort of drawn up into the cleft. Zilch. A scoop-neck cherry-red blouse to go with them. Zilch. What did you have to do to get a tumble from the men here, stand around in black net stockings, swinging your bag as you popped a wad of gum behind crimson lips? Whence came Pembroke's reputation for sexist pressure? Where was its bruited macho? There must be some mistake.

There was.

Pembroke Papers had, since the Diesel's intelligence on the house, been absorbed by a conglomerate headed by a tycoon of the pious breed, Prentiss W. Tremayne, who had wrought a thoroughgoing change in top brass, reflected downward through middle management and then lower-echelon levels, each department pursuing a replacement policy of hiring help so as to "maximize the atmosphere of Christian fellowship" Tremayne encouraged. Of Southern Baptist roots, he was a philanthropist who contributed heavily to both secular and sacred causes, with emphasis on the latter. He made large gifts to Billy Graham. The resulting change made for a milieu on which no temptress, however seductively bent on journalistic crusading, could have made much of a dent. The full weight of implications was borne in on Daisy Dobbin when a petition to bring prayer back into the public schools was circulated in the office. She refused to sign, as a born-again atheist.

"Get me out of this den of rectitude," she told the Diesel over the phone, utilizing a line from a novel she'd read in which a witty fag had called a local Ladies Aid society that.

"Love it," Bobsy said. "But yes, there's been a mixup. I'm sorry. The dope we got on Pembroke was all wrong — or rather the poop was outdated. It's not the reptile cage it used to be, I assure you, where your virtue wouldn't have been intact till noon. Let's have lunch and plan our next strategy. Can you make it to the Straw Hat again by twelve-thirty?"

"I only have an hour and I don't want to get fired if it'll wash out my severance pay. I want to *quit*."

"Let's make it Saturday then. I look forward to seeing you. And love your den of integrity. It's made my day."

"Rectitude."

Why did women always misquote you, get stories wrong, screw up the facts, talk in non sequiturs, lie blue streaks, and backbite till hell won't have it? Ten Betty Friedans.

Before they could meet, there was a turn in developments at the office, unexpectedly relieving the blank eventlessness in which Daisy saw her cause as having become bogged. Unoccupied typists often doubled in the glazed receptionist's cage outside the elevators, and Daisy was on duty there a few days later when the door opened and Leo Pocus stepped inside, swiftly closing the door behind him. There was a furtive, even distracted, air about him.

"How are you doing?" His taut smile indicated he had something more on his mind than passing the time of day.

"O.K. It gets a little boring in here."

He sighed hesitantly, and looked in a flustered way at her desk. He had on a suit of that featureless neither-quite-blue-nor-exactly-gray shade that is for some mysterious reason favored by businessmen.

"I heard about your refusal to sign that petition. Are you really an atheist?"

"As God is my judge," she said, and they both laughed.

"I think it's mainly that you believe in the separation of church and state. Yes, that's it." He nodded to himself, as though solidifying this extenuation in his own mind.

"That's probably it."

He glanced over at the elevator doors, then came a step farther into the cubbyhole. He gulped, and ran a finger under his collar, like an actor portraying a timorous swain.

"How about lunch again?" There was a hoarseness in his voice that made the invitation radically different from what it had meant the first time. It could only denote some intensification of his interest in her. Against her better judgment she said, "Well, all right." A woman lunching alone was always a somewhat pathetic sight, and even eating with God botherers beat brown-bagging it or muddling about in a crock of yogurt in an office where you already spent eight hours. "Sometime."

"How about tomorrow? I'll book a table at the Copper Kettle for twelve."

They got the same cramped corner as last time — Pocus could hardly be greasing any palms. He did something he hadn't before, drank two whiskeys in rapid succession to her single martini. His face became flushed, his voice took on a rasp, like a piece of chalk on a blackboard. At last: "I've been thinking about what you said the other day. On our first date." *"Date?!"* "About branching out and living a little, because you only live once?" His eyes rolled as he brought out, "Extracurricular sex you meant."

"Well, now, I don't . . ." She couldn't remember exactly what she'd said.

"You're a very attractive young woman, and I duh, duh, definitely respond to you. Especially after you . . . I realize that now. Definitely." Again he fidgeted with his collar and gulped like a smitten bumpkin. "I don't think any the less of you for, well, you're the New Woman. Take the aggressive, why not? The old barriers are down," he ranted wildly, as wildly as she listened, "equality between the sexes. One hundred percent. That television commercial, you know, some wine or other, the girl says it's O.K. to ask a man over for a drink. It's downright upright. That's dirty they tell me. A double entendre. Oh, my God."

Daisy laid a hand on top of her head, as though steadying the lid of a kettle about to boil over. "I thought you were religious."

"We're all human. You only go through this world once —"

"What about the afterlife? I thought you believed in that."

"I very much doubt there'll be any sex in that. You've got to pack it in now." He had finished his bourbon — or it had him — and his cheeks had taken on an additional flush when he looked away and said: "I don't know where we'd go."

"That's the trouble, you see," she answered with a calm she found demented. "So we'd best forget about it. Ships that pass in the night sort of thing. I'm going to quit anyway." A sudden decision, this time calmly rational. As though a close friend still in possession of her faculties had made it for her.

"Ah, but it's not so easy, once you, once the fire has been lit, a woman has ignited you, set your blood . . ." His eyes bulged and he gargled his words as he said, "I tossed and turned all night, thinking about you. And I will tonight too, that I promise, with my wife right there beside — Quit? What do you mean?"

Now quite mad, she said, "It would be best."

"Quit Pembroke?"

"Pembroke."

"But you're not — you'll still be around? Where is your apartment?"

"Is there much sex at Pembroke? I hear there used to be."

"It was a cesspool, but Mr. Tremayne put a stop to that. Men using it to get women promotions and so on. Now they'd get fired. I would if they ever got wind of us. Excommunication they call it. The new Moral Majority. So would you, so we've got to be careful." The swizzle stick from his drink cracked in two in his hands, and Daisy felt it might be the sound of her mind snapping as she heard Pocus say: "I'd tell my wife about us."

"Oh?"

"Oh, yes. I made a promise to her and to myself: I would never deceive her. Cheat I wouldn't. Deceive I won't. Lie I can't."

"Have you ever done this sort of thing before?"

He shook his head firmly, his mouth a resolute line. "Never. This is the first time I ever lusted after another woman. Committed adultery in my heart."

Lusted . . . Committed adultery in my heart. That had a familiar ring. Of course. President Carter in the famous *Playboy* interview.

She rose to leave, and not only so as not to see the size of the tip Leo Pocus left this time. She must end a conversation she would in retrospect refuse to believe had taken place. Her recollections must be aberrant. "I must get back to the office. We shouldn't be seen together too much."

"No — not now. The gang will soon realize you've got me running a fever over you, my Daisy."

She got out of the Copper Kettle in a kind of walking sprint, and, having gained the street, consulted her wristwatch. One o'clock exactly. She was due back, but saw no harm in arousing Mrs. Deepshade's disapproval now by returning fifteen or twenty minutes late since she was going to get the hell out of there anyway. She needed a little stroll in the open air to cool her head, sort out her thoughts. As a lame duck in an office that had flunked out as far as her cause was concerned, she had gone back to wool skirts and the sensible shoes in which she could now comfortably stride among the warehouses and parking garages, even then drawing ogles and occasional wolf whistles from truck drivers pulling in and out of them. A feminist as ardent as any in essentials, she was not blind to a few of the movement's idiocies and lunacies. The word sexist was probably its crowning foolishness. Who would not want to be whistled at by truck drivers? She had smiled gratefully back at a few in her time. And "the maternal instinct is a creation of the male brain." Had she not read that in a biography of Colette written by a liberationist? What rubbish. It was girls' mothers who bought them their dolls, not their fathers. Her own had given her dolls that talked, walked, cried, wet, and recited the Lord's Prayer and the Declaration of Independence. Well, anyway the preamble. There was a doll that saluted, another that, let's see, sneezed, there was one that fed itself from a spoon which you filled, which was then raised to its mouth, dumped, and the contents sent down through a tube leading to a disposable diaper. And so now you were supposed to bristle doubly when a man called you a doll. And all this long and winding trail had led to poor dear old Leo Pocus, who had just made her feel like Doll Tearsheet.

Her round-the-block stroll got her back to the office building just as Pocus drew up there himself. Worse than that, there were no others in the elevator when they walked into it, nor in the lobby waiting to get on. Pocus poked the button for their floor, then stepped back, so that they stood side by side, their shoulders touching. Let there be other passengers, at least one, *come, somebody,* Daisy prayed as she watched the starter look down the foyer to the right, then the left. He shrugged, pressed a signal button on the panel behind him, and the door slid shut.

Pocus drew her around with one arm and turned his

face toward hers. The car jerked, and was still. Good God, what if it stalled? The door twitched, hesitated, twitched again, and at last the car rose. Pocus pressed his mouth to hers, one hand clamping her head in what bad fiction writers had once called a vise-like grip. As he kissed, she kept an eye on the lighted numbers overhead, registering the floors past which they slid. Five . . . ten . . . She could just see the figures past his left ear. She mumbled a protest, smothered in something he was saying about brushfires and when it was too late to put them out, the trees had caught. Eleven . . . She'd expected he'd be reeking of whiskey, but such was not the case. There was about him a rather pleasant personal air having nothing to do with after-shave lotion. There floated grotesquely to mind something she'd read in a biography of H. G. Wells. Asked what made the famous womanizer so attractive, a mistress was said to have answered, "He smells like honey." What a lot of truck we collect in a lifetime, to have crop up at what incredible moments. Eighteen, nineteen. The door opened, after another twitch of hesitation giving her another moment of panic.

The receptionist being busy on the phone, there was no one to witness the brief word with which Pocus detained her in the foyer.

"Will you agree to meet my wife, so we can be open and aboveboard about this thing?"

She could not believe her eyes, ears, nose and throat — especially the last-mentioned, which somebody was using to say "All right." In retrospect (two minutes later as she slid in behind her typewriter under the disapproving eye of Mrs. Deepshade), she figured she had responded as she had in order to cut short an exchange Pocus would have continued in the attempt to persuade her, one whose nature the receptionist could ultimately not have mistaken, even without hearing the words. Her reply should keep Pocus quiet for the few days before she would be gone, never to see him again.

She would have liked to meet Mrs. Pocus, the family, in real life, if that's what this was. Plain folks, to be sure, real people, as they themselves would say, possessing rock-solid virtues not to be taken lightly or to go altogether unmourned by those quick with the word corny. They had faith, even in retribution; even their superstitions of some value. They harked back to a time when daughters were still "ruined." How could you ruin a daughter today, with everybody thrashing permissively around in the sack from the age of fourteen? Their daughters were ruined and their sons went blind (or insane) from masturbation. The old values. Relatives got appendicitis from eating grape seeds, dying in thunderstorms they knew would sour the milk and spoil the cheese. Thus Daisy woolgathered at her machine, until the patrolling Mrs. Deepshade sent her into a fresh spasm at the keyboard. How had she ever got into this? Maybe the proper study of mankind wasn't man after all, but woman.

Why had she broken off with Al Morley, Jeff Bolt, and one or two others with whom she'd had reasonably happy interludes? Because she didn't want to marry any. Which must indicate by a subtle inversion that marriage was what she wished, since it operated as a criterion in judging her men along the way, whether as a feminist she admitted it to herself or not. Or, alternatively, that she *didn't* want to marry, because they were all perfectly intelligent, adequately amusing, reasonably solvent, physically palatable men, though none to the best of her recollection smelled precisely like honey. She very much doubted she would have enjoyed being ravished by H. G. Wells, whatever his bouquet. What a lot of slush we pick up in the name of erudition. An aphorism attributed to Lord Chesterfield — "The pleasure is momentary, the position ridiculous, and the expense damnable" — had once or twice come to mind in mid-love, when, not to shortchange the heaving biped grinding her bones in the gloom, she had nevertheless charitably feigned paroxysm, crying "Ah! Ah!" in a diminuendo of counterfeited bliss, so that her glutted rider could dismount, collapsing onto his back like an empty gunnysack.

The Pocuses would all be innocent of this smarmy self-inventory. "Tell me about that there laid-back narcissism," the old grandmother would ask Daisy, after the two wrongdoers had set a spell with Mrs. Pocus and been forgiven. "I read about it in the papers and hear about it on the television panels," shifting a clove in her teeth, "them panels where professors hold conversations about what's going on these days. Tell me about that there laid-back narcissism I hear so much about these days. Tell me about shacking up, and what are items? Two people together are an item, it says in the gossip columns. Two people are a thing. Are you and Leo an item? Are you a thing?"

Daisy now made her trips to the cooler as brief as possible, but this afternoon she sensed somebody behind her as she gulped off a quick belt of water. It was Hearst, staring at her through his dense spectacles like a fish behind aquarium panes.

"When can you have lunch with me?" he said in a voice as thick as his glasses. "Remember we talked about it, when you used to come to the other cooler. I hope you're not avoiding me."

"Oh, no, nothing of the sort." She began another eyeball

headache, counting his white lashes. "It's just that, working mostly at the other end . . ."

"I know you do lunch with men."

"Yes." She lunched with men. A Jezebel. "That would be nice, but I'm going to quit."

"That's too bad. Maybe you'll give me your number, or call me here. I want to give you this pamphlet in any case," Hearst said, pressing into her hand a small booklet entitled *Wise Men Still Seek Him.* She riffled through it. Things about sowing and reaping, making your bed in Sheol.

"Well, thanks a lot. I'll read it tonight, or at the very latest, soon. This will be a nice souvenir from you anyway. Meanwhile, what is Sheol?"

"Hell."

"Ah, yes. I remember now."

·5·

THE DIESEL WAS quite out of sorts over the turn of events, her displeasure with the operative who had fed her false intelligence about the target corporation being so great as to temporarily pollute her relations with everyone, Daisy included. "It's not my fault, you know," Daisy said. *"I'm the real patsy."* She didn't especially look forward to the luncheon at which they would plan their next strategy. She arrived at the Straw Hat a few minutes early, and was shown to the Diesel's table. She improved the wait by listening, as unobtrusively as she could, to the conversation at the next. After a moment, she placed a woman there who had looked tantalizingly familiar. She was to be seen on television blowing manageability into her hair, when not advertising a mattress coming in twenty firmnesses. Dress of black wool jersey, expensive simplicity, a gold necklace surely destined to be snatched. Companion vaguely identifiable as a professional associate. Ruddily handsome man in middle age, thick mop of hair turning the color of February slush. Beard reviving the antique query did he sleep with it over or under the covers. She waved a cigarette holder like a sceptre, clearly accustomed to holding court.

"You must plan everything, not just your will, but the funeral services, how, what, then put it all away and forget about it. Guardians for your children too, in case anything happens to you. Mac and I have even decided on who gets custody of the child if we get divorced."

"You have a child?"

"We're expecting one in November."

Two schnecken floated just above the café curtains in the window, and the Diesel was here, bearing down on their table. Trouble with Rats and Snails and Puppy Dogs' Tails had caused her mood to deteriorate still further. Something about property settlements. They had agreed to divide moneys realized from the sale of the house, but it was still on the market, with R. and S. and P.D.T. trying to keep everything got from the interim rental for himself. "He's married again, have I told you about the Amazon River, and says he needs the money. Well, who doesn't. He claims now that I agreed to this when I did no such thing. With again the old husbands' tale about how women get everything wrong." She had just passed a church where a debouching bridal couple had once more been symbolically sprayed with the male sperm known as rice. "Why is the fertility symbol always masculine? Mistletoe, I guess we all know why *that's* sacred. Huh!"

"It isn't always," Daisy said, to comfort her. "In many countries they break eggs on the bride's head, I think."

"Yolk and albumen all over her? Pretty a sight as you could ask."

"No, no, the shells are stuffed with confetti and so on by the good folk of the village. Here it's one thing, there it's another. I've heard that in certain African tribes for a wedding feast they serve a kind of stringy white soup —"

"*Please*, not while I'm eating. Or hoping to. Where the hell's that waiter? Oh, there you are. Frank, I'm sure my friend will join me in the usual. Two bloody Marys."

The Diesel's spirits were in for another setback. The waiter shook his head with the crimp-mouthed expression of those who take satisfaction in retailing calamity. "There's no bartender."

"What are you talking about?"

The waiter jerked his head toward a large party of women behind him, twenty-five or thirty in bright dress-up best, clearly an office group celebrating "one of them's birthday or either one of them's retirement," as he put it, a bunch of clucking hens whose cocktail order was as follows. "You want to hear it?" the waiter said, and read it aloud from his order pad.

"Three martinis, one on the rocks, two up, with twist, olive and onion respectfully, two Manhattans, two bloody Marys. So far so good, no harm in that, but now hold on to your hats. Three sidecars, a pink lady, two grasshoppers, an angel's kiss, two Margaritas, *one not too much salt*, a gimlet, a between the sheets, a Mamie Taylor, two Alexanders, a bee's knees, Lord give me strength —"

"That's a drink?"

"No, no, that's me crying out. Christ, the bartender don't know what half these things are any more than I do. A Gertie's garter, a blood and sand, a King Alphonse, and two Rob Roys." He flipped the order pad shut and thrust it into a hind pocket. "See that guy going out the door putting on his hat and coat? That's the bartender. That's the last we'll ever see of him here. Of course in a way he's blown his honor, like a soldier chickening out under fire, but still I can't blame him. Whether he'll blow his brains out it's too early to tell. I always knew one of them would crack under the strain of" — again he gestured with his head — "one of them."

"What on earth is a Mamie Taylor, or a between the sheets?" Daisy asked. "I've never heard of them."

"Neither have I. Neither has he, probably, not even in bartender school. And consult a recipe book he won't. That's to a bartender's shame too — looking something up. His honor won't permit it."

Both women craned their necks to observe emergency readjustments behind the bar. The couple who owned and ran the restaurant had apparently flung themselves into the breach and were beckoning the waiter over with the rejected order. He scurried off, promising to see what he could do about their drinks as soon as possible. Daisy and Bobsy got down to business.

The new corporation to be infiltrated was *Metropole*. The go-between was none other than Effie Sniffen Colby, who worked in the business department of the periodical in question. As a fifth-column plant, she thought she could get Daisy a job in the editorial end, by pulling strings with the personnel manager there. Though Daisy was clearly qualified for a post of more importance, they thought she should parachute into the typing pool as a white nigger, a bottom rung from which promotions to higher levels could be offered in return for sexual favors; alternatively, denied if cooperation was.

"There's so much hanky panky going on there that nobody knows how they get the magazine out every week," Bobsy said. She read from notes dug out of her bag. "The all-time, barefaced championship lecher seems to be a guy in the makeup department known as Dog Bokum, who thinks *Playboy* glorifies women, and who glorifies them himself by taking them out for what he calls lunch-hour quickies, or nooners. What in a more genteel age were called matinees. All you have to do to have Dog pay you court by jerking his head toward the elevator at twelve sharp is not be cross-eyed, have not more than two nostrils, and your ears pasted on straight. He has a midtown apartment near the office, which makes it convenient — a sprint down the street and slam-bam-thank-you-ma'am. His female counterpart seems to be a girl so obliging she's known as Immediate Occupancy, but that's neither here nor there, though she'd be among your competition. Now —"

"Hold it. This is something we never got straight with Pembroke either. Just how much am I expected to do for England?"

The Diesel gave her rug-merchant shrug, spreading her hands. "That's up to you. All you do is *research the amount and nature of sexual pressure on women in the American labor market.* How far you want to go personally is up to you. Of course you can recount the experiences of other women. The perks and the penalties, for sleeping with the bosses and not."

"What constitutes a 'boss'? Does Effie have anything more about this — God, I can hardly say it — Dog Bokum?"

"Yes." Bobsy shuffled her notes. "Dog is *head* of makeup, which has traditionally been all-male but has recently been integrated. There's one woman in it now."

"Immediate Occupancy?"

"I think."

"One of Dog's — the words that have to cross your lips — nooners?"

The Diesel nodded weightily. "One of his nooners."

"Why isn't Effie here with us? If she's our vacuum cleaner."

"She mustn't be seen with us. *Metropole* people lunch here."

"And if she's got all the dirt, why doesn't she write the articles herself?"

"Oh, Effie can't write. She splits infinitives like they were kindling wood. And she wants to be kept out of this, so that, and this is important, her name must never be mentioned in connection with it, whether the mission fails or succeeds. She likes her job selling advertising and doesn't want to jeopardize it. Things aren't going too well with Doctor Colby," Bobsy added, a glint in her eye suggesting that her radar had already caught the rumor of another divorce. She stuffed the notes back into her bag, cancelling the fear that they might have to divide them, chew them up and swallow them, like spies disposing of secret documents once their contents have been memorized. Dog Bokum, Immediate Occupancy . . . How would the Diesel herself have fared there as the *Lay Misérable?* Ten Hail Marys.

"Andy Squibb," she said, snapping her bag shut. "He's the personnel head cum office manager in the editorial department. He devotes Wednesday afternoons to interviews. Effie has spoken to him about you, and now you're to write a letter with a yummy resumé, asking to be seen. That part's as good as in the bag. Our drinks, don't tell me. Well, here's luck. Look, I'm really sorry Pembroke was such a washout. I'm still loving your den of righteousness."

"Rectitude."

Why didn't women ever get anything right? Ten Emmeline Goulden Pankhursts.

Andy Squibb responded within ten days to Daisy's letter, and it was with a high heart and every hope of early defilement that she set out to keep an appointment with him scheduled for three o'clock the following Wednesday. Striding down the corridor toward the office to which she was directed by the receptionist, a stringy brunette in overalls eating a Twinkie while reading Gide in the original, she already had a sampling of what she was up against in the way of competition: girls markedly younger than she, casual and assured in an environment where clothes themselves apparently meant nothing. The Twinkie-Gide bit had been no misrepresentation. They swung along, the girls, with their marketable little bottoms snugly encased in dungarees, their breasts galloping in any old thing — shirt, blouse, sweater. One or two chatted in doorways, or tarried in the hall in smiling exchanges with men for the most part in shirt-sleeves, pleasantly detained in the everlasting grind of moving paper from one place to another. Any one might be Immediate Occupancy or Dog Bokum. At the end of the corridor she "hung a left," as the Gide reader had instructed, musing to herself that the prospects for degradation here must be notably better than at Pembroke, despite Leo Pocum's fall from grace and the first signs of fissure in Hearst's moral edifice. She trusted she would never hear from either again. Here was a proper den of iniquity at last, by all accounts.

A secretary pointed her through an open doorway into Squibb's office, which had a couch, from which Squibb, himself in shirt-sleeves, rose. He gallantly waved her to it. He explained that his air conditioner was on the blink, which accounted for the mid-July mugginess in his lair. She must feel free to shed the coat of the raspberry-colored linen suit she was wearing, which she promptly did. He put it on a wire hanger after removing his own coat from it, which he then hung on one of two nails driven into the wall. Reports of this magazine's anti-chic were not exaggerated. It was all the rabbit warren one had been promised.

Squibb had crinkly dark hair, neatly barbered and sideburned, and a thin mustache that seemed like two rivulets of tar running out of his nostrils and spreading symmetrically to the sides of his lip. His desk was a heap of documents, letters and newspapers, one of which, Daisy noted, was a copy of the *National Now Times,* the official journal of the National Organization for Women. His sharp black eyes took in her note of it. He stood with the flat of one hand against a rather dirty wall, so that his tautened red suspender raised his trouser crotch enough to throw into advantageous relief the bulging pouch of jewels within.

"I'm a feminist," he said.

Oh, my God, not another nut. Though most militants welcomed masculine support, Daisy had her doubts about the ilk, who muddled the issues and disheveled battle lines best left cleanly drawn. They turned up on television panels seriously airing the problems of discrimination, and by championing the women's crusade diluted its case and confused people, or so it seemed to Daisy. Bobsy Diesel's view was surprisingly enough that of American foreign policy since World War II: "Take allies where you can find them, however rotten." Well, an ally of that kind here might seriously hamstring Daisy's investigative mission by safeguarding her against precisely the harassment she was here to research. He might even have his own vigilantes in the office. Did the Diesel have a dossier on this character? Did Effie? What was wrong with her intelligence, a second time awry!

But now Squibb, dismantling the macho tableau and putting back into perspective the bully bag, struck a more hopeful note.

"My sister gave me a subscription to this for Christmas. That ardent a camp follower I'm not, though I am for the ERA and equal pay and all that, which I try to foster here, though the bosses in the business tend to drag their heels on it. Enlightened as we are, I still couldn't offer you what a man would get for the same work. Effie Sniffen says you might be interested in work as a copyeditor." For this foul-up in communication she was grateful: it would be better than the typing pool, God knew. "Have you done any of that?"

"Yes, for Rawlins and Healy," she said, deceptively naming a publishing house now safely defunct. What a jungle it all was! Squibb struck the tableau again, throwing the goodies into bas-relief more pronounced than before. Keeping her gaze resolutely raised, she started an eyeball headache.

"You didn't mention it in your résumé." He nodded at the Collier brothers mess on his desk.

"Didn't I? I may have neglected to do so because I basically thought I was just applying for *anything* you might have open, even the typing pool. I can take dictation." Damn, why was she screwing herself up?

"Wow! Do you know that of all the typists we've got out there now, not one can take dictation? This I've got to see."

"As for proofreading, I've got all those marks, the squiggle for delete in vertical parentheses for delete and close up, the tic-tac-toe frame for insert space, the comma cradled in a *V* for insert apostrophe, all floating around in my bloodstream like letters in a bowl of alphabet soup." This was true enough from three years on her college magazine. The fictitious hitch at Rawlins and Healy could have done no more.

Squibb ignored her, having extracted at random a magazine from the compost on his desk. "I'm going to fire a paragraph or so off to you and then you type out what you've taken down — here's a dictation pad — and we'll see what comes out." She readied herself with the pad and a pencil, noting how his little black-raspberry eyes took in her legs when she crossed them in order to prop the pad on her knee. Was this at last the pigsty she had been promised? He was really not unattractive, in a sort of fresh barnyard way. Was she going at last to be hectored by a cofeminist? It was getting a little baroque. He began to rattle off something from a short story.

"Quote apostrophe ello comma apostrophe ello bang close quote. It was Henley open paren the daft Englishman he'd met in the bar last night open second paren and rashly given his number close double paren babbling into the phone Feversham wished he hadn't answered dot. Tina comma the girl he'd picked up in the same bar comma apparently lay beside him dash no cap wasn't that her name Q. Open ital Feversham wasn't even sure close ital double bang. New paragraph —" Squibb laughed. "I won't torture you any more. If you can type that and it comes out looking half like what I've read it from, why, I'll have to give you something. I have to see somebody down the hall a minute. You can use my typewriter here. I'll be right back."

When he returned presently Daisy handed him the typed draft:

> " 'ello, 'ello!" It was Henley (the daft Englishman he'd met in the bar last night (and rashly given his number)) babbling into the phone Feversham wished he hadn't answered. Tina, the girl he'd picked up in the same bar, apparently lay beside him — wasn't that her name? *Feversham wasn't even sure!!*

Squibb smiled as he read it, stroking the pencil mustache with the ball of his finger. He raised his eyebrows in appreciation. "Not a bobble. Not fiction we'd ever print, but anyway. Well, O.K. Would you mind starting with Huxley's monkeys for a bit? I've really nothing in proofreading right now, but if an opening turns up, and of course I'd have to give you a test just as rigid as this. It's done and done as far as the pool is concerned, so if you want to start at our notorious slave wage" — and he named a figure fully deserving the name — "I'll be glad to take you round to Mrs. Gromley, the warden there. Claims to be short of typists, so you can probably start next week. Would you like to have lunch your first day? If you're a good girl I may tell you the meaning of life."

She watched Andy Squibb distribute tartar sauce on his entire filet of sole, dipping his knife into a ramekin in which the sauce had been separately served, and spreading it on as one would butter a slice of bread. The last time she had seen that done had been the occasion when she and her parents decided they could no longer take her grandfather out in polite society. "Gramps, you dab on a forkful at a time, daintily, like so . . ." Squibb sauced his sole neatly, evening the edges, like a bricklayer spreading mortar with a trowel. He twisted around in his chair, as though on the point of looking for the waiter in order to ask for more, but happily did not, falling to instead.

"I was an ardent fisherman once," he said. "Then one day I suddenly gave it up. Decided it wasn't worth it. I remember the afternoon well."

"What happened?"

"I caught sixty-three mackerel."

"And that discouraged you?"

"Wouldn't it you? How would you like to clean sixty-three fish, then eat all you could, phone your friends frantically to get rid of some so they wouldn't sit around smelling the house up, the guts . . . Heads, eyes gazing accusingly up at you. You know who your friends are when you've caught sixty-three fish. I thought, this is a mug's game. But I like to eat fish. Any kind except bluefish. I feel they're too oily."

"I couldn't agree with you more," Daisy answered, with a force aimed at emphasizing areas of compatibility. She had been trying to get the subject around to sex, without any success. They were lunching at the Straw Hat, the Diesel seated at her usual table with Effie, where they couldn't quite see their undercover operative at work. They had exchanged the most covert of nods, Daisy and the Diesel, betraying no familiarity, like compatriot spies feigning total ignorance of one another in a foreign land.

Squibb said: "Who's the dike with Effie Sniffen?"

"I don't know. Has anyone ever told you you have beautiful hands?"

"Do you want to write?"

"What?"

"Most girls with the gleam in their eye you have get a job with us because they want to write for us. Pieces. Stories."

"I used to write poetry, but the *New Yorker* and *Poetry* turned everything down so I quit."

Squibb had laid down his fork and was inspecting his hands with curiosity, as though picking up a pair of vases on which she had commented. "My hands? Really?"

"Look at the way the thumbs taper."

"All right. So have you. Your hands — mine aren't — your hands are like alabaster. I should be doing this like in the Old Testament. Thy hands are like alabaster," taking one in his own and turning it over as though, this time, he was indeed examining a rare work of art.

· 73 ·

"Why, thank you, Andy." She lowered her eyes into her scampi, managing not to flutter the lashes.

"They have the translucence of alabaster, which is, actually, a white, or tinted, fine-grained gypsum. I realize it falls down in a heap there, the gypsum bathos, but I know things like that because I used to work in the checking department, and once there was a piece with a lot about alabaster in it. Your complexion is just as clear, not a blemish on it. The reason I suggested we *meet* somewhere, not leave the office together: I'm not supposed to play favorites, cultivate fondnesses that get in the way of impartial judgments." He relinquished her hand and once more fell on his well-mortared sole. "Of course lunching with men is different, you're bound to make friends in an office. But if you're lunching with a pretty girl the whole thing takes on a different connotation. Especially at *Metropole*. What goes on there! Of course the Puritan ethic is dead as a doornail, and good riddance to it, but maybe the pendulum is swinging too far in the other direction." He lifted a skillfully burdened fork and chewed thoughtfully for a time, gazing off into the distance. When he spoke he was wagging the tines at her. "I personally take a dim view of this in-and-out-of-the-sack stuff, don't you? I mean it trivializes the very sex we want to enjoy."

Ah, at last! This pitch every girl knew. Of all forms of seduction it was the craftiest: seduction by chastity. She might do a whole article on the various masculine techniques. Most of which weren't translucent, either, but downright transparent.

"Anybody would know you couldn't be had casually, and I couldn't be casual about you." How strongly he disapproved of the shenanigans he was trying determinedly to march her toward was expressed by further disquisitions on

· 74 ·

the sanctity of the flesh and the pagan dignity of mating. Predictable quotations from Havelock Ellis, not a little D. H. Lawrence. "And here's where I, well, not part company with the feminists so much as differ with the reigning ideology. There *is* a double standard that's not discriminatory, or is against the man. Like if you and I were lovers, right?"

"Yes?"

"If so, it would be O.K. for you to kiss and tell, but if I did I should be taken out and shot. We don't want your sort in this club, Markham. That's the code. And you're the beneficiary. Don't you agree?"

"Well, yes, you've got me there." Daisy decided to give him his head, though beginning another eyeball headache, attributable again to the already noted problem of how to look at somebody talking to you close up. Her eyes roamed from his mouth to his nose, then hairline, then back to the mouth, with its really fine set of teeth recalling her own father's, which her mother called "consistently rewarding." Consistently rewarding teeth. Well, her own true parents were dancing the night away at Domblémy . . . Squibb warmed to his subject, again putting his fork down for the moment and wriggling forward in his chair. "Woman *is* the object of desire, the chosen vessel, idol of artists, glorified in song and story. So we judge her more harshly than we do the man in a case of sexual, sexual, oh, I mean we come down doubly hard on Immediate Occupancy but who's going to care about Dog Bokum except laugh at him. I rode down in the elevator with him, clutching a bag lunch to grab a bite in bed with some piece in his pad, as he calls it, though I believe the term is passé. Taking *out* sandwiches he's had *sent in,* to save time. Tie that. I said to Dog once, 'Dog, this office is a pigsty,' and do you know

· 75 ·

what he said?" Daisy turned the stem of her wineglass, lowering her gaze in hopes of a moment's relief from the eyeball headache, as she shook her head. "He said, 'Thank God.' " Squibb shook his own head, conveying an entirely different value. "Where were we? Yes." He wagged the fork again to stress his point. "You're censured precisely because you've been put on a pedestal. You *have fallen.* That's corny now, but I mean just as a figure of speech. I mean the double standard is something instinctive with the species. You can't have it both ways — be glorified but not subject to censure. I can't fall because I'm already on the floor, at floor level, on my knees, a man, worshipping you."

How helpless we are to read another's thoughts precisely at those moments when we'd most wish to, Daisy mused. This was one of the decentest men she'd ever met or the intergalactic champion lecher utilizing the great gimmick, sincerity, which ought to be about as low as you could sink. One of her teachers at Kidderminster had been a dehydrated old party who was fond of quoting a mot attributed to Talleyrand, partly for the pleasure of adding that it wasn't original with Talleyrand at all but lifted from a contemporary and retailed without credit: "Man was given the gift of speech in order that he might disguise his thoughts." Animals lacked it, therefore not even buffaloes could buffalo one another, the d.o.p. had added. But here was duplicity eminently worth smoking out, if such it was. She must first nudge the subject around to Sex and the Job. Was there often a quid pro quo in sleeping with a colleague? A higher-up? Had the woman successfully at last integrating makeup's previously male preserve done so by sleeping with Dog Bokum? Andy Squibb would know or confirm things like that if anybody did. The Diesel's data shouldn't be accepted automatically.

"Tell me, did Immediate —"

"Did you read Hart Crane in college?"

"Not in college, no," Daisy said, to imply that she read more than was formally crammed down her throat, "but I've read him of course. Why, what did you have in mind?"

Squibb didn't answer for the moment, being deep in a thoughtful gaze elsewhere. "That dike with Effie. I've seen her somewhere."

"Oh, she's not a dike."

"Why, do you know her?"

"No, no, I mean just because somebody wears bowties and smokes cigars doesn't mean she's a lesbian. You've probably seen her somewhere before, maybe here, is why she looks familiar. Or maybe she reminds you of somebody."

"That's it! Who?"

Daisy turned in her chair, pretending to scrutinize a stranger. How had she got herself into this ridiculous pickle? "Will Rogers?" she said, and the cock crowed twice. Or was it thrice? In any case, ten Our Fathers.

"That's it! You're right. How did you ever —?"

"What were you saying about Hart Crane?"

"For one thing he satisfies the craving for rhetoric, which we're all starved for. It's out today. Begone, rhetoric! Amscray! 'Raus!" Several nearby lunchers looked over as a result of his exclamations. The wine was getting to him. He poured them both some more of the carafe of Chablis between them. "Didn't Yeats say sentiment was fooling other people while rhetoric was fooling yourself?"

No, he didn't, it was just the other way around, if memory served. But like a lady, or even a gentleman, Daisy forbore correcting Squibb, who, after another gulp of wine, looked to be off on another recitative like the pedestal one.

His cheeks were flushed and his eyes glittered. She thought of Leo Pocus.

"One does miss the sheer ink-slinging like you got in Faulkner, and Wallush, Wallace Stevens could still dish out rhetoric, though with a certain . . . a certain . . ."

"Urbanity?"

"Urbanity. Yes. That's it exactly." How they were grooving! Or was that expression out too, like pad?

"I agree." She was agreeing with herself. "Actually, in rereading Hart Crane recently, I found that those sentences that pick you up and send you out through the transom are few and far between." She laughed apologetically as she reached for her own glass. "But it was you who were saying something about Hart Crane."

"Mmm. Now it's slipped my mind. Go back. Woman, pedestal, glorifi — Yes, now I remember. That terrific sentence from the 'Powhatan's Daughter' section of *The Bridge*." He fixed her with a preparatory smile, as though a past as an actor had equipped him with the knack of telegraphing that a zinger was en route. "Ready?"

"Shoot."

" 'And she is virgin to the last of men.' "

His eyes loitered over her face with a kind of pious carnality, as though he was prepared to illustrate the principle he had been enunciating by sinking to his knees, let the other customers think what they would, and worshipping at her shrine then and there. "I take it to mean, probably not what the poet intended, but anyway, to mean that a woman's virginity is renewed for each man she lovingly takes, and he her. That would be you, to any man, to myself, a fresh lover, to any man worthy of the name, each time anew."

Her head swam with visualized commas, but still she

had lost the grip on his syntax, as had he himself, seemingly, but each time *anew?* Had she heard aright? It was like a celluloid collar, the word, like a bustle, a farthingale, whatever that was. It went with "thus we see" and "afresh." She decided he was nice, but probably a little shy and in need of encouragement. By centimeters she had been moving her foot toward his, until now she could, well within the timetable, just, *just* feel the toe of a shoe against the sole of his. All but *not* feel it, as in the case of her knee next queasily edged against his. It was more that the hem of her skirt could sense the fabric of his trousers — leaving any question of actual pressure up to him. That she now felt as, in an experimentation finely calibrated as her own, he tipped the weight of his leg against hers. He looked away as he did so, as though unaware of physical contact in what were certainly extenuatingly cramped quarters. Daisy looked into her glass as again she twirled its stem in her fingers. "You certainly make a woman feel good. *Decent.* 'Virgin to the last of men.' I'd forgotten that line."

"Would you like to get out of the typing pool?"

"Would I!"

At last she felt like a target female. But where would it lead, other than merely out of the typing pool? Andy Squibb said, "I expect an opening in proofreading in a few weeks," which, since it was only proofreading, would make her a white mulatto. A step up. Only copyediting could restore to her her Caucasian pigment. Which was all right, in that almost any change of position was a vantage point from which to observe the price exacted — or no, asked — in a certainly male-dominated corporation.

But to sort out her feelings about Andy Squibb himself had now become all but impossible, since involved in them would be certain variables now forever lost, forever unknowable because of the special circumstances under which an estimate must be made. That is, if she had simply *met* him somewhere, anywhere, under purely social circumstances unvitiated by journalistic motivations, would she have responded to any genuine overtures, seductive or otherwise? He was a reasonably good-looking, physically palatable bloke with a refreshingly old-fashioned quixotic view of women (unless, of course, all that turned out to be a mare's nest of an Oedipal mess). It was worth exploring, her undercover work apart. Was he playing a game? She would find that out soon enough by making it clear that she wasn't playing musical offices with her virtue. There must be no strings. Let him promote her if he wished, and then we'd see. She herself was playing a game, and therefore began to feel a little like those spies in adventure stories who find themselves growing fond of people they are ostensibly planted to use, and thus end up bromidically "torn between love and duty." "Virgin to the last of men" was such a sweet thing for a girl to have fetched up for her, she thought, even as she felt the pressure against her knee become unmistakable. Then he said, "Oh, I'm sorry, am I bumping you? It's pretty snug in here," and withdrew his knee. "Why, I'll have to give you that test for proofreading, which I'm sure you can pass. Hell, you can take it home, easy enough to cheat, so we'll consider it done. Find out when Georgia Walsh is actually leaving, and then see. Look, is Effie Sniffen a lezzy?"

"Good God, no. I lived with her for two years at college, and you should know that much about your roommate. She's married. Not that that's taken to mean much any more these days. Doctor Colby is a top ophthalmologist. Of course you hear they're getting divorced."

They got out with a minimum of regard from the other women, and Squibb asked her to come to his office for the sample galley to proofread. Waving her to the visitor's chair, he sat down on the couch, then after a moment drew his legs up, leaning over with his head propped on an arm, like a decadent Roman at an orgy.

"You married?"

"Not that I know of."

"Attached?"

Daisy shook her head.

Squibb sat up and began to undress. Removing first his left shoe, then his right, he reached under the couch and produced a pair of wedge-shaped rubber lifts, which he inserted one on top of the other into his right shoe, the thick end against the heel. In this shoe and a left stocking foot, he began to hobble around the room, up, down, up, down, as though he were a piece of machinery operating on a camshaft. "I have to do this for five minutes three times a day, to make one leg longer than the other. To correct a spinal, in fact *total skeletal, misalignment* that's pinching a nerve between two vertebrae and causing me great pain. The orthopedist says he's done everything he can for me, and that the next step is surgery. In desperation I'm trying a chiropractor. He's sure I put the whole caboodle out of line ten years ago when I fell on the ice and broke a leg. Came down on my hind pocket in a comic-strip sprawl. One hip is higher than the other, and what we're doing now is *rocking the pelvis into a new alignment.*" He stood in the middle of the room and set his loins to writhing in a circular motion, like a striptease dancer doing the bumps and grinds, the gyration rhythmically throwing the bully bag in and out of bas-relief. As if in synch, Daisy's eyes began to swivel away, reviving the headache. "Would you like to come to my place Saturday night?" Squibb said, ending the demonstration and resuming the march with a glance at his wristwatch.

"Well, that all . . . Why?"

"My brother from Akron is visiting us for the weekend. He's sort of been through the mill lately, his marriage breaking up and all. His wife ran off with another woman. I guess that's why I'm so conscious of this lesbian stuff. Happens more and more these days, with both sexes. People pouring pell-mell out of the closet. I don't know whether *it* or just the *acknowledgment* of it is on the increase — or whether if the latter that's any consolation. Amelioration." Having reached the far wall, Squibb about-faced and marched the other way, reversing himself again when he reached that end of the room, like an infirm sentry pacing off his rounds. "I don't know whether you two would hit it off, but he needs a good time, relax, so my wife is fixing up this small dinner party. Timmie works for a big tire company. He's in the research department, where they're desperately trying to correct the defect in these steel-belted radials that are being recalled by the millions."

Daisy wanted to dive headfirst into the compost heap on Timmie Squibb's brother Andy's desk, and, buried to her chin among the debris, continue this colloquy from there.

"My father had two tires blow out, and my mother, who's a consumer activist, her protection agency is flooded with complaints about them," she said.

"Timmie says they've figured out it's a faulty bonding between the rubber and the metal."

"That so?"

"Yes. They're trying desperately to correct it, and he

thinks they're on the track of it, there in the laboratory. I don't know if he's your type. Who knows whether anybody is anybody's type."

Daisy thought that if she were applying at a computer-dating service and they asked her to fill out a form telling exactly what she was looking for in a mate she would say she wanted a healthy, reasonably attractive, decently groomed chemical research scientist, preferably named Timmie, dedicated to getting to the bottom of the faulty bonding between the rubber and the metal in steel-belted radials, and correcting the situation. Such a man she would follow to the ends of the earth, or Akron, Ohio.

"I have a date for Saturday, Andy, but it's not too important. I'll see if I can break it. If you want to give me that sample galley I'll get back to my chores before Mrs. Gromley gets mad. I'll be in touch with you. And I hope your — skeleton is better."

Seeing the Diesel bearing down on her along a midtown sidewalk, Daisy ducked behind a parked truck, and from there scurried across the street. Ten Hail Marys, plus five more for pretending to window-shop in order to keep her back turned until the Diesel had safely stridden from view, but she didn't want a meeting now, when there was nothing to report, no real progress in any case. She didn't want to be pumped just yet. She could see the Diesel's reflection in plate glass behind which appeared to be sickroom supplies. She was window-shopping among them, thermometers and sipping tubes, wheelchairs, enough elastic bandage to tuck a Pharaoh in for eternity. Some walking sticks and crutches, yes, she must get a line on what they were showing in them this year. Bobsy swam ectoplasmically through it all, in salami-colored tweeds and a porkpie hat, with a shoulder bag that left the arms free to swing in her characteristic purposeful stride. Then she was gone.

Daisy lunched alone. She wanted to be alone today, to think. She went to a recently opened Chinese restaurant, the quality of whose fare turned out to have been grossly exaggerated. It was take-out food eaten *sur place*. She fancied she could taste the carton in the egg foo yung, but that may have been a kind of gustatory hallucination resulting from long conditioning. Sipping her martini and then her tea, she took stock. She had been promoted to proofreading and had her own office, near, as Andy Squibb had said, grinning like Beelzebub, near makeup where Dog Bokum held sway. Repenting the lie about being busy, she had told another about cancelling, and gone to the Squibbs' for dinner. Tim was really quite nice, somewhat resembling Andy, and a fair dancer. The party of ten had rolled up the rug after dinner and put on some phonograph records. Stirring a saccharin pellet into her tea, Daisy smiled at a memory revived by one of the songs. As very small girls, she and Effie had together decided that they would marry the first man who murmured into their ear, as they glided across a ballroom floor, "My dear, you waltz divinely," as suitors were depicted doing in storybook romances, and even in movies of relatively recent vintage. They were going to find men who talked like that. "I'm afraid my tango is a bit rusty, but how divinely you dance, my dear." What were one's chances of doing so? Not very good in this disco day! There was a scene in Willa Cather's *The Old Beauty* which she must reread. The old beauty attends a dance dominated by young people doing their rough best, and stops the show, at least for an awed moment, by demonstrating the old elegance in an exquisite waltz. Wasn't it a waltz? Yes, she must look it up.

In early youth, hadn't Daisy seen the old beauty as an idealization of herself in age to come? If she and Effie Sniffen hadn't remained in such close touch for all these years, would either have been amazed to find the other "so changed" in a sudden chance meeting now? What a series of discarded selves each of us is, or selves we think we have discarded but which lurk, one beneath the other, like successive paintings on a single canvas. Now Daisy as a maturing woman smiled over the young one she had so recently been, who had in turn laughed at the adolescent who had laughed at the child — who sometimes still dominated adult conduct when least acknowledged. One of the pleasures of introspection is the amused tolerance we fancy ourselves as entertaining toward our past identities, little suspecting the successor that will, with equal embarrassment, supplant the reigning favorite. Reincarnation indeed. We die and are resurrected enough times in a full life to satisfy a mystic for eternity.

Another game we play is that of thinking back on a version of ourself still ignorant of something sensational that is just about to happen to us. Daisy was often to muse on the woman she was at that precise moment, in a Chinese restaurant eating take-out food on the premises, totally oblivious of the fact that within five hours she would be waltzing divinely across the floor of the Plaza ballroom in the arms of a merchant prince with wavy blond hair, dazzling teeth and — sole tarnish on the occasion — two left feet.

Dirk Dolfin was the forty-year-old Dutch-born publisher of *Metropole*, who never meddled in the editorial affairs of the magazine, and for that matter seldom came to his office in the business department, being more absorbed in other corporations comprising the conglomerate he headed, such as his chocolate-importing concern, and leaving *Metropole* matters to trusted lieutenants, but he usually showed up at the magazine's annual party. This one celebrated its tenth anniversary with a cocktail and buffet supper bash. She found Dolfin's Dutch accent charming, particularly the habit of making every "a" an "an" — or even something of an "am" when the vowel-and-consonant sequence was right. "You like am piece cake?" was the first thing he ever said to her, offering her a plate with a slice he had himself just ceremonially cut. Daisy's other memory of that pivotal moment was to be the view, just past his left shoulder, of Effie watching them like a hawk in the middle distance.

As he trampled her insteps to the strains of "The Tennessee Waltz," which he seemed to regard as a fox-trot, he hummed the tune in a manner suggesting a tin ear as well, and he would occasionally disengage himself and snap his fingers, to emphasize a democratic rapport with his employees. When they made their way back to his table, her feet feeling like the grapes of wrath, she was again aware of Effie watchfully waiting for them. She had evidently been sitting there since early in the party, giving her the right to view Daisy as an intruder, despite Dolfin's arm at Daisy's back herding her along in a broad welcome. "Another slice cake," he said to Effie, who said she must watch her figure. "Well, I been watching it, so you got nothing to worry about," Dolfin said, and laughed. "I'm a cornball, not?" he said, winking at Daisy an eye bluer than her own. "Nonsense, Dirk," Effie said, darting a glance of quite another sort at Daisy, and as if to stress the fact that as an employee of some importance in the advertising department she had long been on a first-name basis with this boss. "It's just that Dutch humor of yours which is so — robust." "Ja, like an ripe Edam, not? How about some coffee? Girls? Waiter, coffees here."

In the days that followed, much of Daisy's curiosity about Dirk Dolfin was willingly satisfied by Effie, who, however, slanted her information in a manner calculated to throw Daisy off — which only convinced Daisy the more that she was out to snare him for herself, pending her imminent divorce. "A single man of thirty is just that," she observed at one of their Wednesday lunches together, "but a forty-year-old man living alone is a bachelor, and thus suspect."

"What do you mean, suspect?"

"Suspect."

"Oh."

Just then the subject of the conversation himself walked in, and had started to slide onto the last remaining stool at the bar when he spotted the women, and sauntered over. They insisted he join them if alone, moving aside to make room for him at their table. "I just have am beer," he said. "I try not to eat lunch," he added, patting a stomach that testified well enough both to that discipline and to regular workouts at a midtown gymnasium. Daisy told him he had the elegance of the pilsner glass his Heineken was eventually drunk from. "Oh, ja? Tell me more." And smiled uproariously. Some people can do that.

Two women together are either conspirators or rivals. Both here now sensed that their lives together as the former were over: henceforth they were to be the latter. Daisy pressed her pilsner-glass-metaphor advantage by amplifying. "You have those beautiful broad shoulders tapering to that slim waist," she explained. "That's what I meant." Dolfin smiled his gratitude, his fingers stroking the stem of the glass where it tapered to its base.

"He's going to keep it that way," Effie put in, "aren't you,

Dirk? He never touches his own pastilles. But as for me,"
with a sigh, "I've nearly finished that five-pound box you
gave me. Is that a new suit? I haven't seen it before." The
doting note now struck was quite at odds with Effie's earlier
stricture: that Dolfin was said to have twenty-two suits and
always stood as though he was being measured for the
twenty-third. "I like vests for a man, and you obviously do
too, but for that any least sign of a tum-tum is out. Did you
know that Dirk has been named one of the Ten Best
Dressed Men?"

Dolfin had the usual human trouble in managing an
expression for compliments of the kind that were being
rained on him, and after a flustered simper he shifted in
his chair and asked Daisy, "Where do you work?"

"I'm a proofreader in the editorial department. My hour
is almost up, and I really should . . ."

He waved her scruples off. "We go back to the office
together, pretty soon. I'll clear it with your boss."

"You're demoralizing me, Mr. Dolfin."

"Dirk, please. Besides, I should look in on the editorial
department oftener. I like to go slumming." Another up-
roarious smile.

The women laughed, Effie rather immoderately, Daisy
thought. There was little doubt in her mind that Effie had
her cap set for him. With matrimony the object, once her
divorce was final. Since that would be soon, Daisy would
have to act fast.

·6·

Daisy was spared any such unbuttoned aggression when the Dutchman took it himself. He phoned her at her office a few days later and asked her to dinner at his Riverside Drive apartment. An attachment developed with such dizzying speed that she found herself again dodging the Diesel, not by running across the street but flattening herself in a doorway till Bobsy had marched on out of sight along the midtown sidewalk where she had been spotted. Evasion this time was different from the previous occasion, when Daisy had scooted across the street to prevent a meeting. Then, she had felt guilty because she had avoided the Diesel. In this case she avoided her because she felt guilty. She was sleeping with the boss without first having put the masculine integrity to the test: by waiting to see, that is, whether inducements such as a promotion or a raise would have been venally dangled before her, in keeping with crass practices known to be widespread and therefore deserving to be put under hardboiled journalistic scrutiny. That was the reverse of the coin of harassment, of which the obverse was the denial of such perquisites as a penalty for chastity, or at least the profession of it until one saw what one saw. Any undercover operative worth her salt to the Cause would have played that game. Bobsy's words rang in Daisy's ears the more stridently for being imagined rather than physically heard. "He would have shown his true colors, you dumb-dumb." Perhaps even more censurable than all the rest was the fact that Daisy wouldn't have *wanted* to see them shown. It would have tarnished an image she wanted dearly to preserve as taken in the pristine blush of first infatuation. She was a disgrace to the Cause. Any true patriot to it would have smoked out chauvinism in the other. She had, like the schoolgirl she had all too recently been, and apparently still was, quite simply fallen in love, and that with the enchilada himself. She had not even waited to be *torn* between love and duty, had gone right ahead and copped out on duty by letting herself be swept off her feet. Her emotions — it was the hackneyed truth, the rock-bottom, irreducible cliché shame of all espionage — her emotions had become involved. Add to that the fact of its all being a triangle to which her best friend was party, and one would have had quite enough of thickening plot. Of all developments calculated to grieve the Diesel heart, this was the most abysmal. And of course now she was farther than ever from having any copy to show.

The footsteps came nearer, the Diesel's. It was a side street in the Thirties, near Daisy's apartment, a Saturday afternoon in July. She had been on her way to Altman's to shop for a sweater for Dolfin, something in perhaps a yellow cashmere to go with a navy blazer, when she had spotted Bobsy coming along, with stride purposeful (as they would have said during the inversion fad at school), and popped into the doorway. It was that of a private house, and of course locked. She turned around and pretended to be peering into the entranceway, as though watching or waiting for someone whose bell she had rung, a hand to her brow as if shading her eyes. The footsteps came close, passed, marched on. Daisy waited till they were well out of earshot before peeking cautiously out, then stepped back onto the sidewalk, heaving a sigh of relief.

Why had she behaved in this fashion, since she would have to face the Diesel with the facts eventually? She wanted time to frame her approach, decide on precisely how to break the ghastly news, was even mentally trying out openers. Singing flat out that she was in love, in love, in love with a wonderful guy would scarcely have done. She must slide the news in subtly, obliquely, let the true facts be paid out a bit at a time. "I've been seeing Dolfin, I suppose you've heard," said negligently as she paused in the act of lighting a cigarette, that might do it. Or, "A development that might amuse you — I've been dating the boss." She would find the words. But the sight of Bobsy pelting down the street in her quasi-military uniform just now had taken her too much by surprise, and she had elected to duck on impulse, whether for better or worse.

Dirk Dolfin had cooked that first dinner himself. "I understand the way to a woman's heart is through her stomach," he said as he whipped up a Dutch East Indies curry dish that was superb. They had it by candlelight at a window overlooking the river. A white Burgundy that was mother's milk. He called it that himself, ungiven to the jargon of sniffing and swooshing connoisseurs. He had no servants, detesting the infringement on one's privacy that servants brought (and that the Diesel claimed was entailed merely by having a husband).

Not only the dinner was superb. He proved that as a lover too, though the bed was full of paper clips and rubber bands, testimony to much nocturnal corporate homework — like the cracker crumbs and sausage strands to be found in nests of the more sybaritic. Nor did he cease attentions once himself glutted: he remained a wooing protagonist even in the "afterglow," as the sex manuals call it. Perhaps one tiny drawback, his sweet nothings were among the weightiest things in Christendom. "Born in Utrecht in 1878," he murmured "afterward" in Daisy's ear, brushing a curl aside with his lips, "mine grandfather was an rigid Dutch Reformed minister who instilled in mine father the austere Calvinist view he tried in turn to pass on to me. The church . . ." He had that new-car smell we all like, an association she realized had sprung from the after-shave he wore, which apparently had a purposely leathery aura about it, intended to suggest manliness. Her mind wandered pleasantly amid this postlude. Among the dehydrated old parties at Kidderminster had been a psychology professor, Mommsen, whom she could remember defining synesthesia as the word for a phenomenon in which one type of stimulation evokes the sensation of another, the most familiar example of course being the colors that musical sounds make us visualize. Daisy had a synesthesia about Dirk's cologne that the d.o.p. would have hailed as a valid illustration had she raised her hand in class to offer it — in fact a double synesthesia. The scent was auburn in color, and in the bass register pianistically, far from the treble-pitched perfumes the manufacturers are marketing for men these days.

Daisy made to turn, not intending to extricate herself from Dolfin's priapic clasp but simply to get into a more comfortable position, but was restrained by the counterpressure of his arm pinning her to the mattress. She eased her aching wrist just ever so, trying not to disturb the exquisitely languid tableau they made, thus entwined, as Número Uno went on whispering his personal brand of sweet nothings in her ear:

"Mine grandfather, the dominie, was an supralapsarian. You know what that is?"

By the wildest of flukes — and how sweet his breath was, faintly tinged with the Burgundy — by the craziest of coincidences, she knew. The same d.o.p. who had put her into synesthesia took two weeks of every semester lecturing on the psychology of religion, and the repellent little tenet was branded forever on her brain. But she murmured back no, she didn't know, in order not to spoil his, their, post-coital pleasure by undercutting the superior male instructing the little woman. Ten Hail Betty Friedans.

"Supralapsarianism is the doctrine that God's determination of the Elect — those who will be saved —"

"Yes, yes."

"— *preceded* the Fall of man from grace, and in fact that God had predestined the Fall itself."

"Good God."

"As distinguished from infralapsarianism, which says that God only *allowed* the Fall and then elected some to be saved."

By the time the elucidations had been completed she had gingerly managed to extricate her arm, and in fact had equally unobtrusively begun a shift to a sitting position against the headboard, adopting it slowly and drawing the sheet up around her knees to emphasize that she had no wish to disturb the afterglow spell. She remembered rather guiltily how the d.o.p. had himself quite thoroughly defined the distinction between the two doctrines, the terminologies for which had consequently piled up in your head as representative sesquipedalian debris for all the theological slag heaps of human time. But Dolfin had certainly refreshed her grasp of the dogmas, to which she had perhaps not given sufficient thought since the vanished years in that school where they had sung a grace with their meals, slid down winter hills on bobsleds, and hated a pudding dessert called Pastor Plunkett's Treat.

Stroked he now her jackknifed legs beneath the sheet, scratching her underthighs delicately as he smiled his peculiarly fetching smile, with its dazzling teeth. She guessed it to be somehow foxy-folk European, imported with the cocoa. A *volk* thing, like the inhaled "ja," which you also got from other old-country people, such as Scandinavians. She'd even known an Irishman who sucked in his affirmatives. Narrowing his eyes slightly, Dirk would purse his lips in a kind of prolonged pucker, before parting them to reveal his "consistently rewarding teeth." Mom's phrase again. "Now the other one." Almost but not quite "ander one." "Now we draw you down again," making her slide back into the original horizontal position, as though she were being exquisitely persuaded down a chute. For chief among the features of the afterglow were fresh rounds of foreplay, into which they subtly segued. "Now we turn you around, now we get you brown all around, like an sausage." No, he had no humor, which was perhaps just as well, because if he did, *that* would be it, as though laughs could be extracted from whimsies such as that. He wasn't making a joke about doing her to a juicy turn, like a sausage, he was being tender. The only thing remotely mechanical about him might be the way he rotated you through the erotic positions in almost stylized sequence, no doubt like the calisthenics that kept him in such trim. For all his disciplined self-regard, you would hesitate to pin the narcissistic label on him. She learned it again: there is no way for a man to give you pleasure but by taking it himself.

Speaking of positions, which did this put her in? Some balancing of moral books, please. But she couldn't get them to balance, flog herself as she might with introspection. Here she was in the boss's apartment, sleeping with the enchilada himself, and hoping and *praying* he wouldn't offer the occupational favors and emoluments she had slipped into the citadel to inspire and research. On him she didn't want to get the goods — or on herself! The merest sign that she was, awful term, sleeping her way up the corporate ladder would have spoiled it. Spoil it — was there no end to the platitudes hounding her? The merest favor given and her affection for him must rot like a piece of blighted fruit. The merest favor taken and her self-respect must wither with it. She had half decided she half wanted to be proposed to, with no such tarnish on either her or the suitor — *especially* on him!

Such was the pot of fears and hopes and doubts boiling confusedly in her mind as Dolfin rose to draw her a bath. Another of his routines. He himself bathed before embracing her, she after being possessed. It was how, all quixotically, he wanted it. Of the half-dozen men she had slept with, none had ablutions in his ritual, at least not of this order. One or two had made a point of showering afterward, the implications of which she wasn't sure she liked. His routine may have involved some kind of gallantry also old-worldly. Maybe it was plain Dutch cleanliness. With no servant but a day cleaning woman, he cooked most meals taken at home, scrubbing his own pots and pans, as he now was her back — though the caressive way he swung the soaped loofah over her arms and shoulders made her think of the old poetic word *lave* — another forbidden four-letter word long since pensioned off. For the first time in her life she was being laved. What a catch! But was there a catch to the catch? As he knelt beside the tub, in what might be called a kind of obeisance, she thought: But he's sleeping with Effie too, the bastard, I *think.*

"About your job at the office —"

"Rrrnnah!"

There is a scene in Aristophanes' *The Frogs* in which Dionysus and Xanthias must submit to a thrashing in order to substantiate their claims to divinity, since a god would not feel pain, and try to pass off their howls and bellows as ecstatic invocations, exclamations over horsemen glimpsed, and the like. Daisy similarly drowned out any attempt of Dirk's to broach the subject he was trying to introduce with inarticulate shouts about the temperature of the water pouring on a toe held inadvertently under the spigot, spluttered coughs and, when all these failed and when the issue was again raised, protests that she didn't want to talk shop.

"As president of the company I could certainly —"

"*Look* at the crack in that ceiling! Do you think there's a leak in the apartment above? That could raise holy hell in yours if it isn't taken care of. Do you own this apartment or rent it?"

"I rent it. I want am place in the country."

"Who doesn't. Look, do you know I'm starved? Can I fix us some scrambled eggs here, or shall we nip around the corner to that new Greek restaurant? I hear it's pretty good. The most wonderful egg lemon soup."

Helplessly she continued to see herself from the Diesel's point of view, as though mesmerized by those green eyes into self-inventory. Actually would become the *Lay Misér-*

able as she stood before a bedroom mirror dressing herself down, as though rehearsing for the accounting that could not be long postponed.

"So. Now we have a whole nother bucket of worms on the table, as the woodwinds exhale the original theme while the second is announced with a disgusted belch from the brasses. The war between men and women gives way to the war between women over men — these are the two motifs to be somehow intertwined. Interspecific rivalry becomes *intra*specific rivalry." Oh, it would be a learned chewing out. Not a dilapidated old puss at Kidderminster but would have applauded its Unity, Coherence and Emphasis with an A-plus, never mind the mixed metaphor. "What a revolting development this is."

Thus the Diesel.

Effie she avoided too now, feeling like a tight end with the ball as she broken-field ran through traffic to get on the other side of the street — there to fear the sight of an oncoming Bobsy, to make her "buttonhook" back again, if she had that football jargon right. Of course a showdown with Effie was inevitable too. Was there no rest for wandering hearts? And would the two themes really be somehow successfully interplaited, like — well, like the braids comprising the schnecken on the Diesel's troubled head? Poor Diesel. She had been primed and girded for everything but an infestation of romantic love. At least she might have been spared that.

Daisy faced her next lunch date with Effie in a turmoilish mixture of impatience and trepidation. Since they worked on different floors, they never ran into one another at the office except for chance encounters in an elevator, usually with other passengers aboard, so it remained for the ritual Wednesday lunch to offer something more than a casual exchange. The constraint between them was un-mistakable the instant they faced one another across the table. Over drinks ordered as quickly as possible, they chattered nervously about everything but the subject up-permost in their minds. Abhorrent as the thought must be that Dirk became Effie's lover after he was her own, it would at least clear her of the charge of intruder. It was a gritty enough consolation. But wasn't it all up to Dirk? And Effie still technically married to Doctor Colby?

They traded gossip about old schoolmates. Effie brought up Professor Mommsen, the d.o.p. recently sprung to mind under the most unlikely circumstances. "Did you know he once fell asleep at his own lecture?" Effie daintily gobbled the olive from her martini and wiped her fingers on her napkin. "Fact. He was sitting there droning away when his head began to nod, jerk, nod, till off he went. Fast asleep."

"What did the class do?"

"We filed out on tiptoe. It stood in the paper the other day that sleep as a human phenomenon — Incidentally, Dirk says that that, you know, locution, gauche as it is in English, derives from a perfectly correct Dutch, and I sup-pose German, construction. Het stond in de krant. It stands in the paper that the Queen this that or the other. Where was I? Something about something in the paper. Well, no matter."

At least she had put the prime subject on the table, leaving their faces strained caricatures of themselves. Afraid her lips were going to twitch, Daisy took a prolonged sip of her bloody Mary, steadying them against the rim of the glass.

When two people are thrown into romantic contention, everything changes between them. A gulf springs up along with a terrible intimacy. It is a kind of flesh bond itself, so that their physical awareness of each other heightens to an almost unbearable degree. Two women fighting over a man feel this more intensely than two male adversaries over a woman. The latter share, or are locked in, a sort of gladiatorial event; combatants for a prize, they do not necessarily hate each other. Men are rivals; women, enemies. That men commit more jealous murders than women is beside the point; they kill oftener, period. When no open declaration of hostilities has been made, the opponents may seethe the more furiously within. A plain catfight, a good old hair pull right there on the restaurant floor, might in the end have been less hard on the nerves than the icily repressed emotion with which the old friends now exchanged pleasantries about Dirk Dolfin. How amused they were by his accent, particularly the seeming absence of the article "a" in his vocabulary.

"I think it's because both 'a' and 'an' are lumped together into the Dutch 'een,' " Daisy said. "They couldn't care less whether vowels or consonants start the noun to follow."

"Yes! We say 'an apple' but 'a peach,' but Hollanders say 'een appel' and 'een perzik.' Did you know that's the word for peach — oh, and they have an equivalent of our 'peachy.' Did you know that? 'Perzikachtig.' Isn't that something?"

And did she know there were paper clips and rubber bands in his bed too, evidence of as much work as play in it? Had she found any? Had she been run through his erotic routines? Knew she the hammerblows of his sweet nothings?

"He often slurs even the 'an,' so you get 'am piece cake,' sort of," Effie went on. "That was the first thing he said to you at the party — probably ever. I remember. But what I love most is getting slang wrong, it's so charming. Something is a 'great deal' when he means 'big deal.' I haven't the heart to correct him. I mean elected congressmen coming in on the President's shirttails." She shook her head and smiled fondly. "Lamb."

Daisy put her fork down and, elbows cocked on the table, chin resting on her folded hands, said, "Do you know the difference between infralapsarianism and supralapsarianism?"

"Yes." Effie finished chewing something and then swallowed it. A sip of her drink completed her timing. "It has to do with whether God merely foresaw the Fall or actually predestined that too, along with those who were to be the Elect."

The bitch. This was sexual harassment at its worst. Downright bedevilment, of the most galling variety. The same pillow talk!

Lightly Daisy began to ask, "How did you know?" but Effie stepped on her line, as actors say. "What on earth brought that up?"

"Mommsen. We were just talking about him, and, the things that stick in your mind, I remembered that from his lecture on the psychology of religion. Is that where you heard it, the lapsarian business?"

"Probably," Effie said in her teeth, "it must have been. What an odd coinkidinky. That's probably the lecture where he fell asleep. Even now a drowsy numbness floods my senses."

Pains my *sense,* Daisy mentally corrected her. "But that piece cake and cup coffee stuff, that's middle Europe too, of course," she said. "Yiddish and German and probably a lot of other. Well, I'd like an cup coffee, to say nothing of an glass brandy, but I'm afraid I'd fall asleep at the office."

So nothing had really come out into the open. That development remained for a far more eventful, not to say harrowing, lunch with Dirk himself, the following week.

He broke his no-midday-meal rule to the extent of having a shrimp cocktail with her, which he nursed along with an bottle Heineken. He picked at it with a strained, preoccupied air, glancing silently at her from time to time before again lowering his eyes to it. Something was clearly troubling him. He waited till she had finished her own before he spoke up.

"Something has come to my attention that disturbs me deeply. Dat mij zeer beroert." He paused after casting his words into the more baleful Dutch, then went on: "I find you're doing an exposé, an series of articles about sexual exploitation in corporation offices — including ours. That's why you're there. Daisy?"

Her heart didn't "skip a beat." She felt it bounce, burst like a hot ember, explode into sparks, and when she answered, her eyes blazed with such anger that witnesses to the scene must have thought she was railing at him, rather than to him. She writhed, the way a poor earthworm writhes when your shovel has uncovered it.

"I don't know who your informer is," she said, hoping her choice of the word over the milder "informant" had served its acerbic purpose, "but if it's who I think it is, and I think you think you know who I think it —"

"Hup up up, all these thinks. Who do I, let's see, think you think I — Ach!" He gave up trying to retain an even ironic grip on the sequence. "Who, then?"

"If it is Iphigenia Sniffen Colby, Mrs. Colby, then you've got more intrigue on your hands even than you know, my boy. Because she was the *first* plant there — Well, no, I have to be honest. She wasn't planted *as* an undercover agent in the operation, but she cooperated willingly when she was there, when she was asked by my editor, who is a mutual friend of ours."

"How?"

"By helping me get in. Touting me to the personnel manager and arranging the interview for my first job, knowing full well why I wanted to get inside the castle walls. So she's been as much a part of the conspiracy as I, if it's undercover work you're talking about. We're all feminists, and I'm still for the Cause, give my time and money to it, but I'm beginning to think women have got more to fear from each other than from men."

"Whooosh!" Dolfin cast up his arms and eyes both in a flamboyant gesture of concurrence. "You can say dot again."

"But the point is," and Daisy leaned forward and lowered her voice, sensing big ears at a nearby table, "who would you rather be dealing with, a spy or a double agent? And the spy at least quitting, at least this chapter of the story. I would never write about goings-on at *Metropole* now, even using a fictitious name, now that there's this between us. That's a fact. I'll give you my notes if you like, and you can then throw them away or do something about the discrimination there. I don't think you realize how bad it is."

"I leave it to the officers to run. I'm not a literary man. I run a cocoa business and some others I inherited from my father. *Metropole* is just there — the classy star in our crown. Why should I meddle?"

"For reasons I'm telling you. You should meddle enough to clean up the discrimination and the harassment. Do you realize how much less women get there than the men, for the same work? I've been kicked up one step to proofreader without being expected to sleep with anybody because my benefactor is a feminist."

"Would you have otherwise?"

"Certainly not!" Daisy said, still hot with rage but inwardly grateful for a turn in the conversation that got her off the defensive. She pressed her grievance. "I'm no Puritan but I like to think of myself as a woman of virtue, which isn't negotiable, or a bargaining chip. I sleep with you only, because of how I feel about you, which must be obvious by now. Whether the same can be said for you I wouldn't know. But I know who's got her cap set for you."

"I'll look into it. The salaries and molestation and so on. But I can't promise any shakeups as you call them in America. I won't fire anybody, just raise hell as a birthday present for you. Isn't it next month? So what will you do now, quit *Metropole* and go where the ladies' CIA sends you next?"

"I don't know." She fastened the discussion on his own problem. "So now what you've got on your hands is an unhappy agent provocateur and a — I won't balk at the word, which may have no Dutch equivalent — stoolie."

"Come again?"

"Stool pigeon we call them here. Squealers."

"Grote God! Effie is een lokvogel. Foooo!" Dolfin blew out a long breath through puffed cheeks that made him momentarily resemble a wind deity. "You're an charming sisterhood, you girls."

"When we're bitched on we're quite prepared to bitch back. Especially when inflamed by the most noble of emotions — which can get pretty nasty."

"Meaning, if you please?"

"Meaning all's fair in love and war."

"And this seems to be both. Love makes the world go round — I guess dot's why it wobbles on its axis." Dolfin took a pull on his beer and sighed. "I'm going to sell the magazine."

"Oh, you mustn't! At least keep it till you've done the housecleaning and laid down a few rules. Made it a sexual democracy."

"All right. But I'm not exactly bung-ho about all this."

Daisy lowered her head, putting a hand to her brow. "Uh, what did you say, Dirk?"

"I said I'm not exactly bung-ho, as you Americans call it, about all this ruction. Ruzie we call it. I'm a businessman, not a crusader. It's very time-consuming for a man who's got his hands full."

"I'll help you. I mean with the paperwork and all. The directives you'll want to dictate and distribute. There'll be paper clips in bed again, like there used to. I'll be your amanuensis."

"All right. Whatever the hell that is. Verdomme!" Dirk scratched at a crimson stain on his shirtfront with a napkin dipped in his water glass. "Thank God it missed my vest. This cocktail sauce is the devil to get out."

There was a silver lining to this cloud on which Daisy swiftly seized. Now was the time to tell the Diesel how she had fallen in love with her boss, because on the heels of the revelation, too fast for the Diesel long to dwell on her predictable disgust, would come that of Effie's similar infatuation, and perfidy. The onus falling on Daisy would be thus greatly overshadowed by the blame they could jointly lay at Effie's door. It would not be a pretty luncheon, with the Diesel having the whole sorry business dropped in toto on her plate: her two chief operatives squabbling like silly schoolgirls over Plum Number One; but it would be better than the encounter Daisy had been dreading like a tooth extraction, with herself in solo disgrace.

Of course the Diesel was furious. She threw up her hands and rolled her eyes and clattered her bloody Mary before tossing the muddler aside. "How could such a mess be made of it? Letting your emotions get so involved in a place you had dead to rights."

"Do you know Dolfin?"

The Diesel shook her head once from side to side, her eyes shut.

"He's quite nice. He . . ." Daisy dealt with the temptation to emphasize that her affections were quite requited, at which the Diesel might naturally with valid cynicism have smirked with the reminder that her lover was at the same time having it on with her rival, like the swine men could be. He had told Daisy she was "am piece tail all right," with no doubt as to his sincerity. Could Effie say her shrine was being worshipped at on a like scale? For he had been on his knees when making the obeisance, murmuring the endearment into her fleece. Had the Diesel in the course of her amorous career collected any such encomia, abed or afoot? She was talking rapidly, the *Lay Misérable*.

"No but the thing is how the big chance has now been shot. Because you've blown your cover. Other places will hear about it."

"*I* blew my cover."

"All right, Effie blew it, it's been blown, whatever. And I admit it was witchy" — she never used the epithet bitchy except on men — "but the thing is it's been blown in an office where the pickings were as luscious as an investigative journalist could hope to find. That place is Mac-Donald's farm."

"?"

"An oink-oink here, an oink-oink there, here an oink, there an oink —"

"I get it. But the thing is, neither the publisher nor the personnel head is a male chauvinist pig. And the former is going to clean the Augean stable."

Bobsy flung her hands wider than before. "So we'll have nothing left there to expose. We're left with egg on our face. Christ, what will *my* boss say?"

"But hey, look. How about this angle? Won't it be even better to boast that thanks to its crusading endeavors *Femme* magazine has corrected discriminatory evils in at least one very famous office? Woman's lot there has been improved, and of course the fight goes on in other corners of the battlefield."

Bobsy drummed the tabletop, and from her expression she might have been saying "Hmm" just below the audibility threshold. "You may be right," she said, though not without arousing a slight suspicion that she might be one of those moral pugilists who relish their wrongs more than they do their rights — an all-too-human phenomenon that does not necessarily undercut their value to whatever there is of the world's progress. It takes all kinds to goad the mulish race along an inch or two. By their fruits we must know them, not their roots. Those are for psychologists to mess about with.

In any case she relented, even brightened. She impaled on her fork one of the kumquats with which her salads were always liberally garnished here at the Straw Hat, and held it aloft a moment before poking it into her mouth. "Why don't you hammer out something along that line and let me see it. You haven't shown me anything yet, you know. And if you do feel it'd be really too sticky to stay on at *Metropole,* I think I've got another den of iniquity, if we can weasel you into it after this brouhaha. Are you going to pin Effie's ears back? I'd like to be there for *that* catfight."

There wasn't any, just yet. Dolfin recognized that now a state of showdown existed, and he would have to choose. Effie's conduct having left a slightly worse taste than Daisy's deviousness, irrespective of the supposedly equal worth of the passions involved, he settled on Daisy — at least for the time being. He had to fly to Amsterdam just then on business anyway, and possibly on to Curaçao, allowing for a period of semisuspension in which all parties concerned could sort out their feelings.

Daisy resolved to wear her victory well, though intuition warned her that she had won a battle, not the war. That a state of hostility continued between her and Effie was indicated by a suspension of their Wednesday lunch custom. She saw more of Andy Squibb, who now stood high on her list by virtue of not pressing her for amorous rewards after promoting her, not merely to proofreader, but then on to copyeditor, with a slight raise in pay accompanying each hoist. Was his affectionate respect for her to be taken at face value, or was he still deviously weaving his long-term web of seduction by chastity — working the delayed payoff? She retained a grain of suspicion there; men could be so illegible, springing when least expected. Dog Bokum gave her an unmistakable tumble or two, now that he and Immediate Occupancy had evidently banked their midday fires, going so far as to mumble something about lunch. He looked like death warmed over, with eyes bloodshot from the unremitting nooners (and, of course, God knew what insatiate nocturnes as well) and a shaving nick on his chin, its crimson ooze stanched with a tiny scrap of toilet paper pasted into place. All very romantic — a home-from-the-wars look augmented by the soiled trench coat sometimes worn to work. Dog was said to sustain the ceaseless grind of romance by subsisting largely on oysters, rotating his patronage among restaurants known for their indifference to whether there was an "r" in the month or not, and had twice had severe bouts of hepatitis. You wondered whether he shouldn't, at the last, bequeath to some deserving medical school the organs that had stood him in such noble stead, the giblets of liver and spleen and the meatballs and other venereal parts on whose long-suffering endurance he had so long relied. How he managed financially was a puzzle, since in addition to moneys squandered on the women on whom he executed his pushups, he was, as he put it, "paying alimony to two squaws." He was really irresistibly awful, so awful as to round himself out into another, almost epic, dimension, one that somehow safeguarded him from the censure he'd have provoked if he'd been about half as deplorable as he was. Daisy murmured something about "not lunching much these days" but added that she would see him around. No special credit adhered to being a target female of Dog Bokum's, whose prurient interest could be taken for granted; and there was a school of thought that traced his nickname to some of the women he'd resorted to when pickings were slim.

One day during Dirk's absence, Andy Squibb asked her to lunch, issuing the invitation from her office doorway where he stood in one stocking foot and one shod one, the therapeutic lifts in the shoe. In the fevers of topical journalism there'd been no time to take five or ten minutes for the exercise. Daisy said yes. They were sipping white wine at a corner table at the Straw Hat when Effie walked in, alone. Andy waved her over. This was the first time she and Daisy had met since the crisis over Dirk Dolfin, and after the initial shock Daisy found the encounter advantageous. Squibb would be an ideal buffer in a confrontation difficult under any circumstances, and so Daisy civilly chimed in with the invitation.

The chair onto which Effie squeezed herself put her squarely under a sprig of soiled mistletoe left over from the previous Christmas, if not a prior management. It was really quite sooty, certainly in no shape to be held over for the next Yuletide festivities. It prompted a rather pedantic lecture from Squibb, calling to mind in the details of its analysis the Diesel's assurance that she'd had a bellyful of mistletoe, and why.

"No doubt it was considered sacred by the ancients because of its color association with the male sperm," he discoursed.

"Oink-oink," Effie laughed.

"What's oink-oinky about it?" Daisy said, resisting, from Effie, a response she might herself have given. Were they now going to fight over poor Andy Squibb?

"Well, isn't that a male chauvinist point of view?"

"I don't see why, necessarily. These buzz words are all starting to get to me, frankly."

But coming to Andy Squibb's defense only put her into contention with him, since as a Women's Lib devotee he took the feminist side, and insisted that he was really pinning something on the ancients, as perhaps unconsciously guilty of the chauvinism Effie deplored, not offering the analysis as one he approved. Which complication further curdled Daisy's mood and left her slightly irked with both her companions, so that she somehow felt herself to be taking the two of them on — a tension hardly relieved as a result of what Effie said next.

"I don't want to come down too hard on Andy with the Freudian bit about masculine protest, though men by and large do tend to protest their masculinity, methinks, and I do feel he may be a weeny bit guilty of it here, unconsciously or otherwise."

There was old evidence, dating back to the bull sessions in Kidderminster dormitories, that neither Effie nor the Diesel quite understood what the term masculine protest meant, or was all about. In fact they had it completely reversed, in common with many parlor psychoanalysts. This seemed as good a time as any to set the matter straight.

"The masculine protest isn't Freud's term at all," Daisy said. "It was coined by Alfred Adler, and it means 'a striving to escape identification with the feminine role.' So it's something women have, at least for the most part, not men. Those of us who don't want to be submissive housewives blah blah blah, or regarded as childbearing machines expected to blah blah blah, we're the ones with the masculine protest."

Andy's eyes widened in surprised acceptance of this correction, while Effie's narrowed resentfully. Chastening a too feline pleasure in the moment, Daisy hurried on in a more conciliatory tone:

"But I do agree that Andy may be showing the contemporary tendency to psychoanalyze everything too much — including the berries of a parasitic shrub, which is what mistletoe is. Of course the psychological slant is valid up to a point, but it's begun to beat itself to death. We would now call Emma Bovary a neurotic woman. But if the word neurotic had existed in mid-nineteenth-century France, why, I doubt that Flaubert would ever have bothered to write *Madame Bovary*."

"Why do you say that?" This from Andy.

"Because it would have sold the poor woman so far down the river he couldn't have seen her round the bend."

Daisy had lost all faith in the validity of her words before they had quite got out, but both Effie and Andy nodded sagely in response to them, murmuring "Hmm," and saying they saw her point. Well, perhaps she was not such an idiot after all. Yes, it sounded rather subtle, in retrospect. She rejected the premise that now she and Effie were fighting over Andy Squibb; that she would have none of. Sure that Dirk Dolfin loved her and was thinking of her, that very moment, in far-off Curaçao, she clapped her hands and suggested they go Dutch on a bottle of champagne. Andy said he couldn't handle anything like his share of a full bottle, but "a modicum of the bubbly" shouldn't impair their efficiency at the office he was supposed to be running. "They serve it by the glass here. Waiter."

"How much is that?" Effie asked, fishing in her bag for a cigarette.

"How much is what?"

"A modicum."

Daisy and Andy gazed off in opposite directions, not daring to look at one another. How had Effie got through college, even Kidderminster? Had she slept with some of the professors? One of them she had called an oxymoron; Daisy had witnesses.

Out of the goodness of his heart, Andy Squibb said, "I don't know. A magnum is two bottles, a double magnum is a Jeroboam, or is it a Methuselah or a Nebuchadnezzar? Say, isn't it interesting they have these Biblical names. I've never thought of that till now. I wonder why. Waiter! I think you have Lanson's here in splits. We can get three glasses out of that. And then I must away."

*   *   *

Dirk said, "Do you know the American jazz cornetist named Big Spiderbecke?" He punched himself in the stomach like Hemingway, to show how hard it was. Like a rock. He was brown all over, as pan gravy, from head to foot. In Curaçao, he had had a room with a private deck on which he'd sunned himself daily. Not talking cocoa every minute. "The Kuypers, the business connection I dined with an few times, they had a lot of his records, and played them after dinner. What an lip." He picked up these terms. He liked to catch up with new things, keep abreast of American tastes freshly in the wind. "You know Big Spiderbecke?"

"Yes."

"I must buy some of his records."

"Don't do that. I'll get them for you," Daisy said, slipping into the bed she had only just made. "Don't ask for them just like that. I mean I know the good ones, and I have some other things I want to get. I have a record shop I like. There's a recording of a saxophonist named Tram playing with him. With *Bix* . . . . *Beiderbecke.*"

"Well, Big Spiderbecke is certainly an new one on me." Stubborn Dutchman. He was hanging his clothes up in her untidy closet, no doubt with the same loving care with which he put them on. She paused in the bed on her hands and knees, watching him over her shoulder, like a woman in a Thurber drawing. Was he a narcissist after all? Or just another wooden shoe whose ancestors had scrubbed their doorsteps for centuries? His money she could overlook. Most troubling were a few personal traits like the legendary obstinacy which she, personally, had found so amiable as to be past coping with. He seemed to get his way in everything they did with such quiet geniality she scarcely realized she was being manipulated. He was getting his way now by making love before they went out to dine, requiring Daisy to undress, remove her earrings, and subject her hair to the necessary dishevelment. She itched to know whether he had written to Effie, either from Holland or from Curaçao; if so much as one postcard it would be irritating, if a letter very galling indeed. Daisy had received four cards, conveying garden-variety tourist sentiments between "Dear Daisy" and "Love."

"They wanted me back at the office two weeks ago for an sales meeting," he said, advancing on the bed, and rubbing his hands as if about to say, "Now then, Mrs. Pettibone." " 'Well,' I thought, 'great deal. An sales meeting. Why should I hurry home for that?' You got any Big Spiderbecke here?"

"No."

In the afterglow he murmured some more church history, elucidating doctrines grimmer, if possible, than the last, such as infant damnation, and then told her about waddenlopen, walking across the mud at low tide from the Dutch shoreline to some islands in the North Sea where everyone went. "Instead of taking the boat, you see."

"Dirk, we've got to have a talk. Clear the air."

"Silence clears it better, mijn schat. I guarantee it."

If he was going to develop an epigrammatic side, like Mother, it would be hard going indeed. It would throw everything quite off balance. He was much less abrasive without humor.

"I want to know where we stand."

"Why should we stand? Isn't this much better?"

Really! He gave her a squeeze, prolonged to pin her to the mattress when she tried to get up. "Dwergpapagaai."

"What?"

"Lovebird. But you're hungry. So am I. Why don't you bathe and we'll get on our horse."

"I bathed just before you came, obviously, and I'm starved, so why — All right, just a quick shower then, you old ritualist." And punching him in the stomach herself, she popped out of bed and ran to the bathroom, offering him a bobbing view of her "pretty little dish custard."

What am beautiful shambles her life was.

·7·

Of the ever-replenished pool of pencils sharpened and resharpened for distribution by the office boys, it amazed Daisy to note how many were chewed to a fare-thee-well by previous users. Even for a place boasting more than the normal share of neurotics the percentage was astounding. Not just the wood was gnawed; the very metal bands below the erasers were often raddled with anonymous teethmarks. Whose? Someone even apparently poked the point-end into his mouth, judging by the perforations that far down the shaft, which could not otherwise have been made without gagging on the butt. Who might that be? Charlie Kemp, an accredited wretch shackled to a known shrew? Dog Bokum, wondering where his next bout of heavy breathing was coming from? A drive to pump semen into every woman in the five boroughs must take its toll, quite apart from the accomplishments themselves. It had by now become a neurotic compulsion of Daisy's own to immediately sort out from each new batch any pencils that showed signs of having been munched on, and, holding them by the unmasticated edge, gingerly drop them into the waste-basket. Their being handled by human fingers seemed hygienic problem enough, after all. Some were devoid of erasers. Were they bitten off by martyrs to chastity, like poor Charlie Kemp, or priapic obsessives like Dog Bokum? Did pencil chewers suck and chomp only on fresh ones, or were they in their nervous abstraction oblivious to whether previous users had teethed on them?

Dog looked like the moral mongrel he was when, startled in the act of pitching away her culls for the day, Daisy saw him standing in her doorway watching her, his great basset eyes mooching advance assurance that the answer today would be yes. "Can you make lunch?"

It struck her then that his nickname may well after all have derived from his hangdog look, rather than the bio-graphical concept of a cur in perpetual rut — or the idea of there being no limit to what he'd go to bed with. Daisy despised the term for an unprepossessing girl, as perhaps the nastiest in the language after nigger. The humiliations of women! Well, anyway, there he was, rounding the trau-matic turn of forty, no longer the most savory of beasts. There was a pot, slight but observable, this morning em-phasized by a missing shirt button, the thinning hair also detrimental to the amorist's cause, and just now a peeling sunburnt nose, product of a Caribbean weekend. His calling on her coatless meant nothing in these rabbit hutches, where to have your shirttails tucked in was to be formally attired. So nemine that — and the fact that an-other missing button had resulted in his having at some point in his toilet secured his left cuff with a stapling ma-chine. His shoes were shined, though his trousers gave some evidence of that having been accomplished by wiping the insteps across his calves. And one could have liked less of brown shoes with blue suits, quite common at this sophisticated mag. What a periodical for one of the Ten Best Dressed Men to be publisher of! Dog was not your well-turned-out chap, and Daisy would have liked to have turned him out then. But she couldn't. What a lot of pity wrongdoers suck out of you! She felt genuinely sorry for him, the more so — and here was a nice little convolution for you — the more so because of its having suddenly now dawned on her that he was calculatedly pulling a male trick known to almost every woman: the little lost boy look. The eyes were bulbs adjustable to whatever wattage of patheticness was required to exact sympathy from the other. Now he laid the flat of one hand against her doorjamb, crossing one foot over the other, and to delay rejection said, "I do that myself. Sort them out and keep only the long ones. I can't stand stubs."

That one went through the Freudian computer without any programming. His smile seemed to be suggesting other areas of consideration, however. He was trying to tell her that a temperamental distaste for pencil ends was only the beginning of the lot they had in common. She'd see.

"If you're tied up today, use one of those to pencil me in when you can."

"It so happens that I'm busy today, Dog, but maybe some . . ." She had put him off in this vague fashion before. She wanted neither to lunch with him nor to hurt him. She grasped at a bit of data she had collected on his modus operandi. He took you out to lunch properly once, to do a feasibility study on you, as her feminine informant had bluntly put it, "where he'll feel you out, and I can say that again. If you're not interested in 'lunching' next time in his apartment, then that's it. He won't bother you any more." She could avoid being seen leaving the office with him by arranging to meet at some restaurant not frequented by the office crowd, and not return with him by pleading a bit of shopping she must dash off to. That would also cut the meal short. And after all, she was an investigative reporter naturally expected to face occupational hazards.

Dog ordered a dozen oysters while insisting Daisy have the pompano, at a restaurant called Fisherman's Luck. The pompano was fourteen dollars, to which one must also add the white Burgundy selected from a wine list bound in vellum, so that Daisy quickly calculated the guilt she was going to feel when Dog moved to claim his reward. He did his best to amuse her, without concealing the lugubrious undercurrent to his gaiety. They found they shared a fondness for Klee, and Dog recalled how the artist, this playful artist, had said that he painted in order that he might not weep. Daisy started an eyeball headache watching for the corner of his mouth to turn up in a wistful, laugh-clown-laugh expression he had. The more transparent his ploys the more she felt as though she was nursing somebody.

"There's a strain of insanity in my family," he said, by way of recommending himself as a candidate for solace from any woman worthy of the name. "On my mother's side. Her brother tried to kill himself by jumping off the Staten Island ferry. He implored the other passengers not to throw him lifelines because of the natural instinct for preservation that makes a drowning man grasp at anything to save himself. But they threw them to him anyway, of course."

"And did he grab hold of any?"

"Yes, and was hauled aboard again. But later he jumped off a bridge in Wisconsin, and that was that. My mother has terrible fits of depression, so I guess I came by mine honestly." He looked off, turning the stem of his wineglass. "Have you ever wanted to put your head in the oven?"

"I actually have."

He returned his gaze, looking at her with new eyes. They might have more in common than at first supposed. "You actually stuck your head in the oven, my dear?"

"Twice."

"And each time someone . . . Or you changed your . . . Didn't have the . . . Darling."

Daisy shook her head, then drank some more wine. "You see, I had been reviewing books for this Long Island paper I worked for, and once when three or four novels in rapid succession, full of the angst bit, you know —"

"I know, I know." He knew, they were simpatico. They shared a shorthand by which such kindred spirits recognized and decoded one another on the shortest of conceivable acquaintances. The unhappy, happy few.

"There was just this rash of death wish stuff, with characters putting their heads in the oven all the time like so many cakes in a bakery. So one night I jumped out of bed after reading that same line again and went downstairs to check for myself. And just as I expected. It's not all that easy to put your head in an oven. Today practically impossible unless you're a contortionist — to say nothing of us all having electric ones to begin with. Anyway, I was right. I opened my oven — they're now all at chest level you know —"

"I know! Yes, yes!"

"— and laid my head sort of sideways on the lid? Which was as far as I could get it, unless you sort of wedge it halfway inside at one of the corners, and then you have this not hinge exactly to contend with, well, yes, hinge sort of, at the base of the door. Very uncomfortable. Let alone that you have to stand there on your feet till you get the thing done, which you couldn't because you'd topple to the floor before anything happened. Unless you had a barstool. The old-fashioned gas stove did stand on the floor, and so I suppose then you could *sit* on the floor — or on a kitchen chair — till the end came. But you still *can't put your head in an oven.*"

"Sylvia Plath did," Dog protested, not liking the way this topic, so rich in prospects for soul amalgamation, had gone off course.

"That's the way you hear. She probably just sat there with the gas turned on, which is of course what's meant in these cases."

"Well, there you are." Dog spread his hands, then twisted in his chair looking for the waiter. "How about a brandy?"

"Oh, I couldn't. I have some shopping to do, and I'm accountable at the office. You're not — you're the boss there, a law unto yourself." He arrested her move to get her purse from under her napkin by laying a hand on hers. "I hate rushing because this has been so —"

"I know you're not married, but are you attached? Living with anybody?"

"Not living, but rather firmly attached."

He gave her hand a squeeze before releasing it, as a cloud crossed his face. He had drawn a blank. The *Weltschmerz* thing had gone awry and she was firmly attached. He had spent forty clams for nothing. That was not her fault. She hadn't deceived him or encouraged any false expectation. Yet she did experience a vaporous regret on his behalf. There must, then, simply be men in whom the pursuit of women is a kind of sickness. "What's he trying to prove?"

is a cliché not relevant in all such cases, nor is the psychiatric truism unfailingly valid, namely that unremitting Don Juanism is precisely the reverse of what it appears to be. He may legitimately have suffered the misery on which he had found it effective to trade, getting women to rock him on their breasts. Insisting on splitting the check would have been pointless. She had never managed it with a man. This one looked more than ever like a poor dog she should throw a bone.

"You're attractive, I like you, I really do, but it's true that I am — what do the British say? Knit up with someone. If it weren't for that —" She flung up her hands with a pretty little laugh and finished with a pretty little lie. "I might." Let him hold that like a poultice to his aching whatever for the rest of the day — or till something else turned up. She pecked him on the mouth as she slid out from behind the table, then hurried away, turning to wave at the door before dashing through it. But Dog Bokum looked as though he had been sexually harassed.

"We remain a minority group."

"Even though we're half the world's population."

The Diesel was not best pleased by that line of discussion, nit-picking obscurantism all the worse for being frivolous. She glanced at Daisy as she pressed the side of her fork into a kumquat, sending a thin jet of juice into Daisy's butter plate. It reminded Daisy of the time a male dinner companion, who prided himself on his urbanity, had caught her in the eye with a similar spray from a cherry tomato bitten into with his front teeth. The incident had so shattered his aplomb as to be conceivably responsible for his vanishing into a monastery, from which he sent her photographs of himself in hooded vestments that made him look more like a member of the Ku Klux Klan than an ascetic Christian.

"We're a *qualitative* minority is the thing, which in many ways is more insidious than a quantitative," Bobsy explained.

"Of course. That was exactly my point. I was being ironic. We women remain a minority through discrimination even though there are as many of us as of them."

Really the Diesel was like the schnecke that was her logo — all coiled round and around herself, or, to graduate the visual metaphor (more in sorrow than in anger), reptilian, really, a psychic arrangement of concentric circles ready to strike at any moment. Of course that added up to a rather untidy figure of speech, yet not too mixed if you compared the hair coils to an adder in repose. But always ready to strike. Daisy revolved the conceit guiltily in her mind as Bobsy chewed another kumquat whole, with her molars, not like the "intellectual with something missing in his life" whom God knew what other mortifications public and private had driven into the arms of the Church. A restaurant management aware that Bobsy was a kumquat freak so heaped her salad plate with the fruit that it seemed as much an order of kumquats garnished with chicken salad as the other way around. Daisy knew that at some point in the meal the Diesel was going to ask to see some copy, so when she cleared her throat to speak Daisy cut in with, "We always seem to be eating."

Frowned then the Diesel. "Whatever brought that on?"

"Did you have a d.o.p. named Turley for English?"

Bobsy narrowed her eyes suspiciously, sensing a stall, and watched as much as listened to Daisy, her gaze fixed on Daisy's lips as though her words were visibly issuing from her mouth and would ascend into a cartoonist's dialogue balloon over her head. Last week there had been no manuscript either, rough or finished; plenty of notes, some paragraphs sketched out and one rough draft for an article tentatively entitled "Musical Swivel Chairs." But nothing meeting the stern Dieselesque edict: "I want their balls in a nutcracker, and I want it by Christmas." The stuff could be exposé, or about reform, or a combination, but it must be forthcoming.

"He was determined that Galsworthy would not die, Turley. We were assigned not only *The Forsyte Saga,* but *all the plays,* mind you. All. The. Plays, Bo. Of course no one doubts now they were ground-breaking then, well-knit dramas of social protest fighting the ills of the day — flogging horses now long dead. We should have a good playwright waging our fight for us! The plays were forgotten even then, I mean when we went to school, dropped forever into the oubliette of . . . of . . ."

"I understand."

"All I remember from the whole oeuvre is one line. I don't even remember the play. Maybe it was *Windows.* But the family are sitting at dinner in the third act after having been seen at table in the first two, and as the curtain goes up the father says, 'We always seem to be eating.' That brought it on, Bobo. The things that stick in your mind."

Their coffee came, and Bobsy shook into hers two saccharin tablets from a pillbox carried everywhere in her bag. She struck Daisy as a Valkyrie in reverse, having the men in hell rather than conducting them to Valhalla. She drew her cup to her by its saucer. "Have you —"

"Do you suppose he lived long enough to see the television series of the *Saga?*"

"Good God, Galsworthy died in the thirties."

"No, no, I mean Turley. He could still be around."
Daisy scratched the tip of her chin, smiling reminiscently.
"He used to quote Galsworthy's remark: 'The precious has
precious little chance of surviving.' However, sir, Gals-
worthy's dead as a doornail while they keep reviving
Ronald Firbank."

"Is he the wispy one?"

"Too exquisite for this world. Too too, they used to
say. I once read a review of his biography by a critic who
said he was unfit not only for military service but for
civilian life in wartime. He also ended up in the arms of
the Church."

" 'Also'? What do you mean?"

"Oh." Daisy made a flustered gesture. "Just somebody
I was thinking of. A friend of mine. Well, once somebody
saw him off in a cab —"

"Who, your friend?"

"No, no, Firbank. A friend of *his* saw *him* off in a cab,
and as the taxi moved away the friend said, 'Good night,
Firbank,' and Firbank had the taxi stop so he could put
his head out the window and call out, 'I wish you wouldn't
call me Firbank. It gives me a sense of galoshes.' "

The Diesel sighed and sat back, giving the lapels of her
suit a loosening flirt, like a woman caller shaking out her
furs to indicate that she is prepared to stay a long time
indeed. "Now how about it? Do you have anything to
show me?"

Nodding briskly, though about to answer in the nega-
tive, Daisy said, "Well, not anything in the sense of balls
in a nutcracker just yet, until I can get to refine the
material. The thing is, one has got such a wealth of it, in
note form, it's a herculean task to get it into organized
shape. Plus now there's the new angle to integrate it all

with, telling how our crusade has rectified evils, though much remains to be done, so we're dealing with a two-pronged thing."

"But surely first it's easy enough to do a few pieces on the evils. Hell, isn't *anybody* being oppressed?"

"You damn tootin' I am!"

That turned out to be truer than Daisy bargained for. Certainly more prophetic than she could have envisioned just at the time of this watershed session with the Diesel.

She was having drinks with Andy Squibb at the Algonquin after work, and had managed to fend off his suggestion that she join him in a third, pleading a letter to write and an important phone call coming in from her family in Indiana. In fact she was hoping to hear from Dolfin, who hadn't phoned in two weeks. As she rose to leave, she froze. Dolfin walked into the lobby with Effie, whose divorce had just come through. She stepped back behind a partition, then with lowered head, digging into her bag, ducked around to the newsstand and bought herself a package of cigarettes. Stowing it in her bag, she darted out the door and into the street.

In the cab crawling home, she felt as though she had been kicked in the stomach. Once before she had been mistreated by a man, and old scars opened into wounds again. But to be cheated on for someone whose betrayal Dolfin himself had admitted was "am piece treachery." Well, she would show what a woman scorned could really do. The steam was back in her engine. Perhaps she had — what was the line from *Hamlet?* — lacked gall to make oppression bitter. No lack now. To hell with pussyfooting about her lover's possession. She would name the magazine itself if the libel lawyers at *Femme* would let her. That at least would not be her problem to decide on. Before she was finished, what the Diesel wanted in a nutcracker she would have served up on toast, on a platter. What stinkers men could be, snug and smug in their old, old suzerainty. With their certified perfidy and deceit, their quackery and their trumpery. She was glad it was her blood week, it helped stoke up the roaring furnace of resolve. She was grateful for the rage itself: it meant she wouldn't cry into her pillow — at least not tonight.

How could she have been so faint a feminist, she wondered as the cab swerved out of a clot of traffic and shot down Fifth Avenue toward her apartment. Rather, how could she so woefully have backslidden, taken in by the very ills she had got close up to inspect. Torn between love and duty? Torn between *slush* and duty! Seduced in more ways than one, and being brought to bed the least of them. Suckered, snowed, cozened and beguiled. Had on a seed roll. If skepticism was indeed the chastity of the intellect, as Santayana said, then she had been the whore of gullibility. But no more. Now it was that great curtain line of Hamlet's. "O, from this time forth, my thoughts be bloody, or be nothing worth."

·8·

"Dog?"

He was to be her first target male, who God knew had had more target females on his conscience than he could easily count. When asked by Joan Fontaine in *Suspicion* how many women he has kissed, Cary Grant replies that he tried to tally them up one night and fell asleep on seventy-three. Bokum might have supplied the same figure, reading screw for kiss.

Dog stood in Daisy's office doorway, chewing on a pencil. Having called to him as he passed, she rose from her desk and went over. Balls dropping into the slots in a pinball machine were Daisy's association with his eyes rolling down the cleft showing just above her blouse.

"I thought it was nice the other day, Dog. Was it nice for you too?"

The eyes rolled upward again were brimming with reproach. By what parody of an honored postcoital ritual query was he being mocked? Was he the victim of a hoax designed to bring the sacred act of love down in a cheap heap? Nice for him — *lunch?*

He took the pencil from his mouth and thrust it into a shirt pocket. A crisp new white shirt, no missing buttons, nor a stapled cuff testifying to his need for the love of a good woman, someone adept with needle and thread. The home-from-the-wars look derived today principally from a loosened collar, the knot of his knit tie slid down; a fresh shaving nick without the sometime scrap of toilet paper; and a somewhat irregular hair part, running in a wavering line across his scalp like that gnawed on an apple by a child.

"Wasn't what nice?" He was going to make her say it flat out, share the outrage with him, admit the travesty.

"Lunch."

He glanced both ways up the hall, as if to recruit witnesses that the mighty had not yet fallen that low. "It was good for me too" would not be heard crossing his lips vis-à-vis a lunch date, not quite yet.

Daisy went on: "Dog, I've been having second thoughts about what I said then." The eyes, somewhat lacklustre this morning, as though things were really slow and he'd spent the night thrashing in chastity, brightened; his ears pricked up. "About staying here at this job." She gestured to the galleys on her desk. "I think it came up, and I exaggerated being satisfied with it. The fact of the matter is that makeup —"

Andy Squibb hobbled by just then, again one shoe off and one shoe on. His pelvis was gradually being rocked back into line: that was the word around the office. "Swell layout on those illustrated limericks this week, Dog," he threw over his shoulder as he pumped away around a turn in the corridor, *up,* down, *up,* down.

"Thanks, Andy."

"That's what I wanted to talk about," Daisy said when they were alone again. "I've always enjoyed doing the makeup on the papers I worked for. Is it true Doris is leaving and you'll need to break in a new recruit?" That was Immediate Occupancy, now engaged to a boy from a nice family in Tenafly.

"Looks that way. Why? Do you want to talk about it?" With the gleam in his eye he might as well have said, "Lie down and we'll discuss it."

"Yes, I would."

"All right, let's. I'm tied up for lunch. How about dinner?"

"O.K."

He smiled, a smile so finely shaded as to stop just short of arch speculation, and left, chewing on the pencil again.

Daisy's scenario for retribution was strictly plotted in her mind. What she worried about was her moral justification, in a way that explained her obsession just then with *Hamlet*. In college she had written a paper on Eliot's critique of the play, with the famous charge that it lacks an adequate objective correlative. That is, the emotions vented in it exceed the circumstances generating them. In other words, the play is undermotivated. Was she? Was she taking out on one man a vindictiveness inspired by another? By the time of her date with Dog Bokum she had grievance enough. Thanks to a whispered conversation accidentally overheard in the ladies' room she learned that she, too, had acquired an office nickname. Apparently she was known as Daisy May. "Get it? Daisy May — or then again she may not." A tease. The wit who had so dubbed her was Dog Bokum himself. Now she no longer lacked gall to make oppression bitter, where he was concerned. She felt quite justified in proceeding with her plan: to castrate him.

That was the personal side of it. Journalistically, she had her ground rules firmly drawn up. Going to bed with him to get a promotion was of course utterly out of the question. Being denied the advancement because she refused to would be all the evidence she needed. She would have the goods on the corporation as far as this one episode was concerned. Tantalization as a way of making the villain tip his hand she felt perfectly justifiable.

"What will I have to do?"

Over the last of the chicken Kiev that followed the mandatory shellfish, the Dog seemed to give a little twitch of pleasure. He had misunderstood her meaning. She had meant to ask what her duties would be if given the apprenticeship in makeup, but maybe there had been a little unconscious cunning in framing the question so that he might take it his way. After all, don't we have it on the highest authority that we are to be wise as serpents while being harmless as doves? None higher. The Dog rather charmingly contemplated a tender morsel of breast on the tines of his fork, licking his lips. Things had in fact been slow. Immediate Occupancy gathered into the arms of Tenafly convention, he had been seen fleeing at noonday with a widowed newcomer in accounting, a chemical blonde of relatively ripened years, of good repute as a ready and still palatable quick lay, affectionately known as the Jiffy Bag. The office wits slumbered not and never slept. Now this delectable young woman not yet rounding thirty, a woman with real — yes, say it, though people who have it never use the word — real class, falling into his lap?

"Why, naturally, Daisy . . . I mean you'd be a real . . . I mean what man wouldn't —"

"I mean would I be actually entrusted with making up a page, or would it be a matter of understudying the rest of you for a while? Just sort of a looking-on, on-the-job training?"

Some color seeped into Dog's cheeks as he smiled faintly. They ate in silence for a few moments, taking flustered sips of their wine. Could he be fairly regarded as having tipped his hand? Daisy realized she had meticulously to retrace herself to the ticklish moment when he had misunderstood, like a player in a parlor game going back two squares.

"About what you started to say a while ago. Was, is the implication that you intend to fill the job with a playmate?"

He set his fork down and made gestures with both hands that were gems of incomprehensibility. "I mean I'm no hypocrite," he said, as though exhibiting like a flawed but still flashing jewel his One Redeeming Virtue. "I mean why not mix work and pleasure in this worst of all possible worlds. This *vita brevis* that's all too — too —"

"Short?"

"Yes. Exactly." Some more bazaar-haggler gestures from the very shoulders. "This fool's errand to the grave, so full of misery and frustration, I for one make no bones or apologies about using my position to gather the only rosebuds in all this stinking world that make it tolerable. I *live* for it, I admit it. It's all that matters for me — split-tail. I no more than have today's lined up than I'm thinking about tomorrow's. Lorri Lanson wants the job, and she knows herself that whoever takes it will be directly under me, and I don't give a damn that that's the office joke about Dog Bokum. Some people think I'm called Dog because I'm always on the prowl for whatever's in heat, or worse, what I'll go to bed with in a pinch, but that's not it. In school I was called Pooch, I guess because of the basset hound look. Around the eyes? That's how it started. The wine of life keeps oozing drop by drop, the leaves of life keep falling one by one, drink for once dead you never shall return, we only go through once in this . . . this moment's flickering of aggrieved desire . . ."

This no-doubt set seduction recitative, not to be stopped

until run through, seemed on close analysis a triple pastiche of Housman, Omar Khayyám and Thomas Wolfe. The moment's flickering of aggrieved desire sounded to Daisy like a literal heist from *Of Time and the River,* that fat slob of a book some d.o.p. was always assigning one. Dog paused only long enough to gulp some more wine, a drop of which he had to dab from his chin with his napkin before he was off and running with the rhapsody again. He was still in it when dessert arrived, strawberries with a bottle of Barsac. Daisy braced herself through a rain of Lawrence, Henry Miller . . . He was really rather well-read, if a bit chaotically so. And he knew a lot of big words.

"I like my work all right, sure, it's rewarding, but other than that there's only the immemorial inexpressible ineffable ineluctable cunt. I think it, sleep it, dream it. I eat it, drink it, chase it day and night. I see it everywhere — in a flower, when I cut a strawberry in two. Watch."

"I understand. That won't be necessary." Daisy hoped she did not look too demure as she sat with her chin poised on fingers interlaced upside down. One elbow slipped off the table edge when she tried to modify her position, and she dismantled the pose, leaning back in her chair. She watched him halve a strawberry with the side of his spoon.

"You see? There. Two ovoid cavities suggestive of the most succulent fruit in paradise. O cunning crevice! O multifoliate rose! O —"

Daisy made a shushing noise, glancing around to see if they were being overheard. The Dog raved on.

"O incalculable primordial polyphiloprogenitive protoplasmic pink!"

"Pull . . . *lease.*"

He collapsed, exhausted, his arms hanging. Daisy remained amazed at the breadth and variety of his paste-up. Even Eliot was in it — that multifoliate and polyphiloprogenitive stuff sounded like it. A little torn out of the original context of course. Torn and bleeding. His pitches, however prefabricated or boned up on, had ardor, you had to give him that. A girl really felt *courted.* He was gasping from the exertion. After dabbling them in the cream, he popped the strawberry halves into his mouth, smacking his lips with due respect.

"Dog, have you ever thought about marrying again?"

He made a pronounced face, not only his lips curling, but one nostril as well. "Man is not by nature monogamous."

"You could have affairs. Marry a nice girl who'd agree to them. Open and free marriages are coming to be the thing. Maybe by racking up as many conquests as you can you're trying to prove something. This mucho macho stuff is suspect, you know."

He waved the bromide away like a wandering fly, impatient to get the discussion back on the track.

"You asked about where you come in. Well, nobody could think of you as anything but a catch. You're quality."

"Thank you."

"This Barsac is really too sweet, even for a dessert wine. Would you like to stop in for a brandy? I'm just a couple of blocks down."

"All right."

"I don't mean if the right woman came along I'd be adverse to it. To marriage," he said as they strolled along toward his flat. He means averse, Daisy thought, who had more important things on her mind. Was he leading up to that familiar "try" ploy? Let me test-drive the car and maybe I'll buy it? Men were all alike, though, of course, some were more alike than others.

"Since my last divorce there have been a couple I liked

well enough for marriage to cross my mind. One in particular. A dream in bed, and a smashing cook. She had one fault."

"She didn't think broiled wieners in the backyard was eating out?"

"She was — affected. Call it that though it's not the right word. Her walking-on-eggs diction got on your nerves. You can't be happy with a woman who pronounces both d's in Wednesday."

Daisy turned to grin at him, as though accusing him of having made an epigram, like the father turning to his plain daughter in Henry James's *Washington Square*. What had the poor girl said again? She must look that up, as she must the multifoliate rose business in Eliot. That was no doubt religious, making Dog's appropriation of it scabrous.

He was saying, "I mean each of these things, while insignificant in itself, adds up. It — oh, isolates the germ of what bugs you."

"What else did? Can you give some more for-instances?"

"Yes. You heard both r's in February, is what you were up against, day and night, and all the letters in clothes, including the what's it called, a dipthong? The 'th.' "

"Well, it's not a diphthong (which is how *that's* spelled and pronounced), that's something else. The 'ae' in aesthetic and aegis is a diphthong. But I know what you mean. It can be irritating."

"We say Wensday and Febyewary and cloze, for Christ's sake," he said, with such vehemence one would have thought Daisy the perfectionist under rebuke. "We don't say an hotel!"

Dog had a seventh-floor flat in a building of which the elevator was on the blink, so they had to puff on foot up the dimly lighted flights of stairs, each offering its slight variant of the domestic aroma that clings forever to the corridors of such habitations — a "chord" of smells, Daisy often thought, of which the dominant note is human cooking.

There was a long living-dining room at the end of which was a bedroom seen, through an open doorway, to be small, and off to the right a kitchen, to which Dog repaired for some ice after hanging up both their coats in a foyer closet. In his absence she stepped quickly over to a single bookcase and ran an eye over its contents — hardly what you'd call a library. It seemed devoid of the poets and other hymnists on whom he drew for his panting paeans to the flesh. A set of Flaubert, a smattering of Modern Library volumes including Saki and Thomas Mann, some tattered Horatio Algers, obviously family heirlooms of the kind you can neither read nor throw out. *Sonnets for All Occasions* was, as Daisy suspected, a birthday gift inscribed by a bygone aunt. A chapbook of the kind found on supermarket racks entitled *Your Prostate*. She was about to turn away when her eye was caught by the top of an all but invisible paperback tucked away behind a row on a middle shelf, and she quickly fished it out. It was called *Diet and Sex: How to Eat Your Way to a Better Love Life*. She whirred through it, reading snatches at random. "Chemicals in today's food that are retarding men's sexuality while stimulating women's . . . Among the meats necessary for virility . . . also nuts . . . some claim honey . . . asparagus . . . Among the ancients . . . vitamin A . . ." The back cover was devoted to blurbs like "The startling book that explores the close link between food and sexual potency." Then something about "a love philter you can whip up in your own kitchen," that will "cure those bedroom blahs."

Hearing Dog's returning footsteps, she dropped the book back where she'd found it, and was bent over a stack of back *New Yorkers* piled on a stool when he reappeared.

They drank brandy and soda for a while, Daisy seeing to it that his glass remained full. She had read somewhere that excessive drinking impaired and sometimes destroyed the erotic capabilities of middle-aged men. She had seen a wretch on television testify to its ravages through a hole cut in a paper bag worn over his head to safeguard his anonymity in the panel he had been persuaded to join. "Den I got drunk and coon't perform in bed."

Dog was soon tipsy enough to come over to where she sat and, kneeling beside her chair, try to kiss her. She was a little fuzzy herself by now, which enabled her to bear a few moments of it, poised primly and turned in such a way as to make only half of her mouth accessible, without seriously blurring the clarity of her intentions. She watched with almost clinical detachment as he rose unsteadily to his feet and removed his coat and then his shirt, without soliciting permission. He evidently had his code, which was that a girl agreeing to come in was committing herself.

"You spoke of a woman good in bed. I once had an unforgettable man once. The best time I had, something I know will never be topped," she said, admitting another self to play this role for Daisy Dobbin. "My God he was tremendous." She rattled the ice in her tumbler, smiling with an air of dreamy reminiscence as she hiccuped. She had read that what men fear most is that they will suffer by comparison with predecessors, even current husbands, so much as often to be immobilized when up against women boasting of the prowess of previous lovers — washed out, so that no comparison is *possible*. Dog Bokum was glumly silent as he picked at a knot in his shoelace, and, that done, shoes and socks both removed, he came over and started to unbutton her blouse.

She sat stiffly, like your maiden aunt saving her breath to cool her porridge, then decorously continued the improvisation, her words belying the tableau. She looked down at his hand with interest, as though managing detachedly to watch a large arachnid slowly traverse her person.

"And the nozzle on him. Really party size. You know — like the nozzle on a firehose? You've probably seen them in public shower rooms and thought, 'My God, where was I when those were passed out?' How he could plow a girl. Not that that's everything. A woman wants more than a pneumatic drill, but still. It isn't the size, it's the technique, as the French say."

Her blouse unbuttoned but not removed, he began to peel off his trousers, sort of crow-hopping on one foot when the other became snagged in a leg. Still partly mired in the pants lying in a pool at his feet, he reached for his glass and took a last swig of the dregs before stepping conclusively out of his trousers and then shucking off his shorts, which were a bright red-and-green tartan plaid. She was tempted to ask whether he knew what clan they were.

"I never expect to see his like again," she resumed. "It's a once-in-a-lifetime thing." She dropped her eyes halfway down his now naked form, letting them come to rest there. "I wouldn't worry too much about it. Size isn't everything. Thickness is just as important as length — could be more so. It could certainly be a compensation." It shrank under her gaze like a contracting worm, finally all but disappearing from view. "You're probably just tired. Advice to the loveworn: give the poor thing a rest. I mean when the competition is stiff . . ."

He stretched out on a nearby couch with an arm flung across his brow.

"This never happened to me before." The couch springs groaned beneath him as he rose and walked to a row of windows at the front.

"It has to me, and to every woman at some time — hearing that," she said, to console him. She buttoned her blouse again, silently watching him stare out of one of the windows. "It's ignition trouble, not engine," she said at last. "Psychic, rather than physical. There's nothing organically wrong with you. Of course a male reaches his sexual peak at the age of twenty-two or -three, and from there on it's downhill —"

"*Please.*" He didn't turn around, but uttered the cry still gazing out the window. He put his head forward, as though to look down rather than across the street. "There's a jut-out on the fifth floor. The fifth-floor roof is a setback, so you couldn't do it from here on the seventh floor. A two-story drop would only leave you a mass of broken bones you'd regret having to live with. A bundle of kindling. Pills would be the thing. Or a razor."

"I have to go."

He came back and started to dress himself. "I'll get you home in a cab."

"No, don't bother. I can manage."

They were both dead sober now.

"Of course I'll 'bother.' Think I'd let you go home alone at this hour?"

It took him twenty minutes to get a taxi, and when at last he handed her into it she said good night and thanked him for the evening. But he climbed in beside her. He insisted on seeing her home, so they could talk.

"You won't say anything about this at the office?"

"What kind of a girl do you think I am?"

She had started a headache, no doubt from all the wine and the booze, but there was also a feeling of more generalized misery. She had realized her intentions, but success left rather a brackish taste. Sexual surrender itself had never been followed by compunctions of quite this kind. The Dog sat slumped in a corner of the cab, his head on his chest. He looked like a whipped puppy. She slipped a hand into his.

"I had a friend who had a friend who — get this, Dog — failed to make an unsuccessful attempt on his life."

"You mean he banked on being rescued at the last minute, and wasn't."

"You're pretty smart. Yes, he was a failure *manqué*. You see, he took an overdose of barbiturates, planning to be found out cold by a roommate returning from a date, but still alive so he could be plied with black coffee and marched around the room and so forth and so on till the ambulance arrived and rushed him to the hospital. A dramatic bid making him the Tragic Romantic figure he fancied himself. Well, the roommate stayed with his girl all night and came in the next morning, to find him dead as a mackerel. So the moral is, we mustn't try any fancy tricks."

"Life must go on. I forget just why," Dog said, gazing out the window. Daisy smiled out of hers, shaking her head. She had not heard such sophomoric thirty-second-rate Sara Teasdale since, well, she was a sophomore. The creaking histrionics to which men could resort! Women too, she reminded herself fairly. What wouldn't the Diesel have given to see this casualty. It would have made her night.

They ground to a stop before Daisy's address. He stayed her exit with a hand on her arm.

"How did they know that was his intention?"

"Because that's how he was. Pulling things for effect. He would have had some good woman wiping his nose for the rest of his life." She felt Dog physically wince at the thrust, and immediately regretted it. We can't always give people their just deserts, she thought, because where would that leave even the best of us? "He'd done it before, you see, with a — idiotic as the term sounds — safety razor blade. Well, it's been a wonderful evening. Thanks so much."

He told the driver to wait while he saw her to the door. She let him kiss her good night. The hallway was just sufficiently lighted so that, drawing back, she could see the look in his eyes.

"Pay the driver and come on back," Daisy said. "You can stay the night if you'd like. I think you'd better."

They lay rather rigidly side by side on, rather than in, Daisy's double bed, their hands folded on their breasts, staring sightlessly ceilingward like figures on a catafalque doubly monumentalizing the priapic corpse of the one, and kindred responsibility and participatory guilt of the other. Snip-snip had gone her cutting shears, and here they were, locked in a marble mourning. Transversely across the foot of the bed lay the Diesel, a silent and phantasmal accessory both before and after the fact, savoring in her style the obsequies in which they must remain collectively steeped, midwife to the birth of a death. The nutcracker had made its claim. The giblets had been had on toast. Daisy had declined the Dog's offer to stretch out on the living room sofa for what remained of the night. Half-mercies would not do in the present restitution, which must be exacted in full ceremony, until morning broke, and the shadows fled, and the propitiatory tableau could be dismantled. Half-mercies would have rubbed salt into wounds keen enough, however deserved they had seemed at the moment of infliction. What the woman in her had dealt, the woman in her must minister to, though it could hardly heal.

Sedated with a few more belts of bourbon, Dog was soon heard sleeping soundly beside her. It must have been three o'clock before she dropped off, but her heart wasn't in it.

She is back home in Indiana, yet not there, but vizting relatives in Connecticut, as her people would say. It is mid-July, and her aunt's yard is a blizzard of gypsy moths. They flutter everywhere in the balmy air, the white females looking for tree boughs on which to lay eggs that, next year, will be caterpillars ordained to generate yet another infestation, eggs on which the wingèd wives will compose themselves for death, their life cycle peacefully closing. Her aunt, buttered to the belly with sun lotion, lies in a hammock, slapping and brushing away the moths blundering into her skin surface and sticking there. How odd — an actual memory precisely embedded in a dream. Her aunt was a narcissist — not that she knew it. That was for her educated daughter later to fling at her in a hot moment. Fadeout to a lake picnic and little Daisy nearly drowning, another memory. She calls out, rousing herself from her own nightmare. Dog sleeps on, though this is supposedly his Gethsemane, she there only to watch with him one hour. His oblivion nettles her, though God knows she doesn't want him to wake up. What demons may be eating his own heart?

They slept late into that Saturday morning. She awoke with a vague sense of someone waiting for her to do so, even hurrying her along. She felt a hand slipping along her thigh, lifting the hem of her nightgown. Resurrection. The male morning arousal. He drew her over onto her back, wedging a knee between her legs preparatory to mounting her. Since his importunities had scarcely given her time to moisten, his entry was painful for both of them, but he must have his stallion plunge. She winced. It was like being deflowered again. She felt as though she was being hurried along with a cattle prod. As he churned away, her arms dutifully if mechanically encircling his back without her bothering to feign any pleasure of her own, she turned over in her mind a lead for one of her pieces, having to do with masculine approaches and ploys and techniques. "The average American man's approach to sex is junk food for thought," she evolved at last, and couldn't wait for him to finish so she could get up and jot it down. What was she doing here? Rather, what was he doing here? What grotesque emotional and moral convolutions had brought her to this restitutional pass? How could sin be a form of expiation? Something from Dolfin's rather special brand of pillow talk popped into her mind. She thought he'd murmured "parakeet," but it had been "Paraclete." Few even among religious folk knew it was the name for the Holy Ghost seen as Comforter — from old Greek and Latin meaning one called to help. Was that the cockamamy office she was discharging here? A solace bringer like a surgeon sewing back on what she had herself amputated. From woman the immemorial bitch to woman the eternal nourisher, in one fantastic nighttime leap. Woman, old fount of the milk and blood. What would the Diesel have thought of that tenth-rate treacle? Here she was, the crutch under the phallus in a Dali fantasy. No doubt all this would seem clearer in the morning. But it *was* morning. Tonight, then, it would fall into perspective. How? Lying here alone, thank God, while her tears lashed at her like winter rain? Would that be the upshot of her offering her own wound for this wretch's rehabilitation? Men had a bawdy ditty about that. Here's to the wound that never heals, etc. She couldn't remember the rest. Nature had slashed them to her own imperial purposes, offering an eternal gash in which to sheathe the masculine sword. Presently he would be strutting around the kitchen, insisting on fixing her breakfast when all she wanted was to have him dressed and out of the house. His explosion over at last, he rolled onto his back, breathing heavily. "So nice of you to come," she wanted to say, like a hostess glad to see a guest's back.

"So you're all right." She sounded like a nurse prepared to be dismissed from a case.

He cleared his throat huskily, wiping morning tears from his eyes with the hem of the bedsheet. "Daisy, you must know how I —"

"Forget it. Please. I told you it was all right. A man's more relaxed when he wakes up, it's that simple. We all know that. No, never mind, really. I'm all right. Please."

He murmured something she didn't quite catch, muffled as it was in the bedclothes. But she was sure she caught "the act of love." She was tempted to say, "It's a hard act to follow — especially if you're not nineteen any more," but of course she didn't. Instead there was something else on her mind, of some importance. It was her turn to ask it now. "You won't say anything about this at the office?"

"*Me?*" She knew his face would have been something to behold, if she'd cared to remove the arm flung across her eyes. Was he pointing to himself? She felt on the verge of hysterics, though uncertain of what kind, of which direction they might take. "What kind of a guy do you think I am?"

That was when she gave way. She rolled over onto her side, like a dolphin sporting in the water, and, burying her face in the pillow, burst into uncontrollable sobs of laughter.

· 9 ·

DAISY DARTED across Madison Avenue to avoid Bobsy, but Bobsy did the same thing to avoid her, and so she fetched up on the opposite sidewalk directly in the Diesel's line of march. But they were still a good quarter of a block apart, and so when the Diesel realized the situation she popped into the nearest store.

"She doesn't like the copy," Daisy thought aloud, "damn her."

She must not be let get away with this kind of behavior. She'd had the material, two articles and an outline for the rest, almost three weeks now, long enough to have been heard from, even allowing for consultation with colleagues. The store into which she'd scuttled was a camera shop. A sidelong glance as Daisy passed it revealed her to be browsing at one of the display counters, her back to the door. Daisy's mind was made up. She would demand an opinion straight away. A telephone call from the office later would do it.

"It lacks — bite," Bobsy said, then. "Put it that way.

You try to 'understand' these men and their exploitations, rather than attack them. You can't be like that in pamphleteering. You've got to slice it clean and lay it on the line. It's almost as though you were fleshing out characters in a novel. Weren't you working on one?"

Unblown Kisses had aborted, dropped along with the poetry. Daisy could remember having had to phone the publisher-acquaintance to whom she'd submitted three chapters and an outline of *that,* after nearly two months of silence. "It's too statemental," he'd said. Where did one pick up words like that? "Discursive. Exposition rather than the scene creations on which fiction depends." So her fact was too fictional and her fiction too factual. But statemental, for God's sake? She'd soon be ready for a statemental institution at this rate.

"No, Bobsy, I'm not working on any novel. Or anything but this series."

"This isn't just my view. Mrs. Smoot feels the same way. She's the one we're ultimately accountable to. It's too — Look, can you come to dinner Saturday? I'll fix us a beef Wellington, and we'll splurge on a Château Lafite." Rats and Snails and Puppy Dogs' Tails had at last recognized a woman's right to independence, and begun sending her half of the mooted rental money from the still-unsold house. Bobsy was in a mood for celebration. Daisy agreed to come. "I've got a new album we might listen to. The complete *Wozzeck.*"

"I'm not familiar with his work."

"Love it. And I'm still dining out on your den of probity. But while I've got you, what about the blast you promised on *Metropole?* I don't see the magazine under any of these disguises."

"I'm working on that. I may have something by Saturday."

In fact she already had a rough draft of her intended blast at "that pale pastiche of the *New Yorker*," but had held back on it for reasons not quite clear to herself, except insofar as they added up to her continuing ambivalence. She had decided to give Dolfin three weeks to be heard from, the generous span of time allowing for business trips everywhere. The deadline up, the machine gun volleys on her typewriter resumed.

"The subtlety, or lack of it, evinced by the buccaneering male naturally varies, but any woman with the normal amount of features together with a pair of legs converging in the time-honored fashion will experience the full spectrum in short order. There was the crudity of a chap I'll call Charlie Stride, at a periodical named, say, the *Cosmopolite*, who talks frankly to his masculine colleagues about 'making a feasibility study' of this dame or that . . ."

She had the revision ready to show Bobsy by Saturday. She had bathed by seven, and was sitting naked, tailorwise, on her bed rereading it, a cigarette burning in her fingers, when the phone rang.

"Daisy May?"

"Who is this?"

"I didn't know you had a middle name. I like it. Daisy May. Prachtig."

"What's that supposed to mean?"

"Splendid, marvelous. Swell."

"Where are you?"

"Amsterdam." He began to sing a bawdy song with which he'd regaled her before. " 'Amsterdam die grote stad —' " Then he broke off. "Look, don't you have an comic strip over there with an voluptuous girl with that name?"

"Where did you hear it? That middle name for me." Effie again, striking from desperation?

"I don't know. Some guy at the office where your name came up. Look, I haven't called because I had to rush back to Curaçao to clear up a bind there, and then here." His distortions of the American slang he tried to pick up were really quite charming. She liked "clear up a bind." It went with the row of beans something or other didn't amount to. "Can I see you tomorrow night?"

"When are you going to clean up the office? It's still Old MacDonald's Farm as far as I can see."

"Some directives are going out next week. You'll go over them with me, not? How about dinner?"

"I'm tied up then. This is pretty short notice. I'm free Saturday, but you're going to get a good chewing out."

The satisfaction of Dolfin's calling, after the weeks of neglect, made her heart's elation like a balloon tangled in an underbrush of resentment above which it could not soar. Or to revert to the clichés in which she seemed ever more deeply mired, part of her sang while the rest of her brooded. Grinding her way northward in a cab smelling of the cigar smoke similarly awaiting her at Bobsy's, she lowered a window and drew deep drafts of the evening air as she put to herself questions that remained elusively unanswered. Was the cavalier treatment generic masculine arrogance? Was it ethnic — an antique European assumption that women existed for men's disposition, a viewpoint exported here like Dutch cocoa? She could imagine how Dolfin, Senior — Klass yet! — and his vrouw had it. A Doll's House. Stuck like another literary quill in memory's inexplicable hide was a line from *A High Wind in Jamaica*, possibly adducible in evidence against Dolfin? How did it go again? "The captain of the steamer, who was conceited in a way that only certain Dutchmen *can* be conceited . . ." Why had that been retained all these years, to crop up now? She even remembered the italics. And why the italics to begin with? "Conceited" was rarely used any more, today we said "egotistical" instead. Was his brief disappearance to be explained as an inclination on his part to give the indicted Effie one last chance? Human nature is pretty shoddy stuff, and we all need forgiveness and redemption and upward of a thousand second chances. She was giving Dolfin no less, after all. Was the "certain" in the remembered sentence a loophole for him?

Someone should really tell the Diesel culottes were not for her. A movie shot of her walking in them would have reminded her of the seat of her problem. But the blue shot-silk outfit itself was beautiful. She shimmered and hissed as she plowed the living room floor, gesturing with cigarillo and white wine in hand. In expansive form, she rambled on about everything under the sun, as she had in the dormitory bull sessions (by no means a male patent). Some road inevitably led to Rats and Snails and Puppy Dogs' Tails. Now if he hadn't gone and got himself in another stock market jam, and hit her for some margin money he couldn't, just then, cough up himself. "So I let him keep the rent money this month. It was almost worth it showing a man how dependent he can be." Had something of that sardonic element figured in Daisy's own bailing the Dog out, saving his face for him? Mercy could be a perversion of vengeance. Or had she simply been "all woman" in getting him over the hump — or into it, as he would grossly have put it in his own tradition. But no time for private analytical byways as the Diesel jabbered ebulliently on. "He's wearing me thin," she announced. "What are you laughing about?" "I'm not laughing." Daisy had recalled her father complaining about being worn thin, and her mother retorting, "And high time someone did," poking him in the paunch. Bobsy paused in her travels to climax a point by banging a tabletop. "He'll never take my advice *before* a debacle." And she brought her fist carefully down among some bric-a-brac, jangling a last few measures out of a wound-down music box that played "How Dry I Am." "Let's eat. There's the oven buzzer."

There was no beef Wellington after all (and no *Wozzeck* either as it turned out, neither being in any mood for Berg). Instead there was a plump juicy capon, and as Bobsy bent to her task of carving up the eunuch it occurred to Daisy, seated at the other end of the mahogany dining table, how inappropriate was the resemblance to Will Rogers of someone who had apparently never met a man she liked. Certainly not her father, of whom she chatted away as she heaped their plates with light meat and dark, small potatoes roasted in their jackets, and string beans with water chestnuts in them.

"He was a handsome dog, still is at what, fifty-eight, always with a bit on the side, as our British cousins say." She swallowed the "t" in true cockney style. "Bi' on the side," she mimicked, smiling with the kind of loitering, indolent malice characteristic of her when she was off on a recitative, as they had called Bobsy's rambles at college. The flannelly thickness of speech and the faint gauze of remoteness in her eyes, as though she were engaging in a soliloquy of reminiscence rather than chatting with you, told Daisy she'd taken about enough aboard already, and the table wine still to go. Two bottles of white Burgundy stood ready. "Mother just had to put up with it, with nothing of her own but a spot of slap and tickle with the butcher, and maybe that was made up. Now he's apparently got another cookie he's in a swivet over." The Diesel gave a single, hiccup-disrupted chuckle as her power knife came down through a mound of breast meat and struck the platter with a hideous rattle of the electric blades. At last a generously heaped plate was handed across, and she started on her own, still discoursing on her "inequitably handsome" father. "You should move into his paint factory next. A gold mine probably for a pamphleteer working on O.S.H."

"O.S.H.?"

"Occupational sexual harassment. Girls at secretarial school planning to apply at Diesel Paint and Enamel better major in keeping the desk between them and the boss. 'I got a new typist.' 'Oh? Is she fast?' 'Yeah, but I'll catch her one of these days.' Remember that patter routine we did at school?" Having served herself, she poured their glasses full of what turned out to be a Bâtard-Montrachet. Splurge indeed. Daisy watched her worriedly as they lifted their glasses and drank. This might be a rough night, and most of it still to come.

"Did you know my mother was Dutch? One of those poor souls whom years of huisvrouw servitude have left with a taste for searing prison dramas. Cagney, Raft." It was known of old that the Diesel was at her best when her comments, however trenchant, reached borderline gibberish.

"But wasn't your father German?"

She waved the distinction away. "German, Dutch. But the fact might interest you after your episode with that wooden shoe — safely gone over to Effie if we can believe the scuttlebutt. Happy resolution if you ask me. They deserve each other. I'm sure you're not wired for being a featured alternate selection, as the book clubs say. Did you know that Prick was a Holland name? Fact. Mother has an uncle — hence I a granduncle — named Prick Ten Eyck. Can you believe anything so dear? You don't believe it. Well, he edited a Dutch-English anthology of poetry that — Hell, I've got it right here somewhere." Bobsy rose to go fetch it, but Daisy successfully discouraged the search. "Later then. Edited by Prick Ten Eyck, it says. Good name for lots of them, not just Nederlanders. I suppose you think I rather hammer away at it. Well, you have to, to get anywhere. Same with *any* protest movement. How long the wheel has to squeak before they finally grease it! We'll talk about salvaging the series later, but first we have a couple of bottles to capsize. Here, you're not drinking your share."

"Salvage?"

"Well, ginger them up."

"The thing is, at *Metropole* they *are* going to clean it up. I have it on the best authority. So the piece about them will have to be softened up instead of — Wait a minute! And also revised to reflect the idea of *tangible results for our Crusade*. How it's beginning to bear fruit."

"I hope the horse's mouth isn't who I hope it isn't. Always distrust a snappy dresser. A fop is a narciss — narcissist." She sounded like a hissing snake as she got a grip on her diction. And my God, was that word to crop up everywhere? "An inturned sensuality that you can trust less than you can most men, and we know how far you can trust them. Pew is well got up too, but the *Ten Best Dressed?*" Here the Diesel spun out a series of rather slipshod sequiturs concluding with an account of the previous Sunday *Times'* supplement on men's styles. There was an article about the "new executive" going to the office tieless, with a picture of one tycoon who in addition wore his shirt open one button below the collar, "and, so help me, two buttons on weekends. Seriously. The vanity. Ours can't hold a candle to theirs." She lampooned the executive by undoing the tunic of her suit in two illustrative stages, leaving her bosom bare enough to display half of her sumptuous breasts. She didn't fasten the buttons again, all through dinner, so that when they repaired to the living room for their coffee, the décolletage as she bent to pour it was more than a little disconcerting. At last, over a certainly imprudent brandy, she did something that in college days had been frolicsome and amusing, but under the circumstances, these years later, was another matter.

She had joined Daisy on a sofa, and now, loosening still a third button, she lifted her breasts out by cupping her hands under them, and, hefting them, said, "There's the old mangoes. Not bad, eh?"

"No, they're not bad at all," Daisy agreed, laughing nervously.

"Yours were always beautiful too, Daze. You'll never need silicone. I probably will, with bazooms like these. Still firm, though. Feel them. Go ahead, feel."

"Later perhaps."

"Smaller, yours are, but choicer. Yours fill a teacup, these a mixing bowl."

She made no move to tuck them back in when she walked to the piano to sing a duet with herself. " 'She used to like waltzes, so please don't play a waltz. She danced divinely, and I loved her so, Ah, but there I go . . .' " She wheeled around on the stool. "I wonder if those two blokes ever settled that bet about the lyrics."

"What blokes? What bet?"

"Weren't you at that party? At the Colbys'. I did my shtick there with the same song, and when I got through, one of the guys said there was no 'Ah' in the line. Just 'but there I go.' Another guy said there was, and lo and behold Doctor Colby dug out an LP of Gene Austin singing the song, and damned if the 'Ah' wasn't in one chorus but not the next. By that time they'd made a ten-dollar bet — not settled that night of course."

Daisy noted with increased alarm that when Bobsy returned to the sofa to pour them some more coffee, the tips of her breasts were swollen. In a silence portentously altering the atmosphere in the room, Bobsy took a long pull on her coffee, looking at the far wall. She stared straight ahead of her for some time after returning her cup and saucer to the table; then as though abandoning any attempt to recompose herself, she turned her head slowly and directed a gaze at Daisy at once shy and brazen.

"Don't you think we're all bisexual at bottom?" she said, thickly yet gently.

"So it's said. I for one have never —"

"Feel them."

"What?"

"Put your hands on them."

"Perhaps some other time."

"Go ahead, and tell me you don't feel a quiver. Or when I fondle *your* pretty little dumplings."

Daisy laughed, and in a sort of stupor watched Bobsy remove the coffee cup from her hand, set it down, and then take her, Daisy's, two hands and lay them over her breasts. Against her palms the pouting tips seemed to harden further, and reading her thoughts, Bobsy smiled and murmured, "We have *three* erections, don't we. Not just one."

Daisy laughed rather inanely again. "I guess *so.*"

"Why not try it? I'll carry the ball. In bed. You might be given the thrill of your life. Thrills. You yourself needn't — you know. Just be passive. On the receiving

end. I could help you get anywhere you want. Bail you out
of this hole with Mrs. Smoot and the other editors. So if
this series washes out, there could be others. I could throw
a lot your way. It's that kind of world. We all have to live.
Let me touch you — I'll bet your rosebuds are up too."
She became playful as she slipped a hand down Daisy's
blouse and tried to pry a breast out from under a cup of
her brassière.

"Bobsy, I don't think we ought —" Daisy began, trying
to wriggle away without making too much of a scene. As
though the scene weren't already out of control.

"Didn't you do it at school with a roommate — ever?
Come on, don't tell me you didn't fondle one another in
bed, and not just here either."

"Well, that's innocent romping. Half-laughing anyhow
midnight stuff. Scrambling under the sheets, not serious,
deliberate . . ."

Bobsy had given off exploring Daisy's bosom and, abandoning more or less the note of playfulness, slid down to
her knees while running a hand under Daisy's skirt. Daisy
sat stiffly helpless, powerless to decide when exactly to act,
or how, flabbergasted to the point of paralysis as Bobsy
parted her stockingless legs and began to kiss her thighs.
"Bobsy, for God's sake, you're drunk." She felt Bobsy's
hands encircle her hips in a sudden impulsively risked
motion, and then her fingers curl around the elastic waist-
band of her undersilk and try to draw it down. "You're
really so pretty, Daisy. I've always . . . always envied you
your looks . . ."

Daisy rose to her feet with a force that tipped Bobsy
over backwards and to one side, off her knees and onto the
floor. There she sat, so pathetically routed that Daisy,
having started away, turned back and laid a hand on her
head.

"I'm sorry, dear. It's not only not my denomination, well, no, the thing is really, the thing really is, I have no objections to it you understand — it's all sex — breasts are breasts and they're beautiful to play with —"

"Don't you want to try everything on the menu? We only go through this rotten world once."

"I know that." Almost apologetically, as though it were she who had misbehaved and was now discomfited, Daisy tried to get a grip on herself. She made a fresh start, to save everyone's face. Bobsy's had probably caved in, if she'd dared to look. She stared in another direction as, at last, she put it all as best she could.

"I have no objections to it, moral or emotional, but it would have made the situation between us impossible."

"It is anyway, now."

Bobsy got back onto her knees and then climbed to her feet, steadying herself by bracing one hand on the sofa seat.

"You mean —?"

Bobsy nodded, dropping onto the sofa, where she finished off her brandy.

"I don't see how we could work together, now, as we'd have to. Because those pieces do need whipping into shape. Complete revamping. Maybe somebody new taking a fresh heave at the project would be the best all around."

The truth had already quite dawned. Daisy got her coat from the front closet and put it on. She grinned, at least taking some pleasure in the irony recognized and articulated as, backing out the door, and grateful for the anger supplanting the pity she'd have found harder to bear, she said: "Well, it vindicates you in one way. It shows how right you are about sexual harassment on the job. You didn't exaggerate. It's everywhere. Everywhere."

She closed the door behind her as gently as she could, hoping her tears would keep until she got home.

· 10 ·

"The Synod of Dort took place in Dordrecht in the years 1618 and 1619," said Dirk, whose pillow talk held no more surprises, unless that was all it held. "It was an assembly of the Dutch Reformed Church, with deputies from Switzerland, Scotland, England and elsewhere, convened to resolve the theological differences between the strict Calvinists and the Arminians among them. You know what we Calvinists are."

"I do indeed."

"Do you know who the Arminians are? Not the Armenians. The Arminians."

She did indeed, having had the doctrines of Jacobus Arminius well explained to her by the dehydrated old party who'd also stuffed infra- and supralapsarianism down her throat. But she said no, to let him go on. His voice, this intimately close up, sent a pleasurable electric tingle down her spine, like a nervous current she didn't want to short-circuit. Besides, she enjoyed learning the full extent of his qualifications for the ministry he had chucked in favor of strewing the face of the earth with chocolate. What spunk it must have taken to resist parents with their hearts set on having a dominie in the family.

"Jacobus Arminius opposed the strict predestination tenets of official Calvinism with his belief that atonement is for all men and not just the Elect," he said, settling a hand firmly across her left haunch. "The issue of infra and supra was never raised."

"Good."

"Arminius himself died before the Synod convened, but by dot time his liberal views were officially those of the ruling House of Orange, as well as espoused by the bourgeois republican oligarchy led by Oldenbarneveldt and Hugo Grotius, the father of international law. But the Synod went down the line for rigid Calvinism, adopting the five principles summed up in the word Tulip, forming an what do you call it — anagram?"

"No, acronym."

This was ringing a bell. Something about George C. Scott . . . Tulip . . . a hooker. Yes. George C. Scott explaining the acronym to the hooker in the movie *Hardcore,* in the course of his search for his errant porn-flick daughter. But all Daisy could remember was Total Depravity.

"Acronym. Ja. All right. Here I come, ready or not. Total Depravity, Unconditional Election, Limited Atonement, Irresistible Grace and Perseverance of the Saints. There you have it in an nutshell. The heart and soul of the Dutch Reformed Church."

"That you got away from." She gave him a squeeze.

He returned it, murmuring, "Daisy May."

The spell snapped like a bootlace. The pleasurable current reversed itself, a tremor of fear going up her spine. Fear of what? Fear that he might learn what it meant before — before what? Before he could ask her to marry him? Was that what she wanted? Was that the discovery she had suddenly made about herself? Was now the time to tell him she didn't have a middle name, it was just a joke pinned on her by friends playfully marking her resemblance to the comic strip character? But she was hardly anything like that voluptuous! What if in his promised personal investigation of the office he queried some miscreant by then aware of why she had infiltrated the place, and inclined to do her mischief? "It's a gag, Mr. Dolfin. Daisy May — and then again she may not. Get it?" Smirk.

Extricating herself from Dirk's embrace, she settled over onto her back and shook a cigarette from a pack on her bedside table. "I don't have a middle name. It's just a sort of joke that goes back to my schooldays," she fibbed, "when 'L'il Abner' was all the rage. That's the name of the comic strip — which you've probably never even seen. It's spelled M-a-e."

"Oh." He swivelled off the other side of the bed and landed with a jump on the floor. "I'm starved. Zullen wij din-din eten?"

They dined at a new neighborhood place called the Corner House, which advertised itself as a feminist restaurant. Why? How could food be feminist? "Just am bunch women who want to get out of the kitchen," Dirk said, with a guffaw in which Daisy joined. Ten Gloria Steinems. Yet why not? What had any shared orientation among restaurant colleagues to do with the food they served (which in this case was creditable standard fare)? It was like the organic theatres, whose productions presumably contained no additives, or the environmental bookstore downtown where volumes supposedly free of pollutants could be purchased. It was all more evidence of how the basically cogent could self-propel into fatuity. Yet Daisy felt an obscure vexation through most of the meal. But a counterirritant presently came to the rescue.

The Dutchman's spartan middays freed him for indulgences at dinner, and after an unsexist carnivorous meal of roast beef and boiled potatoes he ordered a profiterole, which Daisy wistfully watched him consume. He extended a dripping spoonful across the table, and as Daisy licked her lips she again heard "Verdomme!"

A rather large drop of chocolate sauce had fallen on his vest, and the exasperation with which he tried to scrub it off with a napkin dipped in his water glass was understandable in a man who had made the Ten Best Dressed list, a distinction he clearly enjoyed as much as he pooh-poohed it. It also betrayed the dandiacal self-concern on which the Diesel had possibly accurately put her finger.

The dishonor had befallen a checked beige tweed with a reddish overplaid of which he was obviously fond, and the subtlety of whose fabric Daisy herself had admired. The surviving blotch was a kind of medallion certifying the impeccability it had momentarily compromised. They made love again when they got back to Daisy's place, at nearly midnight, after which Dolfin rose and went over to inspect his suit, which hung on the back of a chair, the trousers neatly folded across the seat. "Still there," he said. "The longer you leave spots the more they 'set,' and then cleaners can't get them out." He was quite anxious.

"No, I think it's the other way around," Daisy assured him from the bed. "It's the *cleaning* that sometimes sets it. No, wait, that's not true either. *Pressing* will set a stain. It'll come out when you have it cleaned. Now I'm all mixed up."

"There are things you can do first. Nasty spots can ruin a garment." He hesitated a moment, thoughtfully pulling on his lower lip, naked on a hooked rug. "I call my mother."

"Your mother is in New York?"

"No, of course not. She's at home. She'll know how to get it out before it's too late. Every stain needs a different treatment. Do it wrong and that's it."

She watched him get into shorts and a shirt, to be decent when he got his mother on the wire. Sitting up in bed, she looked levelly across the room at him. "You're going to telephone your mother in Amsterdam?"

"She's an authority on household hints like that. An genius. My father spills."

"It's one o'clock in the morning."

"Not there. It's seven there, and they're always up at six."

The phone was here, and he sat on the bed to put in the transatlantic call. Perhaps it was worth it, seeing a stubborn Dutchman pitted against a stubborn stain. Worth it financially too — saving a tailor-made suit that must have cost several hundred dollars. Morning in Amsterdam. Soon his mother would be outside on her knees scrubbing the doorstep, or at least a housemaid would. Daisy had actually seen one once from her room in the Amstel Hotel there, as she sat at breakfast gazing across the canal. A woman in a billowing dress, on all fours, with a bucket and brush. They actually did it, then, it was no myth. Sidewalks spotless, floors inside you could eat off of. Daisy wondered now how he'd fared with the shrimp-cocktail blot sustained at lunch that time. Could spilling be hereditary? She had an image of her lover dining at Lutèce or the Côte Basque under a dropcloth like that the barber throws around you, to preserve his Best Dressed status as a man about town.

He scratched his head with one finger, carefully, so as not to ruffle his hair. No, she could not marry him. What was a washing compulsion called in the Netherlands — normal?

The phone rang in a remarkably short time. The operator had his call to Amsterdam.

"Moeke?" Daisy popped decently back under the sheet, in case that meant Mother. "Dirk. Niet, niet. Alles is O.K." Then a series of the inhaled affirmatives. "Ja, ja. Ja. Ja, ja, ja. No, Moeke, ik ben O.K. Niet doodplagen." Did that mean "Don't worry yourself to death?" Then, "Kijk." "Look"? God, how these locutions travelled. "Kijk."

There was an of course unintelligible spate of Dutch in which he briefly stated his problem, a chocolate merchant who had spilled some of his own product on a treasured garment. Then another series of "ja, ja"s as he listened carefully to instructions. Were they coming across three thousand miles of cable, or being bounced off a satellite? "Een ogenblik." A pantomime of scribbling in midair sent Daisy scrambling for pad and pencil with which to jot down the details relayed in translation. Sponge with warm water — the ice water in the tumbler had been bad, then, possibly fatal? — then when dry, remove the remaining spot with a toothbrush, gently tamping the fabric with the bristle tips in a solution of three parts water to one part liquid detergent. Her pencil flew. Let set for a few minutes and then flush out with clear warm water. He thanked Moeke, chatted for a while with Pa, just out of his morning tub, hung up, and threw out his arms, as at the simplicity of it, given the right bloodlines. "You got all that down? Good. Done and done. Let's get at it."

He drew the vest out from under the coat where they hung on the chair, and handed it to her.

She stared at him blankly, as all her principles trembled

in the balance. She had been so unprepared for this . . . steely-bland assumption that for the moment incomprehension forestalled any immediate resentment. When that registered, he had turned and gone back to the telephone, where he asked the operator for the charges on the call. Nineteen dollars and seventy cents. Seeing him return to the chair where the suit was, extract two tens from his wallet, drop them on the telephone stand, thereby chivalrously sparing her having to take the money, momentarily cooled her irritation. Was the principle worth making a scene over? After glancing at the vest in one hand and the directions scribbled on the sheet of paper in the other, she shrugged, turned, and marched into the kitchen, trusting the thud of her bare heels communicated something — perhaps that she was merely acting as the hostess, not a woman knuckling under, or accepting any tradition from Mevrouw Dolfin, who had probably never heard of feminism.

But they watched her as she bent to her chore in the kitchen, all of them: Lucy Stone, Susan B. Anthony, Mrs. Pankhurst, and their no less formidable latter-day reincarnations, Friedan, Steinem, Greer. There they stood, their mouths compressed in disapproval, their brows furrowed, their arms folded on their breasts, rank on rank, the army of unalterable law. He called her a jewel as he stood watching over her shoulder, and they all heard.

The job was top-notch. By morning not a trace of the stain remained, and Dolfin, who had spent the night, was again one of the world's Ten Best Dressed Men. She could be proud of him as a husband, as he of her as a wife — for he did ask her to marry him then and there, at last.

She was naturally pleased, but had her doubts. There would be problems, acute ones. She had her own life to live, her own star to follow. She must continue to work, for one thing. "And, like what about the magazine?" she asked. "You're not going to sell it I hope?"

"Ach. I guess not." This time it was he who shrugged. "I tell you what. I give it to you as a wedding present. Now we see if you can clean *dot* mess up."

·11·

"HENRY STEELE COMMAGER makes the interesting point that great cosmopolitans are also often great provincials. Thomas Jefferson was one. Goethe was another." Dirk's voice in her ear was intimate as the whisper of the bed-sheets themselves. "I heard him say that in a television interview one night when I was stuck in a motel room in Detroit. I was interested in his examples, because when he gave them I said out loud, 'Hugo Grotius.' You remember he came into am previous discussion —"

"Ja, ja." She was beginning to inhale her own yesses.

He resettled himself against her, shifting a hand on her bottom.

"Bone of Holland's bone though he was, blood of her blood, when he was sentenced to life imprisonment for treason he escaped from jail smuggled in a chest of books with the aid of his wife, fled to Paris, and as a man of the world he ended up as — wait for it — Swedish ambassador to the court of France."

Nevertheless, Daisy hesitated to accept a proposal it

would have enraged her not to have had made. She totted up the pros and cons, marshalled the arguments for and against, weighed this with that. Then the tiniest thing tipped the scales, a gesture so simple it was almost impossible in retrospect to credit its effect on her at the time.

They were having dinner with some friends of Dirk's, a party of ten over which the hostess, servantless, presided in something like style with a casserole of *coq au vin* she had cooked herself but had had grandly set before her by her husband, a man "high up" in something the exact identity of which Daisy hadn't quite caught. It could have been seamless gutters or aluminum siding. Given to collar-pin shirts and expressions like "from where I sit," he had the narrowly dedicated air and look of corporate pizzazz of men who are always spearheading something. Like Dirk, he did not like help around because it compromised his privacy. Was he another male turnkey keeping a wife under house arrest? Would Dirk turn out to be of that stripe? One of the guests recalled a woman friend of hers who as a newlywed had once asked her husband to take out the garbage, and been told, "Take it out yourself." *Coq au vin* was not garbage, at least not yet, and the hostess obviously enjoyed ladling it out to guests salivating down the long teak table, from the magnificent Meissen tureen in which the dish was served, a priceless heirloom come down from the oink-oink side. She was middle of the road: neither rooster-pecked nor what Daisy's mother's cleaning woman had called "one dem emaciated women." Thirty Our Fathers. Silently as a tumbler slipping into place in a combination lock somewhere at the back of her mind, Daisy's decision was reached: she would not marry. Not marry Dirk, particularly. Simply not marry. All right. Settled.

It was during "seconds" that the tumbler as simply reversed itself.

She passed her plate along to the hostess for "just a wing if you have one. It's so delicious." A woman on her left handed it to Dirk, who was on the hostess's right, but before relaying it on he scraped onto his own plate the bones from the plump breast Daisy had polished off. The utterly casual stroke of courtesy touched her as few masculine acts ever had. Preposterously slight, indeed infinitesimal, it yet struck a note of chivalry, not a gong blow but a tinkle as from a crystal lustre, important for what it must reveal of the man himself. The gesture seemed all the more genuine for being practically inadvertent: executed while he was conducting an argument with another male guest, who'd said he was being too simplistic about something. Ah, simplistic. The word that picked up the marbles these days. The hostess had also noticed Dirk's unobtrusive consideration, and smiled at Daisy, one of the trade-union smiles women exchange about men, as she passed the wing along, with another generous dollop of sauce.

She would marry Dirk. She knew that as she cleared the table and cleaned and stacked plates in the kitchen with the hostess. Scraping debris into the garbage pail she recalled his charming *politesse,* and, as though pinning a rose on him, mentally quoted the lines from Tennyson. "Manners are not idle, but the fruit of loyal nature and of noble mind."

Unable to hoard her news, she blurted it out to the conspirator who down the gleaming table had, with the smile that needed no decoding, already telegraphed her complicity. "He's so nice," the glance had said. "Don't for God's sake let *him* slip through your fingers."

The two women embraced over the garbage pail, hug-

ging in aprons temporarily donned, spatulas in hand. Tonight she would accept Dirk. What a word! Thank God
the Diesel couldn't see her now, much less read her mind
as it raced along the immemorial platitudinous track that
would make her (so the Diesel said) chattel to an oink-
oink who would — oh, Jesus, wait for this one — "claim
his bride" in a Dutch Reformed Church. The Marble Col-
legiate? Norman Vincent Peale?!

"We honeymoon in Holland," Dirk said with the same
easy grace as that with which he had nudged her bones
onto his plate. He was watching her eradicate a fruit stain
they discovered on his coatsleeve when they got to her
place, a drop from the dessert compote apparently. He
straddled a kitchen chair backwards, his arms folded across
its top, as she sponged the spot with lemon juice and then
flushed it with boiling water, correctives she knew herself
without being put through to Amsterdam.

"You're the nattiest slob I know. There. Never use soap
and water on a fruit stain. It only makes it worse."

"What am prize. And an terrific piece tail into the bargain." He shook his head, unable to believe his luck.

A line from a hymn she'd sung in church as a child
floated to mind. "Praise waits for thee in Zion." She swam
in credit. Drunk with it. Was he going to burst into the
strains of "I want a girl just like the girl that married dear
old dad"? He gave her a grateful peck as he slipped into
the coat, which in the bedroom he would presently again
remove.

"Of course I must meet your folks, but I mean for the
honeymoon, I was thinking like the south of France. Nice
and Cannes and so on. And tearing along the Grande
Corniche in a rented convertible! Or maybe Valencia." She

began to sing aloud as they wandered into the living room. " 'Valencia! In my dreams it always seems I hear you softly call to me-hee, me-hee. Valencia! Where the orange trees forever scent the breeze beside the sea-hee, sea-hee.' "

He stretched out on the sofa with a brandy. She'd had enough to drink.

"You'll like it in Holland."

"I've been there."

"We go waddenlopen."

"What on earth is that?"

"Literally, mudwalking." He went on to explain the lark, chuckling softly like boiling water. It consisted in walking, at low tide, from the Friesland shoreline to some islands in the North Sea. Hadn't he already told her about this? How could she have forgotten? It was widely held to be a treat to beat your feet on the muckflats there. All the posh crowd did it, the set who wouldn't dream of eating before six, maybe six-thirty. Passengers on the ferry boats to those islands would look out and see them walking past the boat. "They'll say, 'Wat is me dit?' Folks walking past the boat."

"How can there be both ferries running and people walking past them? How can they navigate if people can walk because there's no water? Alternatively, how can people walk if there's depth enough to float a boat? In the case of Galilee —"

"That'll be us, waving to them. Waddenlopers."

The term made Daisy think of shadowy gray phantoms, of which she was one, hunching out through cold night mists to semiarctic waters. That was because of the untidy telescoping in her mind of "polder," the word for low-lying land reclaimed from water and embraced by dikes, and "poltergeist," a rowdy house ghost. The two had nothing to do with each other or with this new word, yet she nursed the martyrlike fancy of herself as ending her last erotic holiday as a tag-along wife-hulk floating out across the North Sea, there to sink to a watery oblivion among uncountable quintillions of herring, past, present, and to come.

"St. Tropez —"

"As waddenlopers," Dirk went on, warming enthusiastically to his prothalamion dream, "we'll need the following: an knowledge of the tides — don't want to drown — am map of the sandbars, an compass, sneakers, light windbreakers —"

"A Bible in one pocket."

"— food and water. And an life preserver."

"Don't want to die."

"And an guide of course, unless of course we do a lot of it and get to know the ropes."

"Do people do it a lot? I mean actually trudge across to those islands? I mean we all know about you skating from town to town on the canals, with the children strung out behind like a brood of ducks, but I mean living it up on the intertidal slime in sneakers . . . The sea, our first Mother, gathering us in again at the last, maybe."

"Oh, yes. To Ameland, Terschelling, Schiermonnikoog. Those are some of the islands. Of course Texel is the most fashionable."

"Like the races at Ascot, the film festivals at Cannes. People 'do' them."

She had the key to the puzzle: sandbars. These, then, explained the surrealist juxtaposition of ferryboats and muck trudgers, the latter slogging across them on shanks' mare while waving festively and with all the savoir-faire of the Dutch to passengers on vessels navigating the bound-

ing main a few feet away. Pity to have the fantasy dismantled. Much nicer the weird way.

Dirk kneaded a cushion under his head. "Friesland is
the province mijn ouders were born in, as you know, and
it's high time I made am pilgrimage to their geboorteplaats.
Odd they never took me there for a last look before we all
emigrated to America."

"Why did they go back?"

"Heimwee. Nostalgia. Don't you ever want to go back to
Terre Haute?"

"Very often. Lots of rain, but it's a dry rain."

"Friesland is so special that —" Here he sat up, the
better to choke with laughter, the sight of it restabilizing
an original belief that he had no humor. I mean, she would
explain to herself in elucidating the fine-pointed paradox,
people with a sense of humor properly so called didn't
"rock with laughter," they didn't "slap their thighs" as
they roared, like characters in European novels threatening
to break the chairs on which they did this rocking and
slapping. (There was very little humor in those novels in
which characters rocked with laughter either at the kitchen
table or in fields of ripening grain.) She waited with mis-
giving, possibly already training for future despair, for
his payeroo.

"Frieslanders fancy themselves so special, you see, that
when they talk of foreigners they may very well mean —"
Here some more strangling.

"Yes?"

"They may very well mean the Dutch."

Dolfin rose and helped himself to another dropje brandy,
singing at the top of his voice as he strolled to the liquor
cabinet, " 'Theeeeere's . . . . . theeeee . . . Amsterdam
Dutch and the Rotterdam Dutch, and the Potsdam Dutch
and the other damn Dutch!' "

"Isn't Potsdam in Germany?"

"Yes."

Then for the second time the roof came down.

They were dining at a Greek restaurant, and from the first of the evening Daisy had again realized something was wrong. There had been an unmistakable constraint in his greeting kiss, and he had looked down at the floor when he asked how she was. One of them was guilty of something. Table talk consisted of stretches of labored conversation punctuated by pauses even more strained. It was like a sputtering motor. Stirring a saccharin tablet into her coffee she said: "What is it?"

"It's the Daisy May business."

"Of course in the comic strip it's spelled M-a-e."

"I found out what it means. The gag. Around the office."

For the second time too she felt her heart burst like a hot ember. She spoke in a consuming rage.

"And what little harpy or sniggering sophomore told you this time? Was it our same friend, the kind you don't need an enemy if you've got one?"

"Please, calm yourself."

"*Calm* myself! In the face of this skullduggery? Not that I'm sure who the real culprit is, your lying informant or you with your double standard. Because here we have it again, rearing its ugly head. A man can do what he wants, but a woman, she's to be censured even without a hearing. Well, I'll hold my own hearing, and you'd goddam well better listen."

"Shh. People can hear you. Taxipopoulos over there —"

"That office is nickname-nuts, as you know, and the wit who cooked this one up was almost certainly that treacherous, lecherous, kindless villain in makeup, because I rejected his advances. But if it was our mutual friend, you've had such a dose of her bitchery in the first case that if you've been sleeping with her again my opinion of men plummets to a new low. Have you, since it's been definitely 'us'? *Oh!* To even have to ask the question! You give yourself carte blanche while expecting the woman to keep her skirts clean for the nuptial bed. But believe me, that alone would be promiscuity. Sleeping with one like her is the equivalent of sacking with anybody, every trollop in midtown, because it would take that many to add up to her."

"She has nothing to do with this," Dolfin said quietly.

"Then let's go on to the guy. 'Deliver us from the power of the dog,' it says in the English prayer book. Deliver us indeed. I'm going to tell you the whole story so as to be absolutely honest with you. Whether you believe it or not can't mean much to me now, as this is apparently curtains for us."

"Mijn lieve schat," he said, laying a hand on her wrist, which she twitched away, upsetting a pepper cellar. He righted it, waiting.

"I finally went out to dinner with him, for the sole purpose of humiliating him. Revenge. Scorn isn't the only thing that can give a woman the fury hell hath not." Dolfin rolled his eyes in a gesture of agreement. She plowed forward. "I went back to his apartment solely to make sure he struck out. A woman can cut that thing off very simply, you know. A few of the right words, a taunt — anything to throw off his confidence. Do you follow me?"

Dolfin either nodded or shook his bowed head, it was hard to tell from the way he was rocking it in his two hands. Things were coming at him at too bewildering a rate. He said later it was as though his brain was undergoing an attack of strobe lights.

"But he was such a pathetic spectacle, I relented. I

hadn't meant to go that far. Or say I hadn't bargained for that much reaction. I just wanted to teach him a lesson, not mortify him into suicidal carryings-on. He gives women this man-of-infinite-melancholy bit, you know. I stayed the night, bundled with him as the Puritans said, mainly so he wouldn't throw himself out of the window or slash his wrists. I'd have felt more guilty that way, and come morning — well, you know how the cock crows with you boys then. More relaxed and hence virile, and all that jazz. The machinery apparently works on the sympathetic nervous system, and excitement isn't enough. Have to be relaxed as well. Something like that. Oh, Jesus, deliver me. Is this conversation really taking place? So anyway I wound up giving the poor bastard his nuggets back, and if instead of believing what I'm honestly telling you, you credit a putrid office gag with absolutely no foundation in fact, why . . . If you think I've got round heels then the man I fell for has got a square head." Here she burst into tears and dug in her bag for a handkerchief. "Get the check and let's go. We'll split it down the middle. Clean. You know — symbolic."

He refused to take her home just yet, insisting they stroll a few blocks till she had calmed down. They passed his own apartment in doing so, and he steered her into it with an arm around her waist, murmuring that because of the results, and though he wouldn't divulge the name of the rumormonger, he was now glad he had opened this can peas. Far worse awaited them in his flat.

A door slightly ajar told clearly enough that it had been jimmied. The obvious fear froze them momentarily in the hallway. Dolfin insisted she remain there till he had seen whether the caller might be still inside. Lights were burning that he hadn't left on himself. Cautiously, he took a step forward and pushed the door all the way open. He beckoned her on. "Brace yourself," he said.

The place was a shambles. Either a burglar (or burglars) enraged by the absence of disposable loot, or junkies high on something, or both, had vandalized the entire apartment. Lamps were smashed, vases lay in smithereens, draperies were torn down and up. In the bedroom a sight even more horrendous awaited them. Dolfin's entire wardrobe had been slashed to ribbons. Not a suit, coat or pair of trousers but had been ripped apart with a kitchen knife. That had been thrown down on the floor next to the closet. A coatsleeve lay across a disheveled bed with an eviscerated pillow. Hacked-up shirts were strewn everywhere. Dresser drawers emptied on the carpets. "Grote God," he murmured, ashen. Daisy started to sit down on the bed, then instead walked toward the bathroom door, afraid she was going to be sick. Literally all he had left was the suit on his back.

Pale and shaking, he poured them each a stiff brandy before phoning the police. They came in about fifteen minutes, making the usual observations, writing out the routine reports. Two of them, not unsympathetic. "I've seen worse," the older said, "but this is a lulu. We talk about senseless violence, but is there a sensible kind?" They very kindly gave Daisy a lift home.

She dropped on her bed with her coat still on, and lay there staring at the ceiling for some time. Could catastrophe be providential? Certainly the second had driven out of her mind the evening's earlier hell. A third crisis offered ample distraction from the other two. The phone rang and it was her father. His voice already was portentous, like the jimmied door. And he himself was a little strange.

"I hate to call you from Terre Haute."

Where, indeed, would he call from? That was where he lived. Had he been drinking? Perhaps, and why not?

"That's all right, Daddy."

"How's everything?"

"Fine." Not for long. Misfortunes come in threes, and it never rains . . .

"I tried to telephone you earlier in the evening, but you were out."

"What's the matter?"

He heaved a long sigh, like an eight-hundred-mile lariat intended to loop her smartly back home, that much she sensed in her bones.

"It's your mother. You know she's been acting peculiarly lately. Purse snatching . . ."

"Oh, that was just the shoulder bag of that piano tuner she can't stand. She was trying to make a statement, against the unisex thing which she considers the bane of modern life. One of them. Something gave when she saw him mincing toward her, is all. She gave it right back to him after she made her statement. So let's not go blowing it up out of all —"

"Wait till you hear this 'statement.' I need a little help in handling this thing, so if you could come out just for a few days. You haven't been home in some time, Daisy."

"What's she done now?"

"Are you sitting down?"

"I'm in bed."

"She stole a car."

"I'll try to run out over the weekend."

· 12 ·

"You know your mother takes jelly beans for nervous tension."

Daisy and her father were crouched behind a stone wall separating their property from the Ghookasians'. They looked like snipers, which in a sense was the case with Dobbin, holding at the ready a loaded movie camera trained on the neighbors' back door, from which Ghookasian was expected to emerge any minute for some of his "heathen Sunday gardening," as Dobbin put it. The old feud had boiled off and on for over a decade, and had now reached a stage where something more serious than photographic reconnaissance might erupt — in effect already had.

Polly Esther, the troublesome setter long since gone, had started a train of hostilities currently marked by indignant charges by each party that the other was disposing of brush, weeds and stones by spitefully dumping them on his property — a vendetta further fueled by a kindred dispute over the property line. Ghookasian's two-acre plot was L-shaped, the short leg of it running behind a stone wall set at right angles to the demarcating privet hedge through which Polly Esther had romped, to ravage flower beds. Dobbin claimed his land extended several feet beyond the stone wall Ghookasian insisted separated them, and so he freely disposed of brush cuttings and rocks and the branches of pruned trees in the moot corridor, which Dobbin as freely shoved, pushed and threw back again, only to have it returned again by an irate Ghookasian who next, in escalating the war, took to chucking some of it over the very wall itself. From there it was then thrown, by an equivalently heated Dobbin, proportionately farther onto what was indisputably Ghookasian territory. This almost ritualized Laurel and Hardy reciprocation had now reached a stage where the stones were deliberately picked up and pitched back as far as either could throw them. At the moment, scores of rocks strewed the grass where Ghookasian, turning the purple frequently found in batik fabrics such as he himself merchandised, would surely find them when he presently sallied forth, trundling his garden cart. He could be counted on to pick them up one by one — his mouth indeed pursed in Oliver Hardy–type exasperation — and lob them over the wall as far as he could. It was of this that Dobbin was determined to get a picture, the film of which was to be exhibited in evidence for a complaint to be lodged with the Terre Haute police. Both men were home from church now, and the hostilities were due to commence. Dobbin passed the waiting time by filling Daisy in on the crisis for which he had summoned her home, out of earshot, though not entirely out of view, of its principal. She would be sitting at the window, eating fruit out of the hubcap.

"Your mother thinks jelly beans soothe her, by settling not just her stomach, but her nerves mind you, so O.K.

Who's to differ with it or pooh-pooh it — it's the result that's important, even if it's only in her head. Maybe in some mysterious way — the sugar or glucose or something in them, I don't know. Maybe just the act of eating a favorite sweet. Anyway. They've lost their power to sedate, jelly beans. So have all her favorites. Milk Duds, jujubes, you name it. You remember how Milk Duds always tranquilized her she said. How it quieted her down to suck on one, while Sen-Sens gave her a high. Or so she said, so who are we — Hold it. What have we here? The enemy approacheth."

Dobbin reached for his camera, which he had set on the wall, having glimpsed a figure emerging from the house. It turned out to be Mrs. Ghookasian, scattering meal to the three chickens constituting the bucolic side the Ghookasians claimed for themselves. He set the camera down again. "I'll get that sonofabitch this time. I'll clean his rug-merchant's clock." He resettled his position on the ground and resumed. "You know your mother is immature in some ways," he said, "but that's all mixed in with the good, the way it can be with a crusader like her, even a genius. She has fire in the belly. You've got to give her that. I don't know where the expression comes from. But your mother has never had a day of mental illness in her life. What's the matter?"

"Nothing."

"I thought you were laughing about something. Never a day of mental illness in her life, *but* . . . Now she's well, not unravelling let us hope and pray, but . . . I think this kind of crackup, well, not crackup exactly let's hope, started when her dear friend Laura Conley passed away. Just like that, after a lingering illness. Is there something wrong with your cheek?"

"Keeps twitching. Sort of a neuralgic twinge, maybe a tooth. Go on. I know Laura Conley's death rocked her."

"They served on this Consumers Protective Association together for eight years, gunning for the profiteers. Real activists. Well. You heard what Laura's last words were, I expect."

"Yes. 'Get General Motors.' That's dying with your boots on."

"Huh! That's not the half of it. I think I've got the story here in my —" Dobbin screwed about in order to fish from his coat pocket a local newspaper clipping. "Here's her last words in full. Somebody took them down at the hospital. 'Get General Motors. Now they've unleashed upon us a million thirty-four cars with defective emissions-control devices that may malfunction. Tests by the Environmental Protection Agency showed excessive nitrogen oxide emissions owing to clogging of the exhaust gas recirculation valve by exhaust deposits.' "

"That's something."

" 'The valves, known as EGR valves, recycle a fraction of engine exhaust back into the intake manifold, lowering the temperature of combustion and reducing formation of nitrogen oxides, a principal precursor of smog.' And gave up the ghost."

Dobbin gave a terse nod of emphasis as he solemnly folded and repocketed the clipping.

"That's dedication."

"And your mother's got it too, don't you forget it." He gave his daughter an affectionate smile, lightly touching her arm. "No doubt whose blood you've got flowing in your veins, my little chickadee. Whose genes you got your own fire from, speaking of fire in the belly. The fight you're putting into your women's liberation, what is it but the same as Jennie Dobbin's into consumerism. There's no difference except in what course the current takes. The important thing is going at things in an adult fashion, the mature outlook. That's what psychotherapy is all about, the whole thing in a nutshell. Be grown up, that's the ticket. Ah, here's our rat fink."

Peering over the wall through a pair of binoculars slung round his neck, he watched the enemy come through the back screen door, descend the porch steps, and make his way into the garage, from which he presently reappeared, trundling his cart. He disappeared again into the garage, this time coming out with a pair of canvas gloves. He looked around as he drew them on, apparently searching for something. Quite able to see all this for herself, Daisy said: "Hostilities won't begin for a few minutes, so run through the whole thing again. I know Mother's been under a strain, but stealing a car? Would you call it that?"

"Absolutely. Oh, I don't call it that, and you won't call it that, but the law will — if they ever catch up with her. Here's the dope again in a nutshell. Last March we bought the Chevrolet Citation, right?" Dobbin related, continuing to squint through the binoculars, his wide mouth split in a grimace of concentration. "A demo it was, with eight thousand miles on her. She drove it mostly, I have the old Buick, good enough for me. In early June, couple of months ago, we got a letter from G.M. asking why had we not responded to a recall letter on that model sent out *October of last year,* saying the automatic transmission cooler lines were dangerously defective, could heat up and catch fire. Well, we hadn't owned the heap then, only since last March. We took it back to the dealer pronto for correction, but they didn't have the parts and couldn't get them from surrounding agencies. Very lukewarm about it, owner finally bored with your mother's complaints and threats. The motor vehicle department advised us under no circumstances to drive the car, so here was your mother without transportation to: the Consumers Association, which is herself; the Better Business Bureau; and one or two other protest outfits she keeps in touch with. So she asked Midway Chevrolet for a car she could drive, even a secondhand one, while they got the parts. They laughed at her. So one day she kind of disguised herself — different hairdo, big hat to shield her face, lots of makeup, so they wouldn't recognize that Battle-Ax Pest — and pretended to be shopping for a Chevy. Might she test-drive a demo, take it for a spin around the block? Why, certainly, ma'am. So she climbed into this two-door and that's the last they ever saw of it. Needed it herself till they fixed the one they had sold her *knowing for six months it was from a dangerously defective batch.* She telephoned the agency and said she stopped to make a phone call in a drugstore, and when she came out the car was stolen, their demo. Somebody swiped it, she was sorry. They might wish to report the theft to the police. That's your mother for you, a woman among men." Momentarily lowering the binoculars, Dobbin gave his daughter the same nod of awed appreciation as when relating Laura Conley's resonant last words.

"But didn't they smell something fishy? Tumble to who she is?"

"By now, sure. They've put two and two together, figured out it's her who 'stole' the demo. They tail her, watch the house. It's staked out right now."

"But where does she keep it?"

"Your guess is as good as mine. Most closely guarded secret of the war between General Motors and Jennie Hurlbutt Dobbin. I tell you — Hold it, there's the slime

pot, fresh from singing 'Lead, Kindly Light.' No, still looking for something. Maybe the meaning of life. I'll 'Lead,
Kindly Light' *him*. I tell you your mother's something
else. Anybody still harboring under the delusion that the
male sex is superior should get a load of her. *I* don't even
know where the hell she goes after I drop her off at a
different street corner every morning of the world after
we're sure we've shook the tail Midway Chevrolet has on
us. We veer and rocket through traffic like a bunch of
gangsters I tell you. Bouncing you around town, the crooks
call it. It's a dangerous game, but I must confess I get a
thrill out of it. It's, I shouldn't tell you this, but it's renewed our you-know-what life, the charge I get out of it.
The excitement of being a coconspirator to a — well, let's
face it, crime."

"So she picks up the car where she's hidden it. What
about the license plate?"

"Took the dealer's off and put on her own. She may even
have painted the damn thing by this time, I wouldn't put
it past her. Oh, the game can't last, they'll catch her, but
it's been a week now. She parks blocks from her office and
walks the rest of the way, so staking *that* out won't do them
any good."

" 'Them' being the agency, I gather. Why don't they
press it harder with the police?"

Dobbin laughed hoarsely, still raking his own enemy
battleground with the binoculars. "Because they know
Mama Girl's got the state prosecutor preparing a possible
case against them on a charge of reckless endangerment.
Selling us a car they knew was dangerously defective. So
we're all embroiled in a dangerous adventure. There you
have the whole thing in a nutshell, and the crisis I called
you home for."

"But Mother's happy as a clam!"

"Of course! She might have been killed, in a car catching fire and blowing up with her in it. Wouldn't it make your day to be sexually victimized by some bastard you were trying to get the goods on?" He smiled fondly at her again. "You know the old expression about heredity. The apple doesn't fall far from the tree."

She knew it quite well, even its Old World version. "De appel valt niet ver van de boom." Where was Dirk now? He would have been to his tailor and selected the fabrics for a dozen new suits, bought as many new shirts. The apartment would be tidied up, though half bare. The ravaged garments rammed down the incinerator. The broken bulbs and shards of vases swept away. The cops empty-handed. The episode had offered a fitting accompaniment to the sense of her own life being blown sky-high — or hell-deep. The housebreaker himself had somehow seemed a twisted surrogate for all the enraged and outraged of the world. Is there a sensible violence, the cop had wondered aloud. Violence was built into the universe, the cosmos ran on it. Mad atoms, colliding molecules. Maybe Christian charity was an infinitesimal aberration in a universe that gorged itself on violence. It was all versus. Mother versus General Motors, Father versus Ghookasian, her versus Dirk Dolfin. The welkin rang with versus. She versus herself. What were those lines from Siegfried Sassoon? "Man unguided and self-divided . . . Seek, in seeing your own blind being, Peace, remote, in the morning star." Brushed a tear from his eye, old Turley, when quoting it in class, and well he might. A fat lot of peace you'd find in that old carbuncle, the morning star.

Coming home had completed her sense of total disarray. She felt a vexed, itching fury, a sense of everything gone completely awry. This was not the chaos gorgeously reported to be order unperceived. Ha! The childhood news about her parentage had been completely metabolized by now, yet her father's persistent remarks laid it all open to nagging question. The reopened possibilities seemed the "trauma" the original wrench should have been. There are times in every life when one is plowed over; or, in the metaphor dear to Dog Bokum when mawkishly playing up woes he pretended to be playing down, "sent through the old mangle." Pretending to be a Wodehouse character when in fact he fancied himself a Dostoyevskyan one. Him and his "bliss billy," which she had cut off and sewn back on. The d.o.p. had really taught her a lot. So many favorites she'd found contagious. MacLeish. The poem on reaching thirty. "And I have come upon this place/By lost ways, by a nod, by words . . . And by what way shall I go back?" The labyrinthine joys and pains and absurdities by which she had twisted her way to her own imminent thirtieth birthday! And how had her father learned so much about what she was doing in New York?

"Lights! Action! Camera!"

It turned out to be his rake Ghookasian had been looking for, and now having located it, he chucked it into his cart and began the long descent down a width of lawn toward the scrub growth near the stone wall where the properties kissed in disputed alignment. At last he stopped and began to rake the stones together into neat piles, which he then scooped up in his hands and tossed into the cart, moving forward by stages. Dobbin's camera buzzed as he got his establishing shot, which consisted of short takes of these preparations of Ghookasian's.

"He's coming close," Dobbin whispered. "Let's fall back." He led the way, bent over and ducking from tree to tree for cover, like an infantryman in a movie somebody had already shot. Daisy concealed herself behind a fat maple. Dobbin screened himself similarly, poking his head out and keeping the camera cocked at the ready. At last the rocks started coming, and Dobbin started shooting. Some of them flew among the upper branches of intervening trees, others were hurled lower down, zinging in just over the wall. Some sailed in the clear well into the yard. Though often winding up, like a baseball pitcher bent on accuracy, Ghookasian threw them higgledy-piggledy. He just wanted to get the job done, returning this debris that had been commuting between the two properties for God knew how many weeks. Then an especially large stone came sailing between two trees, and Dobbin ran out to shoot it, like an outfielder keeping a high fly in view. He was taking his last step when it hit a maple bough, bounced upward several feet, and came down straight at him. Engrossed in holding the picture, he seemed completely oblivious to any question of personal danger, so that when it came down, it struck him squarely on the forehead. The camera dropped from his hands and he fell to the ground, where he lay on his back with his arms outflung, in a tableau of crucifixion.

Daisy ran over and knelt beside him. She shook him, calling, "Daddy, are you all right?" He muttered something unintelligible, and was silent. Out like a light.

Daisy turned, and was about to run for the house when she saw her mother hurrying toward them. She chafed his wrists in a standard first-aid scene of the purpose of which she was not sure. One saw it in the movies. "Let's get him inside."

They carried him toward the house, Daisy managing the foot-end while her mother lugged him by the armpits, the camera riding on his stomach. Mrs. Dobbin had hastily snatched it up for fear of confiscation by the ever-crafty Ghookasian. This time, however, seeing what had happened and frightened out of his wits, he had turned tail and was running back to his own house, like a boy who had broken a neighbor's window.

They stretched Dobbin out on a couch, and then Daisy ran for a pitcher of cold water. Lacking the heart to dash the contents on her father entire, she dribbled it in drops on his face — to no avail.

"We better get him to the hospital," Mrs. Dobbin said. Somehow they stowed him into the backseat of the Buick, organizing him there with his feet on the floor and his head on Daisy's lap. An emergency-room examination pointed to a concussion. "Hopefully it's not a fracture," an attendant said, the silly dangler grating on Daisy's nerves even there. X-rays bore him out, but the still-oblivious Dobbin was admitted and put to bed. He lay there quite peacefully, a goose egg precisely that size embossing a brow a steadily retreating hairline had given an almost patrician cast. Once he was heard to mumble in a kind of delirium, "I've got to get to Grand Rapids." Another time: "Boil my feet, somebody." Their family doctor, a man named Beddoes, assured them Dobbin would be all right, though how long he might remain unconscious was anybody's guess.

"Well, all I can say is," Mrs. Dobbin remarked to Daisy when he had gone, "I hope that rock brought your father to his senses."

By evening he had still not come to. The women kept their vigil, enduring the familiar hospital tedium. Daisy read an unpublishable novel selected from a cart trundled from door to door by a Bluebird who herself looked to be grievously in need of medical attention. Mrs. Dobbin knew her, a volunteer named Jessie Protheroe, whose own husband was poorly. Mrs. Dobbin ate jelly beans, whose sedative properties apparently remained unimpaired after all. Her hand rustling in the brown paper sack in her lap made Daisy think of a little plump ferret raiding a prey's nest — a metaphor that, like woodsmoke from a winter chimney for Mrs. Protheroe's wisp of blue-white hair, struck Daisy as better than anything encountered in the unprintable paperback. "The old woman's hands crept like crabs across the wilderness of her breasts" indeed. Why had she given up fiction and poetry? She couldn't easily have said. The dream died, as dreams do, that was all. She might as well give up journalism too, to say nothing of the sex life it had bedeviled, and vice versa. The woman in the unpublishable novel was turning to religion on page a hundred and twelve. That was, for Daisy, a window on which intellect had forever drawn the shutter.

The old paving contractor breathed on. How soundlessly in contrast to his waking respiration. Curious. Daisy remembered her childhood annoyance with the noisy buzz of his inhalations, something about a deviated septum, which a curator of nostrils had never cured. Probably couldn't, short of surgery. Have to be fair. Even to those curators of the integument otherwise known as dermatologists, famous as men whose patients never died and never got better. Snout and skin retainers her mother had ever called them, pondering a husband sitting with medicated sticks up his nose, looking like a walrus. Images and memories flashed and fused for Daisy in a mind both tired and overwrought. The eternal feud with Ghookasian, dating back to Polly Esther. Mother's cracks about how what he really should do was direct. Father having a mid-life fling with Lolly Schramm in temporarily deranged Grand Rapids, and now, as rumor had it, his penitential anguish again assuaged, another canoodle with his first flame, Josie Sniffen, to amuse whom, once in the dear dead past, he had swum back to shore with a mallard in his mouth. Daisy began to shake, two or three convulsive guffaws of sorrow disguised as a coughing fit, lowering her head into a hand. She could not imagine her father and Effie's mother pitching woo. It was grotesque.

"Have a jelly bean."

"No, thanks. I'll be all — Well, maybe a few." She fished in the proffered bag for all the world as though they might pull her together. "I'll take blind. Remember how we used to when I was a kid? Have to play fair, the black if you draw them. Remember?"

"There's no black in this assortment. I get them special from Considine's." They sounded like something flown in.

"You really find they calm your nerves?"

"Peacefully chewing your favorite sweets will almost always do that."

"Where is the car?"

"It would make you an accessory. You've got enough on your mind, and maybe even on your conscience. I wouldn't burden you in this area." She was resting her eyeballs from an anthology of American frontier humor. Humor about jackasses, and whiskey, and britches, and women folks.

"You took the dealer plates off the demo and put your own on it."

"I suppose." Mrs. Dobbin smiled archly. There was no doubt the whole adventure excited her.

"You know it's only a question of time till the cops spot you."

"It's only a question of time till anything. What's that fancy French term for a stink you raise? Cause something."

"Cause célèbre. I think Daddy's coming to."

Dobbin's eyes fluttered open. They rolled blankly around the room, over the ceiling and walls, coming to rest first on Mrs. Dobbin, then Daisy. Without comprehension. He didn't know where he was, who they were, or, in fact, who he was himself. That was obvious after the slightest exchange among the three.

"Wait till you finish with Ghookasian now," Mrs. Dobbin said, trying that as a jog to memory. "He knew what happened, because we caught a glimpse of him scooting back into his house. He was scared. Probably scared he killed you. We'll let him steep in that for a while."

"Who?"

"Ghookasian. The feud? The rocks?" She lifted one of his hands and pressed the fingertips gently against the bruise on his forehead. "Don't you remember the stones you got pictures of? One hit you and knocked you out cold, for a bit. You're in the hospital. Nothing serious, dear. You'll be home in a couple of days."

So he was, none the wiser. He didn't recognize the house any more than he did his family. After a day or two, however, there seemed fleeting wisps of recollection, responses to the rooms, the furniture he sat on, the bed he slept in, that gave hope to the women and to Doctor Beddoes, who, nevertheless, seemed equally excited by the first case of true amnesia within his own memory. Inevitably, he succumbed to the temptation to play shrink.

"He's trying to escape from something. But what? Let's bring this Ghookasian in. That might do the trick."

So the poor neighbor was trotted in, the soul of contrition, spluttering apologies as he was led up to the patient stretched out on a parlor sofa. His great brown eyes molten with misery as he extended a pudgy paw in greeting.

"Hello, Dobbin. I see they've got you in dry dock, huh, fella?"

"I . . . don't believe I . . ." Dobbin said, sitting up to shake hands.

"I'm Ghookasian, from next door. Remember?"

Dobbin shook his head, and after a few minutes of this vain exchange, Mrs. Dobbin drew Ghookasian into the kitchen with a summoning jerk of her own.

"Well, you did a good job," she said as Ghookasian dropped his portly figure into the nearest chair. "Thorough. Here is the result of all this childish behavior, both of you. I don't excuse him for his part in this infantile feud that's been going on now for more years than I can count."

"I know. Of course it might have been the other way around. Me the victim."

"And your wife suing us."

"What?" He looked up with his great poodle eyes, stricken with a dawning apprehension of the worst.

"How much liability do you carry? Are you covered for, say, a million-dollar suit?"

"Oh, my God."

"It could be for that amount, if it turns out he never snaps out of it. A zombie. No longer able to provide, do his work, take his place in society. Finished. A jughead."

"I don't have any liability." The words came out in a strained squeak, as though out of a doll equipped to speak when a string is pulled.

"Oh, my. My, my, my." Mrs. Dobbin had started to sit down at the kitchen table herself, but she rose again to pace the room thoughtfully. "This could wipe you out," she said, sympathetically.

"Oh, Mother, can't we wait until — well, wait and see a bit more?" Daisy interjected.

"We've got to be prepared for the worst. Mr. Ghookasian must know what that would be. His business attached, along with other assets such as his house. I believe that you own two other houses, that you rent, for income. You might give us those."

"Oh, God of Abraham, Isaac and Jacob."

"Naturally we'd be as considerate as the situation allowed."

"Let my cry come unto thee."

"I mean from our point of view, if Dobbin remains incapacitated. I work, but that doesn't bring in much, and I don't mean the final judgment would be anything like a million dollars." Daisy stood looking out the door window, her arms folded. Refusing to believe the testimony of her senses didn't change the fact that the scene was really taking place. "People suing *ask* for that" — Mrs. Dobbin shrugged — "or two million, or three, knowing they're lucky if the court finds for them to the tune of, say, a few hundred thousand. Maybe half a million." Ghookasian's normally swarthy complexion was the color of wet ashes. "Plus all the legal fees — to say nothing of the medical expenses. You certainly expect to pay for the hospitalization?"

"Mother, this can wait. I'm sure Daddy will snap out of it."

"I hope so, for everyone's sake. But I think Mr. Ghookasian realizes now that he's been behaving in anything but an adult fashion."

"Boy, do I. Boy. Oh, boy."

Mrs. Dobbin took a few steps toward him, then stood over him, her manner compassionately pondering. "You just don't want to take that final step into maturity, do you?"

"I guess not." His air was now thoroughly hangdog, as

he sat, elbows on knees, his hat dangling in one hand. He rotated it nervously from time to time, as though schooled by a skillful stage director to delineate apologetic distraction.

"It's exactly as though we never grew up. As though we're still in the third grade, never left it. I'm going to emphasize this immaturity by asking you to get up and stand in the corner. Over there."

Daisy's gasp of incredulity died in her throat as, even more unbelievably, Ghookasian did as he was told. He rose and walked to the corner beside the sink, and stood there with his back to them. Very likely this insane penance was complied with in the hope it would get him off the hook on which his own doings had got him impaled. Anything to evade a litigation not, under the circumstances, a totally unreasonable possibility. After all, Mr. Ghookasian would almost certainly have sued Dobbin if the fortunes of neighborly warfare were reversed, and Dobbin had beaned the Armenian with similar results. Dobbin himself wandered in from the parlor just then and watched from the doorway with his hands in his pockets.

"What's he doing, playing horsey?"

Mrs. Dobbin waved him off with a kindly gesture, not wanting the spell broken. "We're teaching him a lesson. Oh, not that we're not all guilty of petty wrongdoing in some form or other. Let him who has never thrown a rock cast the first stone. Do you understand what I'm saying, Mr. Ghookasian?"

"Well . . ." He had turned his head, and now suddenly whirled around. "For God's sake, recognize me, Dobbin! Ghookasian. From next door. For years. The dog, the property line, brush disposals! Rocks! One of them hit you and now — *Think hard.* It'll all come back soon, and everything will be all right. Here's my hand on it."

Dobbin shook it again, again without comprehension.

"My husband is a jughead," Mrs. Dobbin said softly. Then resuming her lugubrious summation of Ghookasian's life, "And the way you run your store. That 'Going out of Business' sign that's been in your window for twenty years. 'Final Closing Out. Prices Slashed on All Laces and Tablecloths.' Not that you're the only one, you see the same signs in store windows in New York, that ought to be ashamed of themselves too. Not that I'm making an ethnic slur out of it. I wouldn't be vile in that area. That I'm above. But there it is. In a way this might be a blessing in disguise for you. Turn you into the better person you have the potential to be. That's all for now. And as God is my judge, I hope it all blows over without anybody being ruined."

Ghookasian left in a well-earned daze of his own, wearing an expression hardly less glazed than Dobbin's. Learning by phone that the confrontation had yielded no results, Doctor Beddoes repeated his suspicion that the amnesia had implications broader than those of an organic impairment physically produced. "What's he escaping from? Something inclement in his life or environment. I'll look in later, and meanwhile I'll give some thought to a psychiatric referral. We'll discuss it then. The important thing is that he's coming along O.K. medically."

They were waiting for the doctor that afternoon when, seated by the window watching for his car, whom should Mrs. Dobbin see coming up the street but Josie Sniffen, holding upright in a paper bag what must be some nutritive goodie. Daisy sensed her mother growing tense with something other than the irritation expressed with a growl and a hand impatiently upflung. "You might know that Meddlesome Matty would show up. You'd think she'd have the grace to stay away." Mrs. Sniffen at least officially rather deemed it the part of grace to call, judging from the warmth and solicitude of her arrival, which by chance coincided with that of Doctor Beddoes. Dobbin was at the moment upstairs lying in bed, trying to sort himself out, and after tucking into the icebox the lemon meringue pie Mrs. Sniffen had come bearing, Mrs. Dobbin went upstairs to fetch him. A flashback memory of the time when, still a card, he had given everybody nine dollars and eighty-seven cents for Christmas. This being Mrs. Sniffen's first call since the mishap, the question of whether he would recognize *her* engendered the same electrified suspense as in the case of Ghookasian. All four, including the doctor, stood watching as Dobbin descended the stairs, wearing, loose, the same immemorial bathrobe as that in which Mrs. Dobbin, years ago, had toiled about the house saying, "A maid would quit," and "I've tried, God knows I've tried."

The faintest flicker of comprehension seemed, again, to cross Dobbin's face at the sight of Josie Sniffen, but it too vanished as quickly as it came. She was introduced. Mrs. Dobbin brewed a pot of hot coffee, which they all had with a slice of the lemon pie. Mrs. Sniffen chatted with Daisy about Effie and their work together on *Metropole*. "She's coming home for the weekend, maybe with her beau. That will be nice. You must get together. Oh, I have some snapshots she sent me."

"Her beau?"

"I think he's the boss. Dolfin. Do you know him?"

"Quite well. Let's see the pictures."

They were snaps of the *Metropole* softball team playing a rival magazine outfit in Central Park. There was one of Effie hunched at bat, another of Dog Bokum shagging a fly, and one of Andy Squibb sliding into home plate, for better or worse. They all seemed effigies of themselves, weirdly unfamiliar, total strangers she had once apparently known, cavorting antically somewhere years ago. Mrs. Sniffen blessedly returned them to her bag after they had made the rounds, passing under Dobbin's nose without so much as a single comment. Then there was a silence as Mrs. Sniffen, an oddly speculative look on her face, drew another snapshot from the bottom of her bag. She concealed it in her lap for a moment, under one hand, as though undecided about showing it. Her own curiosity got the better of her. She held it out to Dobbin, who was sitting on her left. He gaped at it for a second, then let out a whoop.

"Josie Clapesaddle! At the picnic! The picture you took! Now I remember."

It was the snapshot of Dobbin as a madcap youth swimming toward the riverbank with the duck in his mouth. It had brought back everything — their youth, their gaiety, all the exuberant romance and horseplay of the old days. The time when he had been a card, slipping articles of merchandise into people's supermarket carts, giving you a can of putty or a peck of potatoes for Christmas, you had everything else. It all came back with a rush, a flood of memory like a tidal wave depositing him back on the shore of reality.

"You see," the doctor said an eventful half-hour later, when Mrs. Sniffen had gone, "it resurrected events of a happier time, before the harsh facts and grim truths that grind us all down began to close in, that so cruelly close us all in. Escape, sheer escape. He wanted to forget it all, find asylum from it, as he did, until a picnic memory of one carefree, ecstatic, idyllic day unlocked his identity."

He seemed oblivious, as he rhapsodized, of the dim view

Mrs. Dobbin took of all this. She glowered in her chair as he carried on. Daisy could understand all this more clearly when her mother confirmed rumors she had heard.

"Your father's been seeing that woman again, I'm sure," Mrs. Dobbin said. "That's why it beats me he didn't recognize her right away. You know it's nearly three years since Ed Sniffen passed away, and a widow can get to be a restless thing in short order." She spoke in guardedly low tones, so as not to be overheard by Dobbin, who had repaired to the back porch, where he settled down comfortably with one of his favorite snacks, a can of sardines. She stole on tiptoe from the parlor into the kitchen to have a peek. Yes, he could be seen sitting on the glider, drawing on his eyeglasses before falling to. Returning, she observed rather aphoristically, "Men who have to put on specs to eat sardines shouldn't be fooling around with other women." Something outside on the street had drawn her attention. She stood at the window watching between the curtains. "Well, well, it seems to be the police. To what might we owe the pleasure of this visit?"

·13·

"HE HAS TWENTY-TWO SUITS and always stands as though he's being measured for a twenty-third."

That was one of the wisecracks with which Effie had tried to put Daisy off Dirk Dolfin, early on in their instinctively sensed collision-course rivalry over that catch, recently touched on in a *New York Times* roundup of the city's most eligible bachelors. Whether true or false then, now it wouldn't have held in any case. He owned three or four suits, the three-piece on his back at the time of the crime (had the deranged malcontent who slashed up the wardrobe known his victim was one of the Ten Best Dressed?) and a few bought off the rack until his tailor could run him up a half-dozen from fabrics freshly selected. This modest collection must hold him in the sartorial swim for now.

The metaphor was one that came naturally to Daisy, stretched out as she was in an Adirondack chair beside the Pilbeams' pool. The Pilbeams were brunch-prone Terre Haute department store owners, social leaders throwing what would be their Sunday goodbye-to-summer bash. Smoked goggles afforded Daisy a kind of visual ambush from which she could observe both Dirk, standing near the diving board at the far rim of the pool, and dearest enemy Effie, trotting him out as her own houseguest. How much slighter he seemed now, an observation that struck her as odd even as she made it, for hadn't she seen him with less on than the borrowed blue trunks worn now? But there was always, clothed or unclothed, the authentic sense of wiry health and grace. He could hardly be blamed for the silly word with which events had saddled him, but he seemed more conglomerateurish with each new outfit acquired: a garden tool corporation, a publisher of hymnals and cookbooks, and most recently, a firm with a line of bomb sprays including a spot remover (certainly smile-inducing in itself) and an insect repellent.

Dirk appeared to want to take a dip, but seemed conscious of Daisy's eye on him. He strolled around toward her, smiling down at Effie who was stretched out on a lounge chair chatting with the hostess as he passed her, a smile retained with last-minute changes when he reached Daisy's side.

"I like what I hear about your mother."

Mrs. Dobbin was "languishing in prison" for public consumption, while privately grateful for the seal of martyrdom her arrest had set on the Cause. When the police arrested her, after finding the stolen demo in the abandoned lumberyard where she'd kept it hidden, Daisy and her father had promptly appeared with bail money at the precinct station, but she had refused it — refused, that is, to leave her cell until "stink I consider sufficient has been raised. Show me some newspapers so I can see what coverage we're getting." In an apparently bumper year for documentary cinéma vérité, the cops had movies of her getting in and out of the car, which she drove to within a few blocks of her office, stashing it this time behind a disused warehouse, from where, a porkpie pulled down over one eye, she walked to work. The belief that she was taking on the biggest corporation in the world died hard in face of the fact that G.M. was in this case not responsible for the reckless endangerment of her life, but Midway Chevrolet, who for their part were trying to make it clear to the cops that they were not lodging a complaint, did not after all want her booked on a charge of grand larceny, but wanted the whole thing dropped, running scared, as they were, from the possibility that she might just damn well get the state prosecutor to indict *them* for said reckless endangerment. They had now moved heaven and earth to get the parts needed to correct the recall defect (the agency owner himself flying to Detroit to obtain them), and were ready to make the repairs in the fifteen minutes that were all it would take. But Mrs. Dobbin refused to leave her cell. "I'll rot in this jug till justice is done." They would have to carry her out, like the soldiers bodily carrying Sewell Avery out of Montgomery Ward in the forties. Some such apotheosis seemed to have laid hold of her, keeping her bent on self-immolation.

Daisy explained all this as concisely as she could to the still half-baffled Dutchman. Then she laughed, rather mirthlessly, through her nose. "You'd better be sure there are no harmful toxics in those spray cans you took over."

He turned very gentle. "Come back to work, Daisy. We miss you at the office."

Relaxed as ever, yet with something of the secret tension of a set mousetrap. She suddenly realized how fully she had come around to identifying herself with the mother as fantasized, seeing herself as both privileged and wronged, seduced and abandoned in the smart world to which she had risen — a match girl selling disposable lighters.

As softly she answered, raising her goggles to her forehead, "There is damn little I understand."

" 'Tis an common human woe."

"I want to see this business settled with my mother. It shouldn't take more than a day or two. Have you got your apartment cleared up? Any clues on the criminal?"

"Yes to the one, no to the other. Here come some drinks." A cart was trundled up by a white-jacketed manservant. "You want the usual bloody Mary? Perrier for me. Thank you." They were both sipping when a youth zoomed up the driveway on a bicycle, a knapsack on his back. "What is this?"

There was a new spirit abroad in the land, a fresh excitement stirring the trend-setters, radically different from the "New Ferment" of half a generation ago. In contrast to the expressionistic frenzy that had laid hold of Grand Rapids then, and swept to other parts of the country, this had a more subdued, even disciplined, resonance, as the "New Simplicity." A movement back to the soil was accompanied by a parallel return to folk crafts. People not only baked their own bread, they ground and even grew the grain from which to do it; they made their own clothes from fabrics they had in many instances themselves woven — often from wool sheared from sheep they had themselves raised, from lambs they had helped birth by lanternlight. Wandering minstrels sang for their supper; here and there a beggar poet went from door to door offering a rhyme for a crust of bread. It was one such who had pedalled up to the Pilbeams' on his bicycle, knapsacked.

"A rhyme for a crust of bread?" he asked Netty Pilbeam when she ran inquiringly over from her guests. A fine youth, with blue eyes and a thatch of flaxen hair.

Mrs. Pilbeam looked uncertainly toward the house, where a maid stood in the window watching. "Gee, I don't think I have any bread. Not a slice around, or a roll."

"That's all right. It's only a figure of speech for a morsel of food. Anything will do — hunger is the best sauce, and starvation makes a banquet. A slice of cake, piece of pie or a tart. Leftovers from last night's dinner. What did you have?" Onlookers half expected him to say "my good woman."

"Why," finger at lip, "let me — *coq au vin*. And cherries jubilee. There may be some — No, that was the night before. Last night we had ragoût Bordelaise, that was it, and Hubbard squash."

"That will be fine. And if you have any of the cherries jubilee left."

The maid was ordered to fetch this food, which the youth sat on the doorstoop to eat. He declined an invitation to the kitchen table, as out of key with his vagabond life-style, though gratefully accepting a glass of white Burgundy with which to sluice these goodies down. He thanked them all profusely as he tooled off on his bicycle, as bracing a sight as could be encountered on such a bright summer's day. Mrs. Pilbeam, who had again been attending to her guests, ran up the drive waving and shouting.

"Hey! Where's my rhyme?"

He struck himself apologetically on the brow and wheeled back, fishing a scrap of paper from his shirt pocket. He handed it to her and, wishing her a good day, was once more off, whistling merrily as he vanished up the road. She unfolded the paper and read it:

True wit is Nature to advantage dressed,
What oft was thought, but ne'er so well expressed.

"Pretty nifty," she said to Daisy, who read it over her shoulder. Daisy murmured agreement, deeming it best not to add that it might be especially appreciated by readers of Alexander Pope.

Another guest was leaving, a tall Englishman in his forties named Shrubsole. The hostess protested his not remaining for lunch, but he pleaded no end of neglected Sunday gardening to catch up on, his property a disgrace compared to these beautifully barbered lawns and hedges. "I know what your quiches are like, my dear Netty," he said, and then, clearing his throat with an arch expression telegraphing the fact that a waggery was en route, added, "but I have premises to keep . . ."

"I understand, of course. Things do get ahead of you."

Shrubsole started again, staring wildly from one woman to the other. "I have premises to keep, you see. *Premises to keep*," he repeated, pale with horror.

"Of *course*, Tippy."

"Premises to keep," he went doggedly on with a gulp, "and miles to mow before I sleep . . ." He clutched at his breast, as though a seizure might follow on the laying of this egg. "And miles to mow before I sleep," he finished with a faint moan of despair, rolling his eyes as at a heaven vacant of any providence whatever.

"I understand," Mrs. Pilbeam again assured him, taking his hand in both of hers and giving him a sympathetic peck on the cheek before flying back to her remaining guests. Shrubsole tottered away to his car without cardiac incident, no doubt consoling himself with a few muttered remarks about proper American clods unacquainted with even their own literary heritage, despite Daisy's having registered a smile or two in the course of his ordeal. A gag possibly set up for years, perhaps half a lifetime, is not a pretty thing to see bomb. Daisy shouted an additional word of appreciation, lost, however, as his Saab backfired as well in shooting away in a spray of gravel.

Actually, Shrubsole had returned Daisy to thoughts of her mother, sentiments about whom remained ever wreathed in a smoky guilt. Jennie Dobbin had always said foreigners settling here should make some effort to talk as we did. That included Englishmen. There was no excuse for immigrants who had lived in this country for twenty years speaking with such impeccable diction that they were scarcely less incomprehensible than unreconstructed Italians and Spaniards and Swedes garbling and gobbling their vowels and consonants. "You'd think they'd never left the old country." England the old country, immaculately tongued Oxonians immigrants; that was a rather refreshing thought.

Detachedly casing the party from her reclaimed Adirondack chair, Daisy remembered what she could about the departed Shrubsole, popping homeward in his Saab. He seemed to have gone, long ago, on some sort of cultural safari throughout the country, on a grant jointly provided by the British and American state departments, penetrating the American interior with an interpreter useful for when he reached such heathen backwaters as the Ozarks and darkest Oklahoma. It was probably reciprocal: he needed a translator to understand the natives of Alabama and the Dakotas as much as they — and Jennie Dobbin — him. Even Daisy had sometimes had to chew her cabbage twice, when her Hoosier twang had met with a "Beg pardon?" What on earth was he doing in Indiana? This was where the woman lived whom he'd married for her money, one heard.

Getting a little buzzed on a second bloody Mary, Daisy

daydreamed, glad for the moment to lie neglected in the sun . . .

High noon in Indiana, while dusk gathered over Domblémy. From those castle chambers still sounded revelries of the kind at which her father and mother had met in the long ago, folded into one another's arms as they swept across the ballroom floor to waltz strains spinning through open casements out into the Brittany night. Built on coastal rocks, its turrets reached to the very clouds, silvered by moonlight on the night when they'd met, and conceived the Daisy they would themselves not name. They'd bedded amid scented sheets, hearing distantly the ball from which they'd slipped away. Sea spume. Wind in the boughs of trees rooted somehow in the promontory crevices. Arpeggios of hurrying feet along corridors running with palace intrigues. Dank and far below, dungeons in which only the most reprehensible languish, none in durance vile. Then the music quickens portentously. Bats flit among the smoking sconces, mice scuttle underneath the stairs, clouds obliterate the moon over Domblémy. They quarrel, as lovers ever must. Between spirits so fiery the discord must be as keen as the harmony was sweet. A storm of recrimination brews in Domblémy, for what is that castle but a dour and tortuous symbol for the one we build within ourselves, over oubliettes into which we drop our guilts and shames and like to think they are forgotten, but which arise as ghosts to stalk the twisting passages of memory. And what are those phantoms that, huddled in cloaks impervious to recognition, wander forever along the battlements, what if not the spooks of motivations unclear even to ourselves? And who is this that, deflowered flower, black velvet hurriedly flung about her silken vestments, slips from the bedchamber where she has loved well but not wisely, and then from Domblémy itself — to vanish forever in immortal mists? Who if not the forever Anonymous Mother, Mater Incognita, unnamed and unclaimed. The earth has turned on its appointed course, and now château and sea alike lie shrouded in another twilight, the dusk of dawn . . .

Daisy smiled to herself as she lay back woolgathering in her chair. From where she stretched her lazy length, drink in hand, she could see the real author of that fantasy, facing her across the pool in which the human dolphins splashed. It was hard to tell whether Effie was watching her also, since she sprawled in ambush behind goggles even bigger and darker than Daisy's own. Eyelids open no doubt the merest sliver, enough for the same guarded visibility. Why hadn't the two had their obligatory scene long ago, in New York where it properly belonged? Had they come home to Indiana to wage it? That would be up to Daisy. This was where it all began, the best-chums saga that proved well enough the cynical truth that anyone with a friend doesn't need an enemy. They were a stone's throw from the sycamore-shaded street where Effie had blurted out the story of Daisy's soiled origins, from which the girlish fairy tale had sprung. Why not ask her here and now the question she'd always itched and yet feared to: where she'd heard it. Her source, please. Why not indeed. A little more of this Dutch courage on an empty stomach and she might just damn well sock it to her. And then unload herself about all the rest.

New guests were arriving steadily for a party that, though officially a "brunch," would probably go on till evening and then one of the Pilbeams' extemporaneous suppers. Nearby stood a lean blonde young woman, a local tennis star, named Rex Morley, or so she claimed. One had become accustomed to Merediths and Paiges and even Courtneys in the steadily homogenizing world, but Rex?

Still, those quick to mark the defeminizing effects of feminism were not on too firm ground here. These women had been christened all those things thirty years and more ago, well before the sisterhood came pouring out of the trenches.

Somewhat by himself in the pool stood Dirk Dolfin, severed at the waist and clutching his Perrier. For all the cachet conferred by running sartorially abreast of Cary Grant and Fred Astaire, he surveyed the scene with an awed, foreigner's smile on his lips. Standing in a kidney-shaped vessel of blue chlorined American water, he seemed not so much engaging in revels as conforming to some rumored principle of decadence characteristic of high life in his adoptive land. The dilapidated old puss in the English department at Kidderminster had been so endearingly moth-eaten as to regularly mouth the sonnets of Santayana, fond of reciting one in particular about "the rustic at the play." There was still that quality of unburnished naiveté (by no means in itself to be denigrated) about Dirkie Wirkie. That was not Fitzgeraldian wealth out there in the pool at all; there was no money in the tinkle of his laughter. With Dirkie Wirkie the rich were like us, and some comfort in the thought. In some ways, the glossy poor we abound in could upstage him. Someone called to him from ashore, a trite pleasantry about living it up one need not answer but with a commensurate vapidity such as "Yessiree." Who was he again, the jolly friar in the straw hat *avec* bandana band? Of course, Rex's haberdasher husband, protecting his tomato skin from the sun with one of those rigs that hucksters and ice men of the olden days had put on their horses' heads, as one saw in turn-of-the-century photographs. You half expected to see two long ears protrude through the crown.

Shifting her gaze to the left (and pondering the tyranny

of headgear in dictating human appearance), she saw Effie had moved and was now seated at a garden table with a large umbrella, "Cinzano" emblazoned on its flaps, talking across it to another woman. When the woman rose and left, Daisy felt herself propelled out of her chair and around the noisy pool to Effie's side. Effie was lighting a cigarette when Daisy lowered herself into the vacated seat. Their smiles together were like expressions electrically switched on.

"Your mother is something else," Effie quickly said. "You must be proud of her."

"I certainly am. A hundred like her could straighten the stinking world out."

"I mean what a crusader. It's clear where you got your adrenaline."

It was pumping now, God knew. Her heart hammered. "But the point doesn't hold, does it? If what you told me is true."

"If what I . . . I don't understand."

"That I was adopted. You were the courier."

"What? Whatever in hell are you talking about?"

"Surely you remember. Years ago, we were little girls, roller skating — Oh, my God, what does that have to do with it? Out there." She pointed behind her in the general direction of their street.

Looking off somewhere else, Effie drew on her cigarette, holding the smoke characteristically in one puffed cheek a moment before blowing it slowly out of the corner of her mouth. She shook her head. "I don't understand."

"You have no recollection of blurting out that I was adopted?"

Effie's bewilderment was clearly unfeigned. "As God is my judge. I mean why would I say a thing like that?"

"You mean you never heard tell I was adopted?"

"*Are* you? Daisy, I didn't know that."

"Oh, my God," Daisy whispered, "I'm going crazy. I'm dreaming this. Why would you say a thing like that unless you knew it was the case?"

"Why? Some taunt I tossed off when we were having one of our mads, I suppose. We were always fighting and making up. Kids can be mean. There was the time you — "

"*Gentle Jesus.*" Daisy threw up her hands, rolling her eyes, at the same time trying to keep her voice down amid the hubbub. "Mean is good. It never occurred to you in later years how traumatic such a thing — "

"In later years I'd forgotten it. I forgot it the next day. You mean all these years — Why didn't you ask your parents?"

"To spare them, for Christ's sweet sake! Oh!"

Effie leaned forward, as if impulsively to touch her friend across the table, but Daisy jerked her hand back. "Daze, I'm truly sorry if . . . You must understand. I may be sick. That is, vomit. Vomit, do you hear?"

"I think I understand," Daisy said, ignoring her threats. "I understand now that it was vintage Effie Sniffen. In training for the man the child is father to — in this case the woman the child is mother to, of course."

"What *are* you talking about? Are you sure you're well?"

"It certainly wasn't out of character, judging from what I've learned of it in recent gyrations. Your spiteful behavior about Dirk. Pretty Machiavellian way to conduct a romance I must say, or to screw one up. Blowing my cover at the magazine."

"I did no such thing."

"I don't believe you."

"You were the interloper."

"I don't believe that either."

"I will not sit here and be insulted."

Both women were in bathing suits. On that fact hinged both the resolution of the battle and the outcome of the war — to say nothing of the future course of their lives. Effie punched her cigarette out in an ashtray, breathing smoke. Shucking her terrycloth robe, she drew a bathing cap from her bag on the table, tucked in her hair, fastened the chin strap, and marched toward the pool. Following roughly the same preparations except for a cap she didn't have, Daisy followed her, determined to have this out in whatever element.

Effie headed for the steps at the shallow end. Descending a stairway into water always has a faint element of absurdity about it, hardly mitigated if one is doing it in high dudgeon, and with whatever aspect of wounded hauteur. Diving in herself, heedless of her hair, Daisy was waiting for her adversary near the middle of the pool, not far from Dirk who had by now wandered in nearly up to his chin, so that all one could see was his head like that of John the Baptist on a platter, except for the glass of Perrier water held aloft, like a torch for prudence. He smiled at Daisy, a smile that faded abruptly as he realized from the expression on her face that the two women had a scene in the making. He turned to take in Effie's.

Having immersed herself with a preparatory squat or two at the shallow end, like a prizefighter limbering up at the ropes before a bout, Effie began to swim the length of the pool, trying icily to ignore Daisy. The lap was never completed. With long, vigorous strokes, she headed straight for the other two. She would have shot between them like a torpedo had not Daisy, now in a real rage, grabbed her arm and stopped her cold.

"I don't think we're quite finished, you treacherous little bitch," she said.

Brought up roughly erect by the move, Effie bobbed

between them a moment, alternately trying to get her footing on the bottom and retain her buoyancy in the water. Scrambling to get out of the way, Dirk lost his own footing and began to sink, dropping the glass and making distressed gurgling noises as his head went under water. In tranquil retrospect, if there ever was to be such a thing, the sound he made might be recalled as perfectly conforming to Byron's "bubbling groan," from a rhyme certainly worth a crust of anybody's bread. The sudden realization that he might be a poor swimmer, or couldn't even swim at all, struck Daisy with a panic that drove everything else out of her mind as she dove down after the vanished Dirk.

He was trying to run back to shallow water up the sloping bottom, with the incongruously antic effect inevitable to the effort, his feet slipping ever backward as he effervesced a succession of bubbles indicating a novice without the slightest notion about holding his breath while under water. Getting her hands under his arms, Daisy heaved him upright toward the surface, trying as she did so to remember the lifesaving techniques taught in girlhood summer camps (to some of which she had gone with Effie). What Dirk brought to the scene was the classic danger warned against in such instructions, that of the distressed swimmer bringing his rescuer down with him unless properly dealt with. Except that, with Daisy at his back, it was Effie whom he now faced and at whom he frantically clutched. Finding herself in peril of being dragged under in the mounting confusion, Effie began to beat him off, first prying his arms away and then pummelling him about the head, so that there was every possibility of Dirk's sinking once more, this time senseless. It was only with the greatest effort that Daisy tugged him away, finally getting the grip that enabled her to draw him back to the shallow end. Two of the Pilbeams' teen-aged sons hauled him up, spluttering and coughing. He was stretched out facedown before a cluster of onlookers for artificial respiration, which Daisy was able to administer with more certain efficiency, as recalled from camp days. But it was scarcely needed, and soon the summer scene re-composed itself, Dirk insisting that everything was all right, nothing terrible had happened. "It was am piece pie," he assured them, from his swelling fund of English-speaking slang.

It was all eventually forgotten in the tide of gaiety gen-erated by a sumptuous lunch of quiches, salad and cham-pagne. The party went on through the long midsummer afternoon, and for some of the guests, into evening. The Pilbeams scrounged up supper for the welcome diehards, ham and cold chicken, with potato salad prepared by the maid. Beer and wine flowed. All had, of course, changed back into their dresses and suits in the bathhouse and spare rooms available.

Scarcely another word passed between the sobered Daisy and Effie, and the few spoken were exchanged in anything but anger. They were enveloped in a joint, dense embar-rassment. Daisy felt sympathy if anything for the other, whose shame subdued Dirk Dolfin as well. She averted her face from the constraint obvious between the two. After a supper eaten indoors, someone played the piano, the guests joining in a raucous songfest. Daisy drifted through the open French windows to the garden, then on to the pool. The lights blazed there, though it was deserted. A brisk wind cooled the evening air, and above the always drench-ingly beautiful sound of music from the house could be heard the slap and gurgle of tiny waves against the gleaming tiles. One of the Pilbeam boys had dived down to retrieve the glass Dirk had dropped in the moment's chaos. Now, among a few leaves floating in the pool, only a scrap of lime peel from the drink of Perrier marked the day's adventure, bobbing gently this way and that on the chuckling water.

·14·

"I'D NEVER THOUGHT of myself as matrimonial lumber, as they say."

Daisy felt a familiar tremor of dislodgment, as though for a seismic thousandth of a second, continental creep were discernible through the soles of her feet. "Oh, you never felt yourself matrimonial *timber*, Dirk?" she said, trying to keep to a necessary minimum the italics in her voice, as in bygone attempts to correct the Big Spiderbecke thing. Time was when she and Effie would have shared that as unwittingly endearing. "There's no reason for you to change your mind now, I assure you."

"It was am piece luck you were there at the pool," the Dutchman mused obstinately on.

"But if I hadn't been, it all wouldn't have happened."

We are back in New York. Daisy with her muddler pokes at the wedge of lime in her lunch-time bloody Mary, which sinks every time she raises it, and remains submerged. Why, then, had the lime floated in the Pilbeams' pool? She performs an experiment. She squeezes hers dry, scraping the pulp away with a knife. Now it floats in her drink. That's the solution. The weight of the juice and pulp sink it, the rind alone floats, or might depending on its shape. Some frugal servitor had garnished Dirk's Perrier water with a twist instead of a wedge lime.

"You saved my life."

"But I keep telling you it wouldn't have *been* in danger if I hadn't been there in the first place. You're indulging in circular argumentation. I'm sure there's a Latin term for it, besides being what some would call woman's logic. Do you want to be like that? And even if what you say is true, it's no reason for proposing all over again! Don't for God's sake ask me to marry you because you think you Owe Me Something. You'd have got back to shallow water eventually, or someone else would have fished you out."

"Effie tried to kill me."

"Oh, my God."

Preparatory to throwing up her hands, Daisy flipped her muddler so far away it bounced off the table to the floor. She checked Dirk's move to retrieve it. "We can't always be judged purely by our automatic impulses. She acted on sheer self-preservation without thinking. You might very well *have* pulled her down with you. It's the drowner's natural instinct, just as that was hers. Had she time to think, she'd probably have thought less of herself and more of you."

"She pulled my arms off her and beat me around the head."

"Rescuers are instructed to do that, if aught else fails." Aught else? She sounded like Andy Squibb, that master archaist. She must start anew. "If necessary knock out the swimmer you're trying to save if he endangers both your lives. Knock him cold and then tow him ashore without interference."

"The difference in people," he said, ignoring the testimony, or perhaps marking its magnanimity. "You're better than all of us, Daisy."

"Oh, balls."

He rolled a bread pill in his fingers. "I'm no bargain."

Daisy had mentally invented a smugometer — pronounced with the accent on the second syllable, like speedometer — for measuring the complacency quotient informing self-castigatory comments such as these by men. It was strapped on the psyche most frequently in matters of the heart — the heart in this case being located just under the pelvis. The one with the highest opinion of himself had "guessed he was a rat," by virtue (if that was the word) of his career as a Lothario, naturally. "How stupid of me" was always said by chaps who preened themselves on their intelligence. Hastily strapping Dirk into the smugometer, following the declaration of himself as no bargain, she got a reading worse than some, but, honestly, better than most. She gave him a three on a scale of ten. Naturally his self-deprecation carried with it the inevitable shopping for contradiction. She would not let him dangle there forever, thirsting for reassurance. She would not be obnoxious in this area, as her mother would put it. And how happy she was to learn in the end that they were her real parents after all. The guilt gone, the slate wiped clean.

"In a day when raspberries are four dollars for a half-pint, you're no gyp, Dirk." Having suckled him, she burped him. "And you're better in bed than any man I've ever been there with." Having said that, she could not help adding, not tauntingly, yet not quite otherwise, "And your fancy friends would tell you I'm in a position to judge." Her sardonic expression at the last split second left a shade of irony in her favor.

But a bonus for him was also intended in the wry afterthought: even a lifeline if he found himself floundering, now, in moral seas. The teasing premise that she might just possibly have earned the dreadful Dog-broadcast soubriquet gave him a conceivable out: that much restitution his indebtedness could hardly be construed as calling for. One could be eternally grateful to a Jezebel without marrying her. But with a gesture all the weightier for being so airily given, he waved the loophole away. The double standard was buried deeper than ever plummet sounded. Exquisitely, the roles of debtor and creditor were reversed. She owed him the chance to make, at last by marriage, even that much restitution. She had saved his life, and so was obligated to him for the rest of her own.

He took the menus from the waitress who had roller-skated over to hand them, gave one to Daisy with a smile, and opened the other with a will. Being snatched from the jaws of death had opened his eyes to the importance of living while you may; from now on he was going to eat lunch, and that in the best restaurants, beginning with this newly opened one where half-naked girls darted on wheels from table to table, like carp in the water. The place boasted a choice of seventy-five crêpes, the variations consisting of fillings pocketed in pancakes themselves immutable. She had fish and he had chicken. She a glass of Chablis, he am bottle Heineken.

Daisy's mother had been bodily thrown out of jail. Charges of grand larceny the Chevrolet agency had got successfully quashed, and the Dobbin Citation had been put in safe running order with the parts the proprietor had flown to Detroit to get. The state prosecutor found it impossible to nail him anyway, on the reckless endangerment charge, since he had acquired the agency after the Dobbins had bought the defective automobile, and the previous owner, the prosecutor finally said, could only have been penalized by having his license to sell revoked, a situation now totally academic. Mrs. Dobbin was furious, but vowed a new cause célèbre soon. That it was to be none other than the Dolfin Enterprises lay in a future of which all were for the moment blessedly oblivious.

At *Metropole,* harassment and exploitation were eradicated, without dethroning Eros. Passions flamed and died out; affections rooted and then blew away, like tumbleweed. A faint, subtle air of housekeeping steals unaware over bosses and secretaries occupying furniture and brewing coffee and tea at close quarters, sharing desks in the drawers of which papers are stacked as methodically as shirts and scarves in bureaus and chests of a house, in a proximity easily mistaken for cohabitation. Intimacy is imposed, if not chosen. And once imposed, accepted. One knew of workaday pairs coupling behind closed doors on a couch, the very carpeting. For a week, two. Perhaps a nooner at the Biltmore, a quickie at the Roosevelt. Then nothing more to say to each other. Mysterious. A wind blowing itself away, a sprig of blossom self-wilting. And in an office nickname-crazy, the wits unceasingly at work. Andy Squibb had hired a carnivore named Cliff Poole who, owing to tastes as catholic as Dog Bokum's own, became speedily known, it was inevitable, as Dirty Poole. And women a match for both him and the Dog were called Doggie Bags, or, if choosier consorts for weekends of a more elevated order, Overnight Bags. With everybody rolling in the sack, who will make the beds, who ever? Right wing politicians raise their snouts from the public troughs long enough to call for a return to God. And high time it may well be.

"Verdomme!"

My God, has he spilled again?

Again Dirk scratches at a stain, this time on a necktie, and again Daisy has her fancy of the fashion plate dining at the best restaurants under a barber's dropcloth, insurance against his being bumped from the roster that for the moment keeps him abreast of Cary Grant and Fred Astaire. But it's no great problem in this instance. He removes the cravat for Daisy to slip into her bag and take back to her office, to try out on it a new spray cleaner, Out Damn Spot!, which Dolfin Enterprises is thinking of taking over, to add to its growing chemical acquisitions. They will then slip together into nearby Brooks Brothers where she will help him select another regimental stripe to go with the discreet shepherd's check he's wearing, like the possessive huisvrouw toward which she seems irresistibly driving, or driven.

It's well into Tuesday namiddag, but she still has the Monday morning blahs (recalling the now departed uncle who wrote "black" greeting-card jingles, famous for having them until Thursday). Maybe for her they will have lifted by Thursday, when she is committed to lunch with the Diesel. Dirk, still endearingly vowing eternal gratitude for a salvation any pool idler could have guaranteed him, pressing her hand as he does so, remarks that he has no recollection of his "life flashing before him" as he went down. Daisy smiles at the memory provoked, of a story she had started as a high school sophomore. It was to consist in the *evaluating thoughts* a drowning man would entertain about the past unreeling in his mind, a sort of inventory-taking resolve to be a better person if he is saved. Its title was to be, after Debussy, *Reflets dans l'eau*. Reflections in the water. What had ever happened to the once seemingly unquenchable urge to write poetry, fiction?

What had ever happened to Scudder, her teacher at Meat-loaf? What had ever happened to Grand Rapids? What had ever happened to Domblémy? That she knew. It had been cloven clean to the rock on which it rested, riven by a bolt of lightning that had scattered its components into the ever-wallowing sea. Only a twist of lime peel bobbed forever on the surface of the deep.

The honeymoon was not nearly as bad as Daisy had feared, although instead of marriage to her quickening the tempo of Dirk's Americanization, she began speaking broken English in consequence of her brush with the old country. That arose mainly from attempts to communicate with the elder Dolfins with whom they stayed in Amsterdam. "I get toothpaste," she told them one morning when Dirk was looking in on his office there. "Tandpasta. I get am package Kleenex." To get away. She pointed through the front door and then in a circular sign language around toward the drugstore three blocks away. "I get am package Kleenex, an tube toothpaste, and am bottle aspirin. Back in two shakes." Perhaps that was not an idiom here. Yet she found herself charade-pantomiming "two shakes of a lamb's tail." She held up two fingers, as though her hosts were idiots. "Zwei." That was German. "Twee." She wanted to be alone. "I come snel back." She shot one palm across the other, zzt, signifying a swift return. Mr. Dolfin, who parted his hair in the middle and wore Herbert Hoover collars, and in fact looked a little like Hoover, rose to accompany her, but his wife, who looked like him but not like Herbert Hoover, stayed him with a gesture, murmuring a few words aside, of which Daisy seemed to catch "vrouw" something or other. Possibly "vrouwen dingen." Meaning that Daisy might be off to purchase some woman things, ladies' stuff, hygienic or lunar *matériel* one need not know the language to buy since drugstores stocked them in plain view to be simply pointed at, or for one to help oneself to.

Daisy's "ja" hardly represented much of a seachange, given the habit of Eastern-educated American girls saying practically that with their "yeh" or "yah," or the more or less drawled "yow." More noteworthy was her continuing to inhale the affirmative. When asked by the elder Dolfins, who spoke fair English, whether she knew where the drugstore was, she sucked in her "ja" and was out the door like a shot.

Attending the Reformed Church with the family on Sunday mornings helped fill in whatever gaps in her grasp of Calvinist doctrine had been left by Dirk's pillow talk. She couldn't understand much of the sermons, but they were rehashed in English over enormous midday dinners. One was about Jacob and Esau and the bamboozlement of old Isaac, and she had a wild moment when she was tempted to tell how, during the Depression, critics said American proletarian writers had sold their birthright for a pot of message, not so much in the hope of getting a rise out of the Hoovers as to push to the limit the hypothesis that she was going out of her mind and could no longer be held responsible for her actions. Even speaking English, the elder Dolfins took some keeping up with, not their fault, but once she could have sworn Mr. Dolfin was talking about smokeless dentistry. But here she was, amid authentic burgher style, having, as her mother would have said, hooked a hubby. She had come triumphantly up the middle aisle, from which a woman could go on to rule her world no matter what her husband did. "Didn't Shakespeare say something about this sceptred aisle?" her mother asked. "Yes," Daisy'd said, and gone off somewhere to beat her head against the wall.

Women in Holland must still rule indirectly, apparently. Going to church the elder Mrs. Dolfin walked a step behind her black-suited husband, though Dirk explained that custom was outmoded, in fact a hangover from a couple of generations back, a boyhood memory, in his father's case, of seeing his own grandparents proceeding toward divine worship single-file, like American Indians moving stealthily through underbrush. A vestige of the Pauline principle of women's subjection to the husband. Daisy would sometimes drop a step behind her own groom in more or less sardonic parody of what one trusted had been overcome, secretly smiling at what the Diesel would think of this church-bound sight. There had been — how grotesque one's associations could be — another Hoover, J. Edgar, seen daily going to lunch with a male companion likewise respectfully trailing him by a step. One had seen pictures. What a newt pond was the human mind.

Slogging across the intertidal mud toward Schiermonnikoog with the other waddenlopers, feature of the honeymoon, was even worse. "Was it for this my mother sweated in the cold?" she thought, adapting to her purpose some Millay the d.o.p. had mouthed. She lagged sometimes several paces behind her man, not out of prefeminist stratification but because that was as fast as she could go. Just before they reached the fabled island, a nasty North Sea squall came up and sent their entire party of about twenty, soaked to the skin, dashing for cover at the nearest inn. "Vies weertje," the proprietor greeted them with a smile as they charged through the door. Nasty little weather indeed, a translation that emphasized to Daisy something she had already observed about the Dutch. They were diminutive-crazy. The "je" — little — seemed affixed to half the words in the language. A house was a huisje, a book a boekje. The suffix was even heard for cigarettes, which is a diminutive to begin with. "Sigaretje?" Papa Dolfin had been heard to say on their first day there, extending a pack of his personal brand. Daisy's impulsive reach for one was checked by a frown from Dirk, for whom the invitation had been solely meant. Women did not smoke in that great big huisje. So Daisy had had to puff away in bedroom secrecy, at her own newly adopted menthols, an American make containing only five milligrams tar. It rained buckets. She had a dream in which she was dancing *Swan Lake* in galoshes.

But all journeys end, and home they flew, a beautiful vluchtje on KLM, dining on roast beef and a red Bordeaux possessing what Dirk called "an exquisite boutique." She took another week off from the office of which she was now in charge, having indeed been given *Metropole* as a wedding gift, while they settled into Dirk's apartment, where they would stay till they could find a house in some place like Fairfield County. The honeymoon might be said to have terminated with a telephone call from Daisy's mother.

"The spray cleaner Dolfin Enterprises bought? Out Damn Spot!?"

"Yes."

It was the spot-shot cleaner with which Daisy had deleted, or tried to, the sauce Dirk had spilled on his tie in the seventy-five-crêpes restaurant with the waitresses on roller skates, where they'd had their first meal together after the pool party. The fluid had, ominously, *itself* left a ring on the necktie which other commercial cleaners had in turn been powerless to remove. She had worriedly kept the truth from Dirk, pretending to have lost the striped rep in question. Now Mrs. Dobbin was confirming her worst fears. Her consumer protection agency back in Terre Haute had, after exhaustive analyses, reached the inescapable conclusion that Out Damn Spot! contained an ingredient, apparently not checked out by sufficient laboratory runs, that left stains as stubborn as, if not more stubborn than, those which purchasers were trying to eradicate from soiled fabrics. Little wonder the original manufacturers had been so eager to be taken over.

"Are you sure?" Daisy said.

"Positive. We must ask for nothing less than the recall of three and a half million cans of Out Damn Spot! currently on the market. They must be removed from all supermarket, hardware and drugstore shelves this wide land over."

"Mother."

"I'm sorry. I have my standards. I have my ethics. I'm sorry. The bunch at the office are completely sympathetic, they know what's what, but I have to say forget it. No favorites or nepotism they call it. I'm sorry. How was the Netherlands? We got your card from where you waddenloped, saying 'Wish you were here.'"

It was the beginning of some heavy weather for the Enterprises. In addition to the million-dollar writeoff of the product, there were other reverses. An insecticide performed sluggishly against its predecessors, and a vice-president who suggested they change the name to Let Us Spray was fired. Hardly a fruitful shakeup. Dirk became a workaholic, taking stuffed briefcases home with him almost every night, when, indeed, he wasn't off on a business trip. The bed was once more full of paper clips, and once, in mid-love, Daisy felt a fat rubber band around one toe, like a ringer in a game of quoits. Continuing servantless by choice, they had a Dutch cleaning woman, Mrs. Vander Volk, for whose arrival Daisy was forever tidying up the house. She chased dirt in every way but with a stick. She was willing to come on Saturdays and even, when they were entertaining that evening, on Sundays; she was devout, but after all godliness was next to cleanliness.

Daisy was determined to keep her ties with her two old friends, or at least that they would not be further frayed. Effie she assured that the post in her nook of the advertising department was secure, to be run without interference, with what they hoped would be her old and proven efficiency. The Diesel was a harder case. Fired at *Femme*, she was rumored to be drinking heavily. The first sight of her, at the lunch to which Daisy invited her, confirmed that. She had put on weight, unhealthy bloatage not from food happily tucked in, but alcohol sadly imbibed, most probably in solitude. Her eyes were faintly bloodshot, and there were woeful crimps at the corners of her mouth. She had asked that they meet elsewhere than at the Straw Hat of palmier days, and so they joined up at a new place where the barmaid drank Sazeracs on duty and where the waiters seemed to have been handpicked for their truculence. Theirs sidled up to the table with an air of undergraduate menace, as though they were all in the gym shower and his napkin was a towel with which he was going to snap them in the flanks until it stang like hell. Omelets and a carafe of decent Riesling set them going well. Conning the menu for a calorically tolerable dessert, Bobsy told Daisy she had had Horton Pew, her ex-husband, all wrong. It was *Snakes* and Snails and Puppy Dogs' Tails, not Rats and Snails.

"I think it's optional," Daisy said, laughing along with the joke. "There's also 'Snips and Snails.' "

They ordered sherbet and black coffee. Now was the time for Daisy to state her proposition — as soon as the waiter had finished brushing crumbs onto their laps. At last he went to fill their orders.

"Look, I'm sure you'd be" — she rejected "useful" as too patronizing for one in as rickety shape as her friend — "be valuable at *Metropole*. I mean if you're interested, but what? The woman in administrative charge of the fact department, going over story ideas, is going to retire soon, and meantime is short an assistant. A sort of presifter. That's not too far from what you did at *Femme,* and when Sadie Johnston does ride off into the sunset, why, you might have the whole show. Would you like to come talk to Andy Squibb about it? But you'd have to shape up. No more of this," tapping the Diesel's wineglass with a spoon. "I mean not cold turkey. Just moderation. You know it is written. Cut down so you won't have to quit."

"Yes, of course I —" Bobsy's voice broke, and she brushed at her eyes with her fingertips. "I want you to know that, after what —"

"Oh, balls. Here comes the Sunshine Kid with our sherbet. You don't want to make his day, do you? Well so! Done and done. Of course now that the place is cleaned up you might find it a little dull. There's no more harassment."

Dirk remained a workaholic, and along with that drank a bit more heavily too, not yet necessarily to excess. He reverted to his no-lunch rule, but developed a habit of snacking and sipping into wee hours spent over paperwork. Among his favorites — shades of Daisy's father — was pickled pigs' feet, and there must always be a jar of them in the icebox, with Heineken for companion.

We know that to say your foot hurts is somehow less

gross than to say your feet hurt. A trivial enough truth, but curious. With the eating of pickled pigs' feet this nuance is reversed. Taking such a snack into Dirk's study, Daisy found it nicer to think he was having his nightly ration of pigs' feet, even though there was only one on the plate. "Here's your pig's foot" had a crude, even Neanderthal, ring to it. "Here's your pigs' feet" was much better, even though still slightly jarring to the sensibilities of those who find the fancy incomprehensible. She categorized it as an inversion of Taste. Of a piece with your intellectual's addiction to comics, the sexual connoisseur's corollary descents into practices for which there are names you wished did not exist.

He gained weight, his clothes had to be let out, almost certainly guaranteeing a lifetime's banishment from the Ten Best Dressed list. That made him take greater refuge in food and drink, indulgences further imperilling chances of reinstatement — another vicious circle.

Daisy often Danced Till Dawn, usually for a few minutes around ten o'clock at night or so, generally when he was away, but sometimes when he was home, watching from the sofa where he would stretch out with a report to read and a piece fruit to nibble on. Almost always dancing alone. She remembered her girlish resolve to marry the first man who murmured in her ear, in the classic vein, as they glided across a ballroom floor, that she waltzed divinely. Tonight she kicked off her slippers and to the strains of *Rosenkavalier* set going on the stereo wafted herself in graceful arcs around the room, occasionally grazing a table or chair but in the main missing things by a hair, her own hair streaming like seaweed in the water churning forever at the foot of Domblémy, her arms afloat like seafronds too, her cheeks flushed, her robe or caftan billowing like a ball frock of the olden time. Out of eyes *someone* might in thirty-two years have called periwinkles but none ever had, she caught a glimpse of Número Uno stowing a segment of orange between orange-segment lips, nuzzling his stocking feet together as he did so. It was then it happened. "My dear, you waltz divinely," he called over from the sofa. That was when she felt something snap inside her — or the reverse, a decision secretly born, a resolve stiffened. She wanted a divorce. Oh, not now, or even soon. But eventually. In due time she would divorce. The thought settled quietly in a corner at the back of her mind, to be forgotten, or occasionally savored, as might be, like a lozenge tucked in one cheek.

A fresh business crisis proved both to be a distraction, and to possess a silver lining.

The swallowed company with the spot remover that had caused Dolfin Enterprises such grief had also, among its developed products, an insect repellent that proved truly and beyond all cavil superior. In addition to keeping pests away, it had an odor attractive to the gardeners and patio guests for whom it was principally intended. It wasn't a spray, simply a stick, like a deodorant stick, one rubbed on one's hands and arms and neck, even face. The test-marketing campaign had been a bang-up success. All it needed was a name. That being one of the problems Dirk took home with him, it was always on Daisy's mind as well. She suggested "Fly Away," "Beat it," "Bugaboo," "Scram" — even "Amscray." Having to explain the last to Dirk made it totally preposterous.

He became edgy. Here they had a winner, and no name for it. Worries such as these were matched by anxieties Daisy couldn't leave at her own office, and in their state of fatigue and nerves they mated less and less. They were hardly together except in the restaurants where they dined, when they could. Looking for a house from which to commute was out of the question — neither had the time or inclination. They moved out of Dirk's old apartment into a larger one on the upper East Side, and such dinners as they had there they took turns cooking. Magazine and gossip-column stories about marriages among the glamorous threatened by conflicts over careers had always seemed faintly ludicrous to Daisy. Not so now. And here they were under the same roof, not one partner in Cannes, the other in Vegas. The truth itself was ludicrous, in this case. One night there was a row climaxing an argument neither the gist nor the source of which Daisy could remember, of the continuing thread of which she had even lost her grasp. Something to do with women taking everything personally. Were they to become entangled in bromides such as that? The dispute clanked and wheezed along, more illogical at every step. At one point she found herself standing beside her bedroom dresser in a black nightgown he had bought her, a twist of lime peel bobbing on the waves beneath the remnants of Domblémy, tapping her palm with a hairbrush to emphasize her points.

"We are kind and moderate, we get work done, we do our human best to grind out another generation —"

"My dear, you mean . . . ?"

"No, no. Another generation and launch it on its way into a future of which we can only make the foggiest, most pessimistic guess. I mean when we *do* do that. Women do their best to see to it that their children stand on their own two feet, and their husbands too, if it comes to that. We do our best to have our men pass for a man in this world. Women identify themselves with a man's life more than the other way around. We don't resent his challenges, we like it, we're keen for it. The fact remains we are what we are, and you'd better not sell my sex short. I know of more men than I can count to whom I'd like to say, 'Only a woman would marry you.' We're the foot soldiers in most of the world's charities, ringing doorbells till our fingertips are calloused, pouring tea and going to boring kickoff dinners —"

"Hup up up up. Was that maybe aimed at me? 'Only a woman would marry you'?"

"Aha! Now who's taking everything personally?"

He rose from his report-strewn bed and bent over a low shelf of recordings they kept there. Was he going to put on an LP for nighttime listening? Some Big Spiderbecke? Surely not. No. Changing his mind, he went into the kitchen instead. She followed him, hairbrush still in hand. "Go ahead. Eat a pig's foot. It's your answer to every thing. Never mind what's eating me. That doesn't matter."

"Woman is am born malcontent," he said with his head in the icebox. "Everything is too much and nothing is enough. Diogenes will quicker find an honest man than a woman satisfied with her lot."

"You got that from me! You heard me say it first. That about women."

"Then, my dear . . ." And here, a pickled pig's foot impaled on the tines of a fork, he turned around, nudged the refrigerator door shut with an elbow, and struck a pose against it. She had always been afraid he would try for humor, when it ill suited him, and now her trepidations returned. Crossing one foot over the other, he sucked in his cheeks, puckered his mouth in an arch smile, and squinched up his eyebrows in what she prayed to God Almighty was not to be a conscious paraphrase of Clark Gable, of whom there'd been a recent glut on the Sunday television that was his chief pastime. "In that case, my dear, you can hardly differ with it."

"Oh!"

She took a step forward, and thrust her face into his, so that they stood nose-to-nose as in those baseball rhubarbs one also saw on TV.

"Do you know what I'd like you to do, Dolfin?"

"What?"

"*Bug away!*"

Things were never to be the same again. The wheel of chance had pivoted irreversibly on the mathematical point of a moment. They seemed to give a common gasp of apprehension. They gazed at each other with a wild surmise — changing swiftly to ecstatic certainty. There was no doubt about it. She had hit on the name for the insect repellent.

Bug Away was christened by a unanimously grateful board of directors, and, it being already late winter and getting on for early spring, labeled and marketed with all haste. It was an instant smash success, outselling all other competitors. Gardeners of both sexes — and patio guests too — found they needn't coat the whole of their exposed persons; a dab of the stuff on the backs of their hands sufficed to ward off all winged and walking, flying and creeping pests of summer.

The product's success started an upswing for the entire chemical line, and indeed most subsidiaries of the Dolfin Enterprises. Money matters having eased for Dirk and Daisy, everything else did too. There were stresses and strains of course, waves tossing the matrimonial bark and winds threatening its sails, but no weather in danger of upsetting it. They bought a ten-room Tudor in Cos Cob, and the housewarming was a third-anniversary celebration as well. All their friends came. Effie showed up with her new husband, a chap in his forties who had become quite rich selling mailing lists to charity organizations. The Diesel was escorted by a tall, sad Sicilian youth named Florian who wanted to know whether Time was a fixed entity or whether it ran forever down a bottomless drainpipe somewhere. Cocktails were served on a patio strung with Japanese lanterns, among which Florian wandered disconsolately, remarking on the aching ephemerality of things. The Diesel said he was a wallflower at the mating dance, all to the good from her point of view. Another friend had asked to bring a Hindustani sage named Rabindranath Moolah. Dressed in an awning, he drew on a fine thin cigar and offered an epiphany. The world was not an illusion after all; it only seemed that way. The talk meandered on, as it so charmingly will. Someone mentioned the recent rash of purse-snatchings by women, further evidence of their spreading participation in crime as part of their emergence in all aspects of contemporary life. That very day, a female footpad of indeterminate years had snatched a flight bag from the shoulder of a youth on Fifth Avenue and melted into the noonday throngs. "Change in the wind," a man said, with a sober nod. More and more women could be counted on to melt into the throngs. Had Mrs. Dobbin herself not pioneered in this area, both on foot and motorized? The wrists of the smartly dressed guests were lightly dabbed with Bug Away, rendering them impervious to the mosquitoes. Champagne corks were popping when the phone rang. Daisy streamed indoors to answer it. Her mother was on the other end, wishing them a happy anniversary.

"Thank you, Mom. And love to Daddy. Put him on."

"No, one minute. A little business. Daze, you know I have my code. I'm sorry. I can't be bought, influenced, cajoled or corrupted. I'm sorry. Even to the extent of playing favorites, cutting corners here and there. But harmful side effects are harmful side effects, whether to man or beast. That animal shampoo in your pets line? Hair of the Dog?"

"Just a minute. I'll call the man of the house."

She did, and returned to her guests. They were talking about marriage. A gray-haired man in his sixties named Christian Crocker had the floor.

"I don't for the life of me understand why people keep insisting marriage is doomed," he was saying. "All five of mine worked out."